PERFECT HATRED

PERFECT HATRED

Leighton Gage

Published by
Soho Press, Inc.
853 Broadway
New York, NY 10003

Library of Congress Cataloging-in-Publication Data
Gage, Leighton.
Perfect hatred / Leighton Gage.
p. cm.
ISBN 978-1-61695-176-4
eISBN 978-1-61695-177-1
1. Silva, Mario (Fictitious character)—Fiction.
2. Police—Brazil—Fiction. 3. Politicians—Crimes against—Fiction.
4. Terrorism—Fiction. 5. Revenge—Fiction. 6. Brazil—Fiction. I. Title.
PS3607.A3575P47 2012
813'.6—dc23   2012023877

Printed in the United States of America

10 9 8 7 6 5 4 3 2 1

For Heni Puósso de Britto,
And her husband, Joel de Britto,
The kindest people I have ever known.

I hate them with perfect hatred: I count them mine enemies.
Psalm 139:22 (KJV)

Chapter One

THE ACTION BEGAN AUSPICIOUSLY.

Salem Nabulsi had prayed for good weather—and God had rewarded him with a day of brilliant sunshine.

He'd hoped the woman's husband would leave at his accustomed hour—and the husband had departed fifteen minutes early.

He'd feared the woman would not admit him to her apartment—but she had.

And he'd feared she wouldn't die quietly—but she did.

By 8:15 A.M., he'd already washed her blood from his hands, injected her baby with the contents of the syringe and chosen, from among her clothing, the *hijab* and *abaya* that were to become his shroud.

God further smiled on their enterprise when He sent a taxi driver, punctual to the minute, but also so unobservant that he failed to notice how heavy the baby's carriage was when he folded it and stowed it in the cab.

The crowd, too, exceeded all expectations. It wasn't yet a quarter to nine when they reached the consulate, and yet the line already stretched to half the length of the security fence.

But then it all began to go wrong.

How could they have known, how could they *possibly* have known that babies attract Brazilians like flowers attract bees?

Salem hadn't been in place for more than two minutes before a grey-haired lady stuck her nose under the sunshade to have a look at the sleeping child.

She cooed at the infant and started talking about her grandchildren. Salem gave her no encouragement, but it still seemed an eternity before she abandoned her attempt to elicit a response and returned to her place in line.

Next to interfere was a fat sergeant from the Civil Police. Salem, fearing the cop's suspicions would be aroused by the difference in skin tones between himself and the baby, edged his hand closer to the detonation switch.

But the sergeant was wearing dark sunglasses and the baby was in deep shadow, so perhaps he didn't notice. After a few complimentary remarks, which Salem didn't respond to, the cop gave up and moved on.

He'd no sooner disappeared into an alcove fronting a leather goods shop when a third busybody appeared.

Salem was never to know it, but her name was Dorotea Candida. She was a sharp-eyed lawyer, the mother of three and the grandmother of two.

She was smiling when she bent over, but the smile quickly faded.

"Yours?" she asked, standing upright.

The mullah hadn't prepared him for such a question.

"Yes," Salem blurted.

Her eyes narrowed.

"Uh-huh," she said.

Salem didn't like the way she said it.

Then, without another word, she turned and headed toward a cop, not the same one as before, another one. And this one looked a lot smarter. She spoke and pointed. The cop nodded and walked toward Salem.

Wait until nine, the mullah had said. *The crowd will be biggest then.*

And it would have been. At least ten people had queued up behind him. More were arriving every minute. But Salem could wait no longer. Discovery was imminent. He put his hand on the button.

And pushed it, just as the cop reached him.

IN DUDU Fonseca's law offices, a little more than three kilometers away, the shockwave from the explosion rattled the glass in the windows.

Fonseca held up a hand to silence his client.

"What was that?" he said.

"I don't give a damn what it was," Orlando Muniz said. "Answer my question."

The question had been *what's our next move?* And Muniz was sitting on the other side of Fonseca's desk, with his arms crossed, awaiting Fonseca's response.

Fonseca was the best defense lawyer in São Paulo. Not *one* of the best, *the* best, but on Muniz's murder charge, he'd been unable to deliver an acquittal, and Muniz was mightily displeased.

Fonseca picked up the mock-Georgian coffee pot and poured the last of its contents into his cup.

An honest answer would have been that further moves were a waste of effort. The hard truth was that Muniz would be spending the rest of his days in a prison cell.

But, at the moment, Muniz was still laying golden eggs, so an honest answer wasn't in the cards.

"I'll have to give the situation some deep thought," Fonseca said, taking a sip of the (cold) coffee. "Frankly, we're in a bit of a quandary."

"Quandary, my ass," Muniz said. "I can't believe this is happening."

Indeed, he couldn't. In his world, the rich didn't go to jail. Not in Brazil. Not even if they killed an unarmed, penniless priest, in the presence of a federal cop, as he had done.

The initial judgment, one that resulted in a conviction, carried with it an automatic appeal. Fonseca had arranged to plead the first instance before one of the best judges money could buy. He was about to do the same with the second.

But a public prosecutor named Zanon Parma, in a spectacular show of legal tour de force, had checked the man on the bench at every turn.

Parma was to prosecutors what Fonseca was to defense attorneys. The best. Muniz's remaining days of freedom were surely numbered. But this, Fonseca thought, was no time to be candid.

"How important is this guy Parma to the prosecution's case?" Muniz asked.

Fonseca didn't like where his client was going with this. He smelled trouble. But he was being paid for his advice, so he gave it.

"Very. Parma is brilliant, he's dedicated, and he can't be bought."

"And that federal cop? That Chief Inspector Silva? How important is he?"

"Perhaps even more important than Parma. In addition to being the principal witness against you, he's spearheading—"

"The witch hunt. It's a fucking witch hunt. But any witch hunt needs guys up in front with scythes and pitchforks, right? You take those guys out of the picture and—"

Fonseca, once again, held up a hand. "Stop right there, Orlando. I don't want to hear it."

Muniz stood up. "Then we're done. I won't thank you for your time. I'm sure you're gonna bill me for every fucking second of it."

Fonseca, as was his custom with departing clients, struggled to his feet. He was grossly overweight, and it was never easy for him to get out of a chair.

Muniz ignored the lawyer's outstretched hand. "One thing more," he said. "Keep your fucking mouth shut about this conversation."

He departed so quickly that Fonseca's hand was still hanging in the air when the office door slammed shut.

THE BLAST had been the loudest thing Sergeant Flavio Correia had ever heard, louder than a crack of thunder, louder, even, than the stun grenades from his training days.

He rubbed his ears with his palms. One came away wet. He held the hand out in front of him and stared at it. It was red with blood.

His ears still ringing, Flavio stepped into the street.

A crater smoked where once a length of sidewalk had been. The windows in the buildings facing the American Consulate were blown out. The trees on both sides of the security fence were denuded. Small fires were everywhere.

A gas tank exploded, ruffling his hair with a pressure wave of hot air, as another vehicle joined the others already in flames. The woman slumped over the wheel didn't react. She was either dead or unconscious. Either way, she was a goner. There was no way he'd be able to get her out of there.

Flavio shuffled forward and stumbled over a severed foot still wearing a man's brown oxford.

A woman ran past him, her hair on fire, her mouth open in a silent scream.

A few meters away, a bloody arm rose from a legless trunk, waved once in wordless appeal, and fell back onto what looked like a pile of offal.

Flavio, his hands trembling, detached the transceiver from his belt, turned the volume to maximum, and put it to his ear.

But he couldn't hear a damned thing.

Chapter Two

CURITIBA, THE CAPITAL OF the Brazilian State of Paraná, is a city without streetcars or a Metro system. Public transportation depends entirely upon buses, but they don't run between the hours of midnight and five in the morning.

Nora Tasca didn't want to spend a sleepless night in the open air, so she did the next best thing: she got up at 4:30 A.M. to make sure she'd be able to catch the first bus of the day.

It arrived in Tiradentes Square, as scheduled, at three minutes to seven, already too late. All of the best places had been taken. By dint of considerable pushing and shoving she was finally able to wedge herself into a spot in the fifth row from the podium on the right. Not what she'd hoped for, but it was up against a security tape that had been stretched on stanchions to keep a path clear for the approach of the politicians. She'd never seen her hero, Plínio Saldana, *really* close up. This, she realized, was going to be her chance.

The woman to her left was also a great fan of the Man of the Hour, and she, too, had brought a collapsible chair. Nora sensed kinship and, before long, they were seated side-by-side, heads together, heaping praise on Plínio and pouring vitriol on his opponent.

At a few minutes past nine, shortly after Salem Nabulsi had detonated his bomb some 350 kilometers to the northeast, the sun appeared over the surrounding buildings and banished the last of the shadows. The day was cloudless—and likely to be a scorcher. The two women shared their sandwiches, and Nora fought against her inclination to empty her entire bottle of water.

A small group of workmen appeared and draped the platform with bunting, emblazoned with the State flag, and interspersed with Plínio's campaign slogan, *SWEEP PARANÁ CLEAN*. A little later, a squad from the Civil Police arrived and inspected the platform for explosives; then a crew of technicians started tinkering with the microphones and speakers, creating a number of pops and a few ear-shattering squeals.

All the while, people continued to flock into the square. They were, as a TV reporter with a mane of blonde hair and an overbite gushed into her microphone, *turning out in record numbers for this, Plínio Saldana's last major speech of the campaign.*

The camera panned in Nora's direction. She and her companion picked up their brooms and gave them an enthusiastic wave. Nora's broom had a stick two meters long and bristles half the height of a man. She'd crafted it herself, and she'd had a devil of a time getting it onto the bus, but the effort had been worth it. The broom had proven to be an object of admiration. And it was a powerful statement of political allegiance. By 11:30, the entire square, all the way back to the twin spires of the Cathedral of Our Lady of Light, was a sea of brooms, but few were as attractive as hers. Her companion told her so.

The turnout that day was unprecedented. People had flocked into the city from all over the state. The Civil Police later estimated the size of the crowd to have been somewhere between 250 and 300 thousand—the largest ever to witness the assassination of a Brazilian politician.

BY THE time Hector Costa and Danusa Marcus arrived at the scene of Salem Nabulsi's martyrdom, the Civil Police had blocked off the street.

Janus Prado, his face intermittently illuminated by the flashing red and blue lights of a nearby ambulance, was on the lookout. He waved when he spotted them.

Shattered glass crunching under their feet, they walked to meet him.

"Women," Janus said. "Kids. What kind of a sick fuck blows up women and kids?" He was badly shaken.

"Christ," Hector said. "What a God-awful mess. Any sign of Lefkowitz?"

Janus, who headed up the homicide division of São Paulo's Civil Police, pointed at the crater. "Poking around in there," he said. "You ever see anything like this?"

Hector shook his head.

"Once," Danusa said. "In Tel-Aviv."

"Well, I thank Christ I never have, and I hope I never do again. There should be a special place in hell reserved for people who do things like this."

"I agree," Hector said. "Who called it in?"

"One of our uniformed guys."

"He was on duty here?"

"Three of them were."

"Why three?"

"Crowd control. The Americans only admit a few at a time. The rest of them have to queue up here on the street."

"Queue up for what?"

"Visas, mostly. There's always a crowd."

"Have you spoken to your men about what they saw?"

"There are no *men*, Hector. Not anymore. Two of them were blown into little, tiny bits." Janus pointed in the direction of a leather goods shop. "The senior guy, a sergeant, was standing in that alcove over there. He survived."

"Badly hurt?" Danusa asked.

Janus shook his head.

"He's one lucky guy. Eardrums punctured, but that appears to be about it."

"Where is he?" Hector asked.

Janus pointed him out.

"But it's better if we go just the two of us," he said to Danusa. "No offense, but I already know his story, and he's going to be more forthcoming without a woman present."

"No problem," she said. "I'll go see how Lefkowitz is getting on."

"That woman," Janus said, admiring the view as she walked away, "is a knockout."

"She is," Hector agreed.

"You work with her much?"

"All the time."

"Doesn't Gilda get jealous?"

"She does," Hector said.

THE SURVIVING cop looked to be in his mid-thirties, and was fatter than any cop should be. A small trickle of blood, now dried, traced an irregular path from his right ear to his chin. He was pale, his hands still shaking. Janus introduced him as Flavio Correia.

"Flavio," he said, "this is Delegado Hector Costa. He heads up the Federal Police's São Paulo field office."

"You gotta talk louder," Correia said. "The explosion fucked up my ears. I can't hear for shit."

Janus raised his voice and repeated what he'd just said.

Correia stiffened his spine and snapped Hector a salute.

Hector acknowledged it with a nod. "Delegado Prado tells me you're a lucky guy."

"It's a miracle," Correia said. "And all because I fucked my wife's sister. Ironic, huh?"

Hector wasn't sure he'd heard him correctly.

"What? What are you talking about, Sergeant?"

Correia looked at Janus. "You didn't tell him?"

Janus shook his head. "I thought it would be better coming from you."

Thus prompted, Correia told Hector the story:

He would almost certainly have been killed, he said, if his wife, Marilla, hadn't taken the kids and flown to Rio to visit her mother. Flavio and his sister-in-law had been left alone in the house. They'd emptied a bottle of *cachaça*. One thing led to another, and they'd woken-up, nude, in the marital bed. Mutual recrimination and mutual repentance followed. And a pact of silence.

Marilla was unlikely ever to know what happened, but Flavio's guilt lay heavy upon him, and like many a wayward husband before him, he thought a present for his wife might help to alleviate it. Marilla, it seemed, was a handbag fiend. She could never have enough of them. Thus it was that, scant seconds before the blast, Flavio had stepped into the alcove leading to the front door of the boutique. He was, as he told it, admiring a cute little number in burgundy leather, with a brass clasp and zipper, when the bomb went off. The shock wave had toppled him, but the alcove had sheltered him from much of the blast and all of the shrapnel.

"I can't believe it," he concluded. "I thought God was supposed to hate adulterers."

"The Lord works in mysterious ways," Janus intoned.

Hector recognized the remark as sarcasm, but the sergeant took it at face value.

"He sure as hell does," he said. "Here I am alive, and that poor baby—"

"Baby?" Hector said.

Correia looked at Janus. "You didn't tell him about the baby either?"

"No," Janus said. "Tell him."

"It didn't fit," the sergeant said.

"What didn't fit?" Hector said.

"There was this woman, and she was pushing a carriage with a baby inside."

"Uh-huh. And?"

"And the mother, she was dark. Almost like a *mulata*. But the kid wasn't. The kid had really pale skin. Thinking back, I shoulda noticed there was something strange about it. But I didn't. It only hit me afterwards."

A baby carriage made sense. A bomb large enough to do the damage this one had done might have been too big to conceal on a person. Putting it within a carriage could have been the bomber's solution. And, if she was heartless enough, she might have used a child to complete her deception.

Hector was revolted by the thought, but he had to ask. "A doll, maybe," he said.

"No. I'm telling you, it was a baby."

"You're sure?"

The sergeant threw up his arms in exasperation. "Of course, I'm sure. I leaned over and had a good look. My kids are in Rio, and I miss them. And I like kids anyway. This particular kid not only looked like a baby, it smelled like a baby. It was sound asleep, but it was no doll."

Hector ran a hand through his hair. "So what did you do?" he said.

Correia frowned and blinked, as if he hadn't understood the question. "Do?"

"Yes. What did you do next?"

The sergeant scratched his head, vigorously, as if he was trying to kick-start his memory. "I looked at the baby, and I smiled at the mother. I tried to start a conversation, but she wasn't having it, so I walked away. That was all."

"Tell me more about her."

"What?" Correia pointed at one of his ears. "You gotta speak up. I can't—"

Hector raised his voice. "I said, tell me more about her."

"She was a Muslim."

"What made you think so?"

"She was dressed like one, that's what."

"Describe her. What did she have on?"

"One of those headscarf things. And a . . . dress, I guess you'd call it. It went all the way down to the ground. There was no shape to it at all."

"What do you mean by 'no shape'?"

"It was loose. You couldn't see what kind of a body she had. Why would a woman choose a dress like that? I mean, they usually want to show what they've got, right? Especially the young ones."

"And this was a young one?"

"Uh-huh."

"Where was she standing?"

"Behind the carriage."

"And where was the carriage?"

Correia pointed at the crater.

"Right there," he said, "where that big hole is."

AFTER SPEAKING with the sergeant, Hector went in search of Danusa and found her talking to Lefkowitz, the Federal Police's chief crime scene technician.

"Listen to this," she said and hooked a thumb toward her companion.

Lefkowitz turned to Hector. "I talked to one of the consulate's security guys," he said. "There were two video cameras on top of the building."

Hector looked up at the façade. "Well, they're not there now."

"Blown off," the diminutive crime scene tech said, "but it didn't affect the recordings."

His horn-rimmed glasses were slipping down his nose. He put a finger on the bridge and pushed them back into place.

"Two of them, huh?" Hector said. "Both pointed this way?"

"Uh-huh."

"Thank you, God, for small favors. Have you asked for copies of the tapes?"

"They're not tapes, they're video disks. And copies are being made as we speak."

"You find anything down in that crater?"

"I sure as hell did."

"What?"

"Let me have a look at the recordings first. Then we'll talk."

"I'm about to call the boss. He'll want to assemble a task force. And I guarantee you that you'll be on it. Keep your cell phone on."

"I never turn it off."

Hector withdrew to the alcove where sergeant Correia had been standing at the time of the explosion. There, somewhat sheltered from the noise, he took out his cell phone and called Chief Inspector Mario Silva at his office in Brasilia.

Silva was the Federal Police's Chief Investigator for Criminal Matters.

And Hector's uncle.

"You heard?" he said when he had him on the line.

"On the radio," Silva said. "On my way to work. Information is still sketchy. How many dead?"

"They're still counting."

"I've already reserved the jet. I'm leaving now. I'll swing by the house, pack a bag and go straight to the airport. I'll be in your office by noon at the latest."

"Good. Who do you want on this?"

"You, of course. Also Danusa, Lefkowitz, Mara and Babyface. I'll bring Arnaldo."

Mara Carta was Hector's Chief of Intelligence. Haraldo "Babyface" Gonçalves, so-called because he looked at least ten years younger than his chronological age, was one of the best investigators in the São Paulo field office. Arnaldo Nunes was Silva's longtime sidekick. The Chief Inspector seldom went anywhere without him.

Chapter Three

AT FIVE MINUTES TO twelve, Nora heard sirens. Seconds later, a cheer erupted. She got to her feet and leaned over the security tape.

About fifty meters away, Plínio Saldana, wind tousling his jet-black locks, was stepping out of a dark-blue SUV. Some claimed his hair was colored. Nora regarded such remarks as heresy.

Plínio raised his hands over his head and clasped them together. The people close enough to see the gesture went wild.

Plínio! Plínio! Plínio!

Their cries set off the rest of the crowd. The sound was deafening. Nora's heart swelled in her chest. To a rolling wave of cheers, the candidate began to move forward, approaching the podium on the *far* side of the walkway.

That would put him a good three meters from her when he passed by. And, what was worse, at least half his entourage would be walking between them.

Nora expressed her disappointment in an oath so coarse and in a voice so loud that several people across the corridor turned their heads to cast denigrating looks in her direction —and as swiftly looked away when Nora's new friend joined in. The woman was almost as formidable as Nora herself, and the two together formed a front no one wanted to tangle with.

Plínio passed them and climbed the steps. The two women stopped cursing and looked at each other.

"He'll walk on this side on the way back," the woman said. "I just know he will."

"From your mouth to God's ear," Nora said and resumed her seat.

She remained there throughout the preliminaries, but was on her feet again when Plínio stepped forward to speak.

She'd heard it all before. So had her neighbor. So had most of the crowd. And, since they all knew what was coming, they were able to lift their brooms and wave them at just the right moments. Those moments, the high points of any speech Saldana made, were always when he attacked Governor Abbas, and when he talked about sweeping him, and his whole corrupt crew, from the corridors of power.

Nora was inspired. She felt herself at one with the multitude. Mostly.

Every now and then, however, some selfish *filho da puta* tried to shove his way between her and the security tape.

Woe befell those who did. Nora wasn't a particularly tall woman, but she was stout, and many years of carrying heavy boxes of vegetables around Curitiba's Municipal Market had made her strong. No other woman in the crowd would have been a match for her in a fight—and few men.

She set her feet, as if bracing herself against a wind—and the wind would have to be a hurricane to dislodge her.

But it wasn't her physical strength alone that made her well-nigh invincible. She also had her broom. The handle was of peroba, and peroba, one of the hardest of all Brazilian woods, was so heavy it sank in water. Once, just as Plínio was launching into his peroration, she'd slammed it down on an interloper's instep—and had the satisfaction of hearing him yelp.

Too soon, the speech was over. The loudspeakers on the platform erupted into a recorded chorus of two hundred voices singing *Entre os astros do Cruzeiro*, accompanied by drum ruffles and trumpet flourishes. And to that, the music of his state's anthem, a smiling, waving Plínio Saldana started for the stairs.

As he descended the platform, Nora's excitement climbed to fever pitch. She almost forgot she had to pee.

And, yes, he chose her side of the walkway!

Nora turned to tell her companion she'd been right, but the woman was gone, her position usurped by an apelike man, with hairy arms and a low forehead, holding an infant he was offering for a kiss. The infant, obviously his son or daughter, looked not unlike a small chimpanzee.

Over the sound of the music, and from somewhere behind her, Nora could hear her ex-neighbor cursing a blue streak at having been forced out of her place. But it was every woman for herself now. There was nothing she could do to help her erstwhile friend.

Plínio moved closer, shaking hands, smiling, accepting congratulations. An athletic brunette with a bouquet of flowers tried to invade from the left. Nora broomsticked her. The woman staggered back, dropping the flowers. Before she could recover, they were trampled underfoot.

Nora was reaching out to Plínio when she felt, rather than saw, someone trying to displace her on the right.

She butted with her shoulder, dug her elbow into the interloper's ribs—and was nearly deafened by an explosion.

He'd fired a gun centimeters from her right ear. She knew it was a gun because the bullet punched a round hole in Plínio's forehead. His mouth opened in an "O" of surprise. A pistol appeared in the hand of one of his bodyguards.

The people around her started to scream.

Chapter Four

THE TASK FORCE MET in the second floor conference room of the Federal Police building on the Rua Hugo D'Antola.

Promptly at noon, Silva took a seat at the head of the long table, called them to order, and pointed at Lefkowitz. "Hector tells me you've got a video."

Lefkowitz nodded. "From the security cameras on the roof of the building."

He opened his notebook computer, waited until his colleagues had positioned themselves for a good view of the screen and clicked a button.

The image was time-coded. He let it run for four or five seconds and froze it.

"Right here," he said, "we're at two minutes prior to the detonation." He tapped the screen. "I draw your special attention to the individual behind the baby carriage."

He let it run until the explosion took place and the image dissolved.

"Too fast," Mara said.

"I've got another recording where I've doctored the image to slow it down," Lefkowitz said. "We'll look at that in a minute. But, right now, concentrate on what's going on. A woman comes over and looks into the carriage. Then she looks up at the person behind it. Then she turns around, spots a cop, and goes over and talks to him. He's walking toward the carriage when the explosion occurs. Here. Let's look again."

He replayed the scene.

"You're tying yourself into knots," Silva said, "not to refer to the individual behind the carriage as a woman. Would I be correct in assuming it was a man?"

"Hell, Chief Inspector, you're raining on my parade. That was going to be my big surprise."

"How can you be sure?"

"Because, down in the bomb crater, I found some of his body parts still wrapped in pieces of that outfit he was wearing."

"A hijab and abaya," Danusa put in.

"If that means a penis and a scrotum," Lefkowitz said, "you're right."

"I was referring to the outfit," she said. "A hijab covers the head and neck. An abaya covers the rest of the body."

"Thanks for the lesson," Lefkowitz said. "Hijab and abaya. Right. I'll remember that. Anyway, a fragment of this particular abaya had part of his trunk, including his sexual organs, wrapped in it. The bomber was a male. No question."

"How about a hand?" Arnaldo asked. "Did you find one?"

"You're thinking fingerprints, right?"

Arnaldo nodded.

"In fact," Lefkowitz went on, "we found two, one completely charred, but Gilda was able to get three partials off the other one."

Gilda, a pathologist and Hector's fiancé, was São Paulo's Deputy Chief Medical Examiner.

"Put a priority on running them through the database and get copies to the neighbors and the Americans," Silva said.

"Will do," Mara said.

That sort of thing fell into her realm of responsibility.

"How come you're so sure the bomb was in the carriage?"

"I'll show you," Lefkowitz said.

He changed the disk and played the last two seconds of

the previous scene in extreme slow motion. The quality of the image was poor, but it was clear the carriage had been at the epicenter of the blast.

"Why did he put the bomb in the carriage?" Gonçalves asked. "Why not simply strap it on? Isn't that what they normally do?"

"I don't know about normally," Lefkowitz said. "This is a first for me, but this was a bulky and heavy piece of ordinance. The explosive was seeded with stuff from a hardware store, bolts, nuts and washers, all of it designed to act as shrapnel. That, and the sheer amount of explosive, plus the battery, and the detonators, would have made it a heavy proposition to carry."

"And yet," Silva said, "using a carriage without a baby would have been risky. What did he use instead? A doll?"

"Not a doll," Hector said.

Silva narrowed his eyes. "What?" he said.

Hector related what the sergeant had told him and added, "The cop we saw approaching the carriage at the time of the explosion, and the woman who appeared to have tipped him off, were both killed, so we'll never really know. But our assumption is that the difference in skin coloration between the bomber and the child aroused her suspicion."

"I cannot imagine," Silva said, with steel in his voice, "that any mother would willingly sacrifice her own baby for something like this."

"No," Danusa said. "We don't either. We're operating under the assumption the child was kidnapped."

"Any reports of missing babies filed with the Civil Police?"

Mara shook her head.

"Not yet," she said, "but we have a flag on it."

"Do we have a freeze frame of the bomber's face?"

"We do," Lefkowitz said.

He opened an envelope and distributed prints.

"Get a half-dozen of these over to Janus Prado," Silva said. "If someone reports a missing baby, they'll need them to show."

"He has them already," Hector said.

"This kid," Arnaldo said, studying the face of the bomber, "looks even younger than a certain colleague of ours."

"Don't think for a moment," Gonçalves said, "that I didn't recognize that as a veiled reference to my appearance."

"No way," Arnaldo said.

"Way," Gonçalves said, "and I gotta say the constant humor at my expense is getting rather thin."

"On the contrary," Arnaldo said. "I continue to regard it as a thick vein with a great deal more to be mined."

"Don't encourage him, Haraldo," Mara said to Gonçalves. "You know how he is."

Banter about Gonçalves's youthful appearance was a constant in the São Paulo field office, and Arnaldo, on his frequent visits, always contributed to it. There were even those, Gonçalves himself being one, who believed that Arnaldo had started it all in the first place.

Silva, however, seldom joined-in. He turned to Danusa. "You're the one who knows the most about this stuff. The bomber, would you typify him as unusually young?"

"Maybe a little," she said, "but, statistically, more than eighty percent of suicide bombers are under twenty-four."

"How do they do it?" Mara asked. "How do they convince a young man, with his whole life before him, to sacrifice himself?"

"Like the Nazis did," Danusa said, "enlist them when they're young and brainwash them. For all the praise they heap upon them, they really regard the kids as fodder, no more than dupes to the leadership and the cause. The real criminals are the ones who twist their minds.

"How about the explosive?" Silva asked. "Any taggants?"

"Yes," Lefkowitz said. "And we'll know more within a few hours."

"Anyone take credit?"

Mara shook her head. "Not yet," she said.

Silva looked at Danusa. "Your Arabic? Is it still fluent?"

"It is," she said. "I keep it up."

"Then I want you to take that photo and go around to the mosques and madrasas here in São Paulo. See if anyone recognizes him. Mara?"

"Chief Inspector?"

"Put the photo through our facial recognition software and ask the Americans to do the same thing."

"Already being done."

"Lefkowitz?"

"Senhor?"

"Any chance you can recover any of the baby's DNA?"

"Not likely. He, or she, was right on top of the bomb. And, remember, it was chock-full of pieces of steel. The child would have been. . . ."

He didn't finish. Silva winced at the implication. "Bastards," he said, to no one in particular.

The door to the conference room opened. They all turned to look. Lidia, Hector's secretary, stuck her head in.

"A call for the Chief Inspector," she said. "Ana Tavares."

Ana Tavares was the personal assistant to Nelson Sampaio, the Director of the Federal Police.

"Tell her I'll call her back."

Lidia shook her head. "She told me you were going to say that. She also said it's very important, and you have to talk to her right now."

Silva gave an exasperated snort. "I'll take it in Hector's office." Then, to the others: "I'll be back in five minutes."

It took him more than ten. When he returned, he was radiating anger.

"I want all of you to know," he said, "that nothing is more important to me than this case. I'd hoped to accompany each and every development in this investigation, but. . ."

"But what?" Hector said, peeved.

"It's not going to happen."

"Why not?"

"Some politician has been shot, a candidate for the governorship of Paraná by the name of Plínio Saldana."

"Never heard of him," Arnaldo said.

Neither had any of the others. They showed it by shaking their heads.

Silva wasn't surprised. Few state politicians had national projection.

"Unfortunately," he said, "Pontes *has* heard of him, and he's furious." Sergio Pontes was Brazil's Minister of Justice. "He called Sampaio and ordered him to put his best men on the case."

"Good," Arnaldo said, going for the joke. "So we're out of it."

No one laughed. They were all too annoyed.

"We are most definitely *not* out of it," Silva said. He turned to Hector. "Keep me posted on all developments. If you don't have this one wrapped up before Arnaldo and I finish in Curitiba, we'll be back."

"Pontes has his priorities wrong," Hector said, rising to his feet. "We've got sixty-seven known dead as of this moment. What's one man's life compared to that?"

"I've been explaining that to our Maximum Leader for the last ten minutes," Silva said, "but he isn't having it. It appears Pontes owes the incumbent governor a favor. My apologies to you all, but we have to go."

"So it's just politics and favoritism," Hector snapped.

"Just politics and favoritism," Silva agreed. "Let's go, Arnaldo. I've already turned the jet around. It'll be at the Campo do Marte by the time we get there."

BY MID-AFTERNOON, even before Silva and Arnaldo had completed their short flight to Curitiba, the three partial fingerprints lifted from the bomber's severed hand had been circulated to the "neighbors"—the ten countries sharing borders with Brazil.

Based upon past experience, responses from Argentina, Colombia, Venezuela, French Guyana and Uruguay could be expected within forty-eight hours.

Responses from Guyana, Suriname, Paraguay, Peru and Bolivia customarily took much longer.

The baby carriage turned out to be of Brazilian manufacture, one of many thousands produced. It was untraceable.

But the explosive was not.

Manufacturers don't necessarily put post-detonation taggants into all the explosives they make—but they had in this one. It was C4, produced by an English firm called Ribbands Explosives.

This Lefkowitz imparted when he showed up in Hector's office bearing a brown manila envelope.

"And shipped to?" Hector asked.

"The Paraguayan Army," Lefkowitz said. "They bought a container full of the stuff, sixteen metric tons."

"Sixteen metric *tons*? What the hell is the Paraguayan Army going to do with sixteen metric tons of C4?"

"The greater question is: why is there a Paraguayan Army at all? It's not like anyone would want to annex the place."

"Did you contact them?"

"Mara did. To hear her tell it, they were astounded, simply

astounded. Three entire drums, a total of seventy-five kilos, have mysteriously gone missing. Until she asked them to check, they didn't even know they were gone. That's their story, anyway, and they're sticking to it."

"Of course they are."

The response from the Paraguayans didn't come as a surprise. Smuggling and the arms trade are to Paraguay what banking and cuckoo clocks are to Switzerland. And the Paraguayan military was known to be thoroughly corrupt.

"We should have finished the job back in 1870," Lefkowitz said. His expression was sour.

"Harsh, Lefkowitz, very harsh."

A nineteenth-century war with Brazil had been devastating for Paraguay. By the time it ended, seventy percent of the country's total population, and almost all its adult males, were dead. There were those who believed the Paraguayans had been trying to get back at the Brazilians ever since. Lefkowitz was one of them.

"Harsh, my ass," he said. "Do you have any idea how much stuff Mara has traced back to those people? She's called them so often that she and her contacts in Asunción are on a first-name basis, and I swear to God I'm not kidding."

"Believe me," Hector said, "I didn't think, even for a moment, that you were kidding. Any estimation of how many of those seventy-five kilos were used in the bombing?"

"Probably a little over a third."

"So they've got almost fifty kilos left. What's the shelf life of C4?"

"At least ten years."

"Damn. Nothing but bad news."

"Not really," Lefkowitz said and took a photo out of the envelope. Next to a ruler with gradations in millimeters, it showed a twisted piece of steel.

"What's this?" Hector said.

"A part of the frame that held up the shade on the baby's carriage."

"The shade? You mean that collapsible thing, the one that works like a hood on a convertible?"

"Exactly."

Hector remembered the image from the video. "It was up when the bomb went off."

"It was. Now, look at this." Lefkowitz pointed to where the blackened strip was bent around a little donut-shaped piece of steel.

"Is that a washer?" Hector asked.

Lefkowitz nodded. "It's a washer all right," he said. "Now follow my reasoning: the washers were embedded in the explosive. The explosive was *under* the baby. The shade was *over* the baby. When the bomb was detonated, the washers were blown in all directions. This particular washer went straight up and impacted the frame of the shade. The force of the explosion caused the frame to wrap around the washer and hold it fast."

"But to get to the frame it would have had to have passed through the bedclothes and. . ."

"Through the baby. That's correct."

"So, when you pry the frame and the washer apart, you might be able to extract—"

"DNA," Lefkowitz said.

Chapter Five

"LOOKS LIKE A FUCKING street sweepers' convention, doesn't it?" Braulio Serpa said. Serpa was Paraná's Secretary of Security, the top law-enforcement official in the State. He reported directly to Governor Abbas.

Arnaldo Nunes yawned. "*Plus ça change*," he said.

The three of them, Serpa, Arnaldo and Silva, were in Serpa's office looking at a shot of Tiradentes Square. It had been recorded by a news camera only minutes before Plínio's assassination.

Brooms were everywhere: big brooms, small brooms, brooms with dark bristles, brooms with light bristles, brooms with short handles, brooms with long handles, all being waved above the crowd like banners at a football match.

Serpa pushed the pause button and froze the image. "Plusa what?" he said.

"*Plus ça change, plus c'est la même chose*," Silva said. "It's French. Let's move on, Braulio. Unfreeze it."

But Serpa didn't unfreeze it. "French which means what?" he said suspiciously.

"Which means," Arnaldo said, "The more things change, the more they remain the same."

"So, all of a sudden, you speak French, do you?"

"*Un peu*," Arnaldo said with false modesty.

"Well, I don't. So why don't you explain to me, in good Portuguese, what the fuck you're talking about?"

"The brooms," Silva said with a sigh. "He's talking about the brooms."

"Plínio's campaign slogan," Serpa said, "was *sweep Paraná clean*. His symbol was a broom."

"We know that," Silva said.

"So what—"

"He stole it," Arnaldo said.

"Whaddayamean, he stole it?"

"From Jânio Quadros. Quadros invented the slogan. And he invented the symbol. And he got himself elected. That was back in the forties."

"Everybody around here thinks it was Plínio who invented that slogan," Serpa said, impressed. It sounded as if he admired the man for being able to steal something and get away with it.

"Probably not everybody," Arnaldo said. "Probably just the lesser-educated."

"Fuck you, too, Nunes."

Their relationship with the secretary was tenuous at best, but he and Arnaldo were going to have to work with the man, so Silva elected to pour oil on the troubled waters.

"I'm sure it wasn't Arnaldo's intention to offend you, Braulio. Was it, Arnaldo?"

"Perish the thought," Arnaldo said.

Serpa decided not to pursue the issue, a sure sign he needed them even more than they needed him—or thought he did.

"Plínio Saldana," he said, redirecting his anger, "was a fucking hypocrite."

"Hypocrite?" Silva asked, steering the conversation onto safer ground.

"He was a politician, wasn't he?" Serpa said. "They're all hypocrites." Then, realizing what he'd just said, he backpedaled. "Not my boss, of course. Abbas is a stand-up guy. He tells you something, you can take it to the bank."

"How about we go back to the video?" Silva said, breaking the short silence that followed.

Serpa started to say something, thought better of it and reached for the remote.

The broom-waving continued, both on the platform and off. It was still underway when Plínio took leave of his audience and made a beeline for the steps.

"Here it comes," Serpa said.

Plínio approached the camera. His image continued to grow, culminating in a tight close up.

"Wait for it," Serpa said. "Wait for it. . . ."

There was a POP on the soundtrack. A hole appeared in the candidate's forehead. Erupting out of the exit wound, blood and brain matter splattered several bystanders.

The scene, considered too graphic for television, had never been aired. Serpa, however, had seen it many times before. When the bullet went home, he wasn't looking at the screen, he was studying Silva and Arnaldo, probably in the hope they'd recoil.

"How about that, huh?" he said when neither did.

Someone jostled the camera, or the cameraman, and the image skewed to the left. Then someone else obscured the view by stepping in front of the lens.

The two federal cops remained impassive.

Serpa moved on. "Now we jump back in time," he said. "This was shot by a camera from another channel. It's the same action, but taken from the other side."

Three or four seconds into the sequence he pushed the pause button.

"That guy there," he said, tapping the screen, "is Nestor Cambria, Saldana's bodyguard. You get to see more of him in the next shot."

"I know Nestor," Silva said. "We both do."

"So do I," Serpa said. "He worked for me before he joined you guys."

"We were glad to get him," Arnaldo said.

"And I was glad to lose him."

Neither Silva nor Arnaldo commented on that. They already knew Nestor's side of the story—and they weren't interested in Serpa's.

"Have you worked on the sound?" Silva asked.

"You mean, filtered it? Tried to isolate individual voices?"

"Yes."

"We did. But there was just too damn much noise, too much screaming going on. Doesn't matter anyway. No matter what anybody said, it doesn't change anything."

"Maybe not," Silva said, but he didn't sound convinced. "Maybe we should have a crack at it in Brasilia."

Serpa shrugged. "Suit yourself, but it's gonna be a waste of time."

"Sure of that, are you?"

"One hundred percent. Ask that Lefkowitz of yours. Ask anybody. My guys are good."

"All right, go ahead."

Serpa unfroze the image.

Plínio's back was to the camera. Facing him, a squat, powerfully-built woman was reaching out to grasp his hand.

"Nora Tasca," Serpa said. "Our best eyewitness."

A man edged into the frame and tried to shove her out of the way.

"Enter the killer, Julio Cataldo," Serpa said.

Cataldo raised a pistol. Nora elbowed him in the ribs. A fraction of a second later a flash erupted from the handgun's muzzle. Nora whipped her head around to look at Cataldo's face. Saldana, mortally wounded, dropped out of frame.

Again the angle changed. Serpa rustled his papers but didn't say anything. This time, the sequence had been filmed from farther away, or with a shorter lens, and consequently showed more of the surrounding action. Nestor was seen to draw his weapon, shoot, be shot, shoot again and go down.

"Ouch," Arnaldo said.

"Ouch is right," Serpa said, "but your friend Nestor still got the best of it. Plínio and Cataldo are dead. Of the three of them, he's the only one who didn't get a mortal wound. And now, gentlemen, the best coverage of all, which is why I left it for last."

"Why the best coverage of all?" Silva wanted to know.

"Plínio had a personal videographer, a guy who followed him around. He was inside the security perimeter. Nobody got in his way while he was recording. Watch."

The clip began ten seconds before the attack. Plínio and his bodyguard, Nestor, were on the right-hand side of the frame, Cataldo on the left. It was almost as if the assassination had been staged for the camera.

"Whoa!" Arnaldo said, when Nestor fired for the second time, and a jet of blood spouted from Cataldo's neck. "Carotid artery. Game over. He would have bled out in no time."

"He did," Serpa said.

"How's Nestor doing?" Silva asked.

"The doctors say he's going to be fine."

"Did you interview him?"

Serpa shook his head. "What could he tell us that we don't already know?"

"Go back to the beginning of the previous shot," Silva said, "and I'll show you."

"What?"

"Keep your hand on the remote. Freeze the image when I tell you. Pay special attention to where Nestor's hand is just before the assassin's gun appears."

"What are you talking about? What am I looking for?"

"Do as I suggest, and you'll see for yourself."

Serpa shrugged, rewound the video and hit the play button.

"Now," Silva said, leaning forward. Then: "Inch it back a bit. There. That's it."

On the screen, Nestor's gun was clearing his holster, but Cataldo's wasn't yet visible.

"Jesus Christ," Serpa said. "Nestor *knew*. He knew what was coming."

"It appears he did."

"I don't know how I missed it."

"Neither do I."

Silva meant it as a reproach, but Serpa was oblivious to the criticism.

"We gotta get to the hospital," he said. "Time to have a little chat with Senhor Nestor Cambria."

"Go back to the beginning of the tape," Silva said, ignoring him. "This time, pay attention to the expressions on Cataldo's face."

"Why? What am I going to see?"

"You want me to tell you?"

"Tell me. We'll look at it afterwards."

"When he approaches Plínio," Silva said, "Cataldo looks nervous, but determined. He's grim, but his jaw is set. After he shoots, his expression turns to one of horror."

"That doesn't make sense."

"No, it doesn't. He drops his gun hand to his side and stares. Nestor shoots him. He looks down at his chest, and looks up at Nestor, as if he can't believe what Nestor has done to him. Surprise turns to anger. He lifts the gun again and shoots Nestor."

"You saw that? You saw all of that?"

"You'll see it, too, if you watch the tape again."

"It's just . . . that it all happened so fast."

"So aren't we lucky we have it on video?" Arnaldo said. "You got slow-motion on that thing?"

"I do," Serpa said.

"So let's see it that way," Silva said.

They watched it again.

"Plain as the nose on your face," Arnaldo said when it was over. He stressed the word *your*. Serpa had a nose as prominent as the bowsprit on an old-time clipper ship, but the secretary of security didn't react to the dig. He was too intrigued by what he'd just seen.

"How about this?" he said, after a few seconds of thought.

"How about if Cataldo and Nestor were in it together?"

"Go on," Silva said.

"Yeah," Serpa said, warming to his theme. "Cataldo was set up to kill Plínio, see? And, afterwards, Nestor was supposed to hold him at gunpoint so the crowd wouldn't tear him apart."

"I don't think so," Silva said.

"No, wait. Let me finish. It all makes sense. Afterward, Nestor was supposed to let him escape, at least that's what Cataldo expected. But Nestor's plan, all along, was to kill Cataldo as soon as he'd taken Plínio out. Plínio dead. The killer dead. The bodyguard just doing his job. The perfect crime."

"Not impossible," Silva said.

"But you don't buy it."

"No."

"Why not?"

"It doesn't seem like the Nestor I know."

"Everybody's got his price."

Arnaldo turned his head and looked at him.

"What?" Serpa said.

"Nothing."

"Why are we wasting time?" Serpa said. "Nestor is the key to the whole business. Let's—"

Silva held up a hand. "I'll get back to Nestor in a moment. Right now, I'm interested in Cataldo. What else can you tell us about him?"

"What's to tell?"

"Any history of violence? Any criminal record? Any indication he might have been mentally ill?"

"No, no and no. He was a family man, born and bred in Curitiba. His friends, his neighbors, everybody we talked to said he was the last guy they would have expected to do something like this."

"And you don't find that suspicious?"

"Not when you know the rest of the story."

"Which is?"

"He was broke. He had debts. He needed money."

"So he took on a kill-for-hire. That's the way you figure it?"

Serpa shrugged. "Like I said, everybody has his price. All we gotta do is figure out who picked up the tab."

"Okay," Arnaldo said, "so let's talk about the elephant in the room."

"What elephant?"

"Lots of people seem to think your boss had the best motive."

"Lots of people have got it wrong. Governor Abbas is a smart politician. Even if he wasn't, even if he'd been dumb enough to try to knock off Plínio, Madalena wouldn't have let him."

"Who's Madalena?" Arnaldo asked. "His wife?"

"Hell no. That's Esmeralda, and she's as dumb as a post. I'm talking about Madalena Torres. She's his campaign manager, and she's fucking brilliant."

"And the Governor wouldn't have acted without consulting her?"

"He consults her about everything. When to have breakfast, when to go to sleep, when to take a—"

Silva cut him short. "So you're sure the governor isn't
mixed up in this?"

"One hundred percent. Think about it. If Abbas had anything to do with it, why would he have agreed to call you
guys in? Answer me that."

"Agreed?" Silva said. "What do you mean *agreed*? The way
I heard it, it was his idea. It started with him."

Serpa shook his head. "It started with me. It was *my* idea.
I told the governor I needed help."

Silva raised an eyebrow. "You mean to tell me, Braulio,
that we're here because you actually *wanted* us here? The last
time we were in Paraná, I got the impression you couldn't get
us out of your state quick enough."

"Hey, that was then. This is now. This time, it's different.
This time, I'm your new best friend."

"And with friends like you, who needs enem—"

"Shut up, Nunes. I'm talking to your boss."

"Why the change of heart?" Silva said.

"I'm forty-eight years old. I got three kids. I got responsi-
bilities. I got expenses. I leave this job without finding out
who bankrolled Plínio's murder, I'm not gonna find another
one paying half as well. I solve the case, I'm going to be a
hero, and I can write my ticket in the civilian security world."

"So you don't see yourself staying on after Abbas leaves?"

"Are you kidding? You know who's running in Plínio's
place?"

"No. Who?"

"His widow, Stella."

"His widow?"

"That's right. Stella Saldana announced her candidacy
about two hours ago. With the backlash, with half the state

thinking Abbas was behind her husband's killing, she's sure to win. She'll take office on the third of January, and by the fourth, every Abbas appointee in this state will be out on his ass, me included. Happy New Year, right? Anyway, that only gives me another nine weeks to crack this thing, and I'd take help from the Devil himself."

"Yeah, we've been looking forward to working with you too," Arnaldo said. "Just the thought gives me a warm, cuddly feeling."

"I told you to shut up."

"If not Abbas," Silva said, "who?"

"I don't know," Serpa said, "but it's got to be non-political."

"How do you figure?"

"Simple. Up until the time Plínio got shot, it was a two-horse race. Either Saldana, or Abbas, was gonna win this election. Nobody else. No other candidate had a ghost of a chance. And, since nobody in Saldana's camp would have wanted to kill him, and nobody in Abbas's camp would have been stupid enough to. . . ."

"We should be concentrating on people outside the world of politics. Is that the way you figure it?"

"That's the way I figure it."

"All right, understood. Any suspects?"

"None," Serpa said. "Well, okay, maybe one. But it's a stretch."

"Who?"

"You didn't get this from me, okay?"

"Okay. Who?"

"Plínio's brother."

"Explain."

"Plínio's old man, Orestes Saldana, is richer than God. His wife is dead, and he only has—make that *had*—two kids, Lúcio and Plínio."

"So?"

"So, before Plínio got himself killed, Orestes's estate, when he died, would have been split equally."

"I see."

"And it didn't matter a damn that Orestes hated Plínio's guts, which he did. The law prohibited him from disinheriting a son, so Plínio would have gotten half the money, unless—"

"He predeceased the old man."

"Exactly."

"Likes money, does he? This Lúcio?"

"I don't know if he likes it, but he sure as hell needs it. Word on the street is his business is going down the tubes."

"What business? What does he do for a living?"

"He's a financial consultant. But I wouldn't call it a living, because it isn't."

Silva shook his head as if to clear it. "Say that again," he said. "This Lúcio's a financial consultant, yet he can't make a success of his own business?"

Serpa gave a sardonic grin. "Doesn't exactly inspire confidence, does it? So it's no surprise that the folks in this town who have money aren't likely to trust him with any of it."

"You just said his father was richer than God."

"So?"

"So why doesn't he help him out? Pump some money into the business? Use his influence to get his son some clients?"

"You wouldn't ask that question if you knew the old man. Orestes Saldana doesn't put a *centavo* into anything that isn't guaranteed to give him a return."

"Like that, is he?"

"He's the biggest tightwad that ever there was. Every charity in this town has had a go at him at one time or another, and he's sent every one of them packing. The only thing he ever contributes to is Governor Abbas's campaigns."

"And what is there about Governor Abbas that inspires the generosity of Senhor Saldana?"

"It's not generosity. It's an investment. Orestes owns a construction company that does about ninety percent of its business with the State."

"How cozy," Arnaldo said.

Serpa didn't look at him, acted as if it had been Silva who'd spoken.

"Very cozy. Abbas and Saldana are like this"—Serpa held up a hand with his forefinger and middle finger crossed—"and the governor is going to want to keep it that way."

"And therefore," Silva said, "if we should subject Orestes, or his son, to interrogation—"

"Orestes is gonna squawk. And who is he gonna squawk to? Abbas that's who! And the next thing you know the governor will be on my ass. There's no way he's gonna believe Orestes, or Lúcio, had anything to do with Plínio's death, not unless we can prove it to him beyond a shadow of a doubt."

"How do we prove it, if we can't question them?"

"Yeah, that's a problem, isn't it? Put your thinking cap on, and maybe you'll come up with a solution. But I never said a word to you about either Lúcio *or* his old man. Are we clear?"

Silva didn't reply.

"You want to visit the crime scene?"

"That won't be necessary."

"No, I didn't think so. You wouldn't get anything out of it anyway. It's already been trampled over by everybody and his brother—and it's knee-deep in flowers."

"Have you spoken to Cataldo's wife?"

"Sure. She sang the same tune as their friends and neighbors. She claimed to be mystified, said what her husband did came as a complete surprise. At first, I didn't buy it."

"But you do now?"

"I hooked her up to a lie detector. She passed with flying colors."

"Lie detectors can be fooled."

"You telling me something I don't know? But that takes a cool customer, and this lady is an emotional wreck."

"I'd like to talk to her anyway."

Braulio shrugged. "Suit yourself. What else?"

"We'd like a copy of everything you've got. Everything."

Serpa opened his drawer, removed a ring binder and put it on his desk. "I figured you would."

"Not very thick," Arnaldo said.

Serpa chose to take the observation as criticism. "What the fuck did you expect?" he said. "It just happened a few hours ago."

"Medical examiner's reports?" Silva asked.

"Tomorrow morning. But they're not gonna tell us anything we don't know already."

"Names? Addresses?"

Serpa nodded. "Plínio's father, his brother, Cataldo's wife, even Nestor's wife, they're all in the book."

"And the governor?"

"Him too. And the governor's chief-of-staff, Rodrigo Fabiano. And Madalena Torres. But you're going to be wasting your time with that lot. No way any of those people are involved in this."

He pushed the binder in Silva's direction.

"Then we're done for the moment," Silva said, picking it up and rising to his feet. "Next stop, the hospital."

"I'll go with you," Serpa said, standing up and reaching for his coat.

While his back was turned, Silva and Arnaldo exchanged a glance. The last thing they wanted was to have Serpa dogging their footsteps.

"Not a good idea," Silva said to Serpa's back, knowing he wouldn't take kindly to being excluded.

The secretary turned to face him. "Why the hell not?"

"We're friends of Nestor's," Silva said, reasonably. "You're not. Without you, we're likely to get more out of him."

It wasn't a strong argument, but it was the best he could think of on the spur of the moment.

Serpa stood there for a few seconds, trying to think of a way to refute it—but he couldn't, so he mumbled something inaudible, scowled and sat down.

He was still scowling when they closed the door behind them.

Chapter Six

A TWENTY-MINUTE CAB RIDE took Silva and Arnaldo to Santa Cruz Hospital. They arrived to find a horde of people exiting the front door.

"Shift change," Arnaldo said.

But it wasn't.

"The afternoon visiting hours just ended," the woman at the reception desk told them. She was elderly, long past retirement age, probably a volunteer. Her thick glasses magnified friendly brown eyes.

Silva showed her his warrant card. "Police business," he said.

"Well, that's different, isn't it? The patient's name?"

Silva told her.

She opened a folder and ran an index finger down a list. "Here it is. Cambria, Nestor. Room 542."

They boarded the elevator and pressed the button for the fifth floor. It stopped on the second.

The door opened to reveal two young women engaged in conversation.

"So then I told her," one was saying, "that, with a boyfriend like that, she'd be better off if she just—" She stopped abruptly when she saw the elevator wasn't empty.

Both women were dressed in identical pink frocks, and both were pushing carts laden with trays. Arnaldo put out a hand to prevent the door from closing as they climbed on board.

"Thanks," the one who'd been speaking said, but she

didn't resume her conversation. The elevator filled with the smell of overcooked vegetables.

One woman got off on the fourth floor; the other on the fifth where she turned left and moved off at a brisk pace.

Arnaldo and Silva stopped at the desk directly in front of the elevator doors. From behind it, a no-nonsense type with a pencil protruding from her hair like an antenna was staring daggers. Silva looked for a name tag. She wasn't wearing one.

When they asked her how to find room 542 she raised her chin.

"Visiting hours just ended," she said.

"Yes," Silva said. "We're aware of that."

"We're serving dinner. We don't admit visitors during mealtimes."

"Sorry. You're going to have to make an exception. This is police business."

"Can't it wait?"

"No, Senhora," Silva said, keeping a tight rein on his temper, "I'm afraid it can't."

"Credentials, please," she said.

Both cops showed her their warrant cards. She took her time studying them, then pointed and said, "It's that way, at the end of the hall."

"The life of the party, that one," Arnaldo muttered after they'd turned their backs and were walking away. "Remind me never to get shot in Curitiba."

"Never get shot in Curitiba," Silva said.

Just then, there was a scream followed by a crash. The woman who'd exited the elevator with them hurried out of a room and passed them on the run. She stopped at the nurses' station and leaned over the desk.

Silva and Arnaldo quickened their pace, reached the door

from which she'd emerged and stepped over the tray of food and crockery she'd let fall to the floor.

Nestor was lying across the bed, his pajamas and sheets soaked with blood. More had pooled on the floor.

The PA system burst into life.

Code Blue. Room 542. Code Blue. Room 542.

"Closet and bathroom," Silva snapped.

Arnaldo, gun already in hand, went to check both places.

Silva holstered his Glock and put his index and middle fingers on Nestor's carotid artery.

Their friend's eyes were open. An ugly gash was in his forehead, a bloody pillow next to his body. His pulse was nonexistent.

"Whoever did it is gone," Arnaldo said, returning from the bathroom. "Nestor?"

"Also gone," Silva said.

There was a commotion in the hallway. A young man wearing green scrubs appeared at the door. He spotted the pistol in Arnaldo's hand and stopped so abruptly that both of the nurses behind him ran into his back.

"Police," Silva said and stepped aside.

Reassured, they entered the room, followed by a third nurse pushing a cart heaped with instruments and medical supplies. The first two women went to the bed and bent over Nestor.

"I'm Doctor Sobel," the man in scrubs said. "What happened?"

"Senhor Cambria is dead," Silva said. "Murdered."

The young doctor raised an eyebrow. "I think I'd be the better judge of that."

"I don't give a damn what you think," Silva said, annoyed. "Tell your security people to block off this floor and to send their senior man to the nurse's station near the elevator."

"I'm a doctor. I'm not—"

"Just do it!"

Sobel grimaced and, apparently better at giving orders than taking them, addressed one of the nurses.

"Do as he says."

She moved toward the telephone. The two cops hurried back in the direction of the elevators.

"Senhor Cambria?" the no-nonsense woman asked before either one of them could get a word out.

"Murdered," Arnaldo said.

His bluntness would have rattled most people. Not her.

"Murdered, eh?" she said. "You seem very sure of yourself. Don't you think Doctor Sobel should make a call like that?"

"No, I don't."

That took her aback. "No? Why not?"

"Because I've examined more murdered people than that arrogant little prig ever did," Arnaldo said.

Silva stepped-in before the altercation could escalate. "Your name, Senhora?"

She shot a nasty look at Arnaldo, but responded civilly enough. "Telles. Celia Telles."

"Tell me, Senhora Telles, is it possible to get onto this floor by way of the stairwell?"

"Stairwells," she corrected him. "There are two, and, no, it isn't. You can *leave* the floor, but you can't *enter* the floor."

"What happens if you get trapped in the stairwell?"

"You have to descend to the lobby. Down there, the door isn't locked."

"So any visitor to this floor would have to use the elevator to get here?"

"Unless he had a key, or someone admitted him."

"Or unless someone left one of the doors propped open," Arnaldo said.

She obviously would have preferred to ignore him, or refute him, but was forced to give a reluctant nod.

"Who has keys?" Silva said. "The nursing staff? The doctors?"

She shook her head. "Only the security people."

"How long have you been on duty?"

"Since ten. I'm doing a double shift."

"How much of that time have you spent here, in this location?"

"Most of it. Someone has to keep a constant eye on the monitors. Unless I'm on a break, that's me."

"When was the last time you were on a break?"

She glanced at the clock on the wall. "I returned from the last one an hour and . . . twenty-six minutes ago."

"Where are the monitors?"

"Come around to this side."

Silva stepped behind the desk. Below the level of the surface, out of the sight of visitors, was a bank of small computer screens. Sharply-defined peaks were springing into existence on one side of each and trailing-off to disappear on the other. Above the pulsing green tracings, and in the same color, there were numbers. Some changed as he watched.

"Vital signs," she said, and then pointed them out, "heartbeat, respiration, blood pressure."

"Was Senhor Cambria hooked up to one of these?"

She shook her head.

"Why not?"

"We don't have enough units for everyone. His wound wasn't serious. We had other priorities for the equipment."

"What kind of priorities?"

"Patients over sixty, or those with special problems. Senhor Cambria didn't fall into either category."

"You keep a list of visitors?" Arnaldo asked.

"No," she said.

"Why not?"

"We do that in intensive care, and in maternity, where it's necessary."

"Meaning that here it isn't?"

"Meaning exactly that."

Her tone was getting sharper with each successive reply.

Once again, Silva stepped in, "How many patients on this floor?"

"Forty-two. Every room is occupied."

"Forty-two," Silva repeated. "That must generate a great deal of coming and going."

"It does."

"So you'd have a hard time remembering all the visitors."

"It's not my job to remember visitors."

Silva betrayed no irritation, although he certainly felt it, and persisted: "But Nestor would have been different, right? He was a special patient. Somewhat of a celebrity. Someone whose visitors you'd be more likely to remember."

"Yes," she conceded, "he was. Senhor Cambria was a hero. Everyone saw him on television. Everyone. They kept playing the scenes over and over."

"So who were they? Who came to visit him?"

She reflected for a moment, then said, "Well, his wife, of course. She was here this morning just after they brought him in. She said she'd be back after dinner."

"Who else?"

"A gang of reporters."

"Who else?"

"Stella Saldana, Plínio's wife. She arrived with a whole entourage. They all trooped down to Senhor Cambria's room. After a while, the others all came back and hung around here, waiting for her."

"Let me get this straight. You're saying Senhora Saldana remained alone in the room with Senhor Cambria?"

"That's correct, but surely you're not suggesting that she had anything to do with—"

"I'm not suggesting anything, Senhora. I'm just trying to get a feel for the timeline. How long did Senhora Saldana stay with Senhor Cambria?"

"Ten minutes? Fifteen? I really can't be sure. I didn't keep an eye on the clock."

"But you don't think it was more than fifteen minutes?"

"Probably less."

"At about what time did she leave?"

"Shortly before you arrived. When the visiting hours ended."

The elevator door opened, and a man in a uniform stepped out.

"Just one more question, Senhora," Silva said. "How many of those reporters were there?"

"Seventeen," the newcomer said, injecting himself into the conversation, "most of them idiots."

He was a slim young man, about a hand's breadth shorter than Arnaldo, with a mole on his left cheek and intelligent gray eyes.

Silva turned to face him. "What makes you say that?"

"They kept asking him how it *felt*. How it *felt* to be shot. How it *felt* to lose a friend. How it *felt* to kill a man. They weren't really after answers, just sound bites and visuals. The newspaper people were the only ones who asked intelligent questions. And there were damned few."

"Newspaper people or intelligent questions?"

"Both."

"Sounds like you were there," Arnaldo said.

"I was. Bunch of ghouls. Hell, how did they expect him to

feel when a friend was murdered? A friend he was supposed to be protecting? And right in front of him too. I'm Raul Sintra, by the way, Head of Security here at Santa Cruz. Who are you?"

Silva showed his gold Chief Inspector's badge. Sintra looked suitably impressed.

"And this is?"

"Agent Nunes," Arnaldo answered for himself.

"Did I understand you to say Saldana and Nestor were friends?" Silva said.

"Close friends, ever since they were in law school. Didn't you know?"

Silva shook his head.

"Tell me this, Senhor Sintra, did you ask for credentials from all those reporters?"

"No. I didn't deem it necessary."

"Fair enough. Did you take their names?"

"Nope. I didn't think that was necessary either. I just told them to assemble in the lobby, and we'd take the whole gang upstairs at once, which we did. My turn. What's going on?"

Silva told him.

Sintra reddened with anger. "Murdered him?" he said. "Someone *murdered* him? On my watch?"

"I see you're taking it personally."

"Goddamned right I'm taking it personally. Nobody warned me his life was in danger. Nobody said so much as a goddamned word. If they had, I would have had people inside and outside his room. I would have had a camera installed in there."

"You sound like you might have been a law-enforcement officer."

"I was. I was a delegado with the Civil Police here in Curitiba."

"And?"

Sintra's jaw tightened. "I resigned."

"Because?"

"Because I had a boss I couldn't stomach."

"Braulio Serpa?"

"Bingo."

"Good. We can't stomach him either."

Sintra smiled. "You sound like my kind of people. What can I do to help?"

Silva pointed toward the elevator bank. "I spotted a security camera when we were coming up. How many have you got and how many actually work?"

"There are security cameras in every elevator in the building. They all work. And we record all the images and keep them for seventy-two hours."

"Excellent. And the stairwells? Also covered?"

"Both stairwells. Ground floor only. And, before you ask, all the exits and entrances to the building."

"And, if you're on this floor, there's no other way to leave other than via those elevators"—Silva pointed—"or the two stairwells?"

"Correct."

"And the video recordings are date and time-stamped?"

"They are."

"Excellent. I'd like you to go through the videos and make a photo of every person who used an elevator, or one of those stairwells, in the past hour. Will you do that for me?"

Sintra nodded. "Sure. No problem. Why only the past hour?"

"Senhor Cambria's body is still warm. He hasn't been dead for more than a few minutes. So, in the interest of speed, let's start with that. We can always expand the envelope if we don't come up with anything. Are your men trained to use firearms?"

"They're all ex-cops, except for one who's an ex-army NCO."

"Do they carry?"

Sintra shook his head. "Not normally, but there's a locker downstairs where I keep some weapons for emergencies." He fished a notebook and a ballpoint pen out of his hip pocket. "You want me to cover the exits, right? Just in case he's still in the building?"

"Exactly," Silva said. "Two armed men on each of the exits, make a record of everyone who leaves, detain anyone who's suspicious and carry out a complete search of the building. Have you got enough staff to do all that?"

Sintra nodded.

"Enough on duty," he said, "to cover the doors with two in reserve. I'll call in people from home to do the search. What else?"

"You want me to call Serpa and get backup?"

"If that bastard's in," Sintra said, "I'm out."

"Then he's not in," Silva said.

"Good," Sintra said. "What else?"

Show the photos to the staff and the patients. See if there's someone none of them recognizes."

"Okay. Who do I call if I get a hit?"

"Me. Take this."

Silva offered his card.

"The number for the phone I carry is on the back," he said. "If Serpa shows up, don't give it to him."

Sintra flipped the card over to check the number.

"I can already see it's going to be a pleasure to work with you, Chief Inspector," he said.

Chapter Seven

THE FOLLOWING MORNING, JUST before ten, Hector got a call from São Paulo's Head of Homicide.

"Late last night," Janus began without preamble, "this salesman for a media company got back from a trip to Rio and found his wife dead in their apartment."

"And this is significant because?" Hector asked.

"Because they had a baby, a son about four months old—and he's missing."

Hector grabbed his pen. "Name?" he said.

"Adnan Chehab." Janus spelled it. "His wife was Carlotta with two Ts."

"Chehab? What kind of a name is that?"

"Lebanese, I think. Anyway, the guy sells space in magazines, has a number of clients in Rio and goes there once a week. Yesterday morning, at around quarter past seven, he kissed his wife goodbye and left. When he got home, at ten that night, he found a bloodbath, and she was in the middle of it. Somebody cut her throat and left her body on the living room floor."

"The father's story check out?"

"He had ticket stubs for the shuttle. He met a colleague at Congonhas. They flew together. We called his business contacts, had a look at the passenger lists. He was in Rio all right."

"Could he have killed her before he left?"

"The M.E. says he *could* have, but the first responders found him sitting on the floor, with her head in his lap, babbling like an idiot. If he was putting on a performance, they said, he deserves an Academy Award. So I don't think it's likely."

"Yesterday, Lefkowitz told me he might be able to recover DNA from the baby. We'll need a sample of the woman's blood."

"I'll get one for you. But I'm not finished."

"Sorry. Go on."

"Chehab kept getting more and more hysterical, and the paramedics finally had to shoot him full of sedatives. But, before they did, my guys got him to take them around his apartment."

"And?"

"And it wasn't a robbery. Other than the kid, nothing was missing."

"Nothing?"

"You're about to ask me about a baby carriage, right?"

"I was, yes."

"Like I said, nothing. The Chehabs' carriage was still there, and they only had the one."

"Where is Chehab now?"

"At the Sírio-Libanês Hospital. We won't get any more access to him until sometime this afternoon, if that."

"You have people there?"

"Two. Sitting just outside his room."

"How about the Chehabs' neighbors?"

"My guys held off until this morning before they did the canvassing. They wanted to do it at the same time of day the wife had her throat cut."

"And?"

"They struck pay dirt. It's a small building, only twenty-two apartments. A lady who lives on the floor above goes out every morning to buy fresh bread. Yesterday, Adnan joined her when she was going down in the elevator. He was off to Rio, he said. She wished him a pleasant trip and went to the *padaria* on the corner. It isn't fifty meters from the front door of her building. When she got back a young guy, *pushing a baby carriage*, was talking to Chehab's wife on the intercom."

"Description?"

"Dark-skinned, she said. A middle-eastern type."

"Your man show her a photograph of the bomber?"

"The damned fool wasn't expecting to get lucky, so he didn't have one with him. I chewed up one side of his ass and down the other. He's on his way back as we speak, but I haven't got much doubt about what she's going to tell him. You?"

"No. Did she hear their exchange? Over the intercom?"

"Carlotta seemed to know him and had no qualms about buzzing him in, only that."

"Did she introduce herself to him? Get a name?"

"They rode up together in the elevator, and she tried to initiate some friendly chit-chat, but he wouldn't have it. His attitude put her nose out of joint. She thought he was rude."

"Baby in the carriage?"

"No baby. The carriage was new. She thought the guy was delivering it."

THE *Centro Islamico*, on the Avenida do Estado, was São Paulo's oldest mosque and the one with the largest congregation. It was, therefore, the logical place for Danusa to initiate her inquires.

She was just arriving for her appointment with Sheikh Ahmad, the worship leader, when Hector called her cell phone and filled her in on the conversation with Janus Prado.

"With a name like that," she said, "I think Janus is right about him being Lebanese. What's the wife's first name?"

"Carlotta."

"Carlotta? That doesn't fit."

"I didn't think so either."

"Is the husband a practicing Muslim?"

"No idea."

"I'll ask the Sheikh about him. Maybe we'll get lucky."

THE AGED cleric, a hunger-thin man with a kindly face and sad eyes, received her in his office.

"I must admit to a certain degree of curiosity about all this urgency," he said. "I was to have spoken, this morning, at a school, and I hate to disappoint children."

He'd used the word *curiosity*. What he really meant was *irritation*, but he was too polite to say it.

"I'm sorry," Danusa said, "but when you know the facts, I think you'll agree that there was no time to lose. Tell me, what percentage of the city's Muslims worship here at the Centro Islamico?"

"Fifty percent . . . or thereabouts."

"So it follows that you probably know half the Muslims in São Paulo?"

"Probably. We're not a very large community."

"Are you, by any chance, acquainted with a couple by the name of Chehab?"

"I know two couples named Chehab. Why all these questions?"

"The people I'm referring to are Adnan and Carlotta."

"Adnan and Carlotta? Yes, I know them."

"Are you aware that Carlotta recently gave birth?"

"Yes. God blessed them with a little boy. They named him Fadi. Again, why all these questions?"

The murder of Carlotta would be in the morning papers. There was no need for secrecy. Danusa told him.

The Sheikh's mouth opened in surprise, and his eyes became even sadder. "What kind of a monster would do something like that?"

"That's a question for psychiatrists," Danusa said. "Our job is to *identify* the monster. You've heard about the bombing in front of the American Consulate?"

"Yes. A terrible thing."

"More terrible, even, than the newspapers are letting on." She told him about the baby.

"And that baby . . . was Fadi?"

"We don't know that for certain, but it's a distinct possibility."

The Sheikh looked at his hands. He was quiet for a long moment.

"And Adnan?" he said, looking up again. "What of him?"

"He's overwrought. He's being treated at the Sírio-Libanês Hospital."

The Sheikh began straightening the things on his desk. "I must go to him."

Danusa shook her head. "He's under heavy sedation, and he's not being allowed any visits, even from the police."

"Oh," he said, becoming still. "Until when?"

"Sorry, I don't know."

"I shall call the hospital to check. And I shall pray for him. He's a good man, who loved his wife and child very deeply. He will be heartbroken."

"So you can't see him using his baby for something like this?"

"Adnan Chehab? Never!" He accompanied his words with an emphatic shake of his head.

"No chance he could be involved with an extremist group?"

"Adnan's positions against radicalism and violence are well-known. He is moderate in all things, extreme in none."

"You're sure?"

The Sheikh's nod was equally emphatic.

"Ask anyone in the congregation. If Adnan hates anyone, it's the people who bring our religion into disrepute by misinterpreting the word of God. Further proof of his tolerance, if any is required, is that he married a Christian."

"Carlotta is a Christian?"

The Sheikh waved a finger in denial. "Carlotta *was* a Christian. She converted to Islam."

"At his behest?"

"Certainly not. Of her own free will. Because she wanted to."

Danusa showed him one of the photos. "Do you recognize this man?" she said.

He gave it only a cursory glance. "That's a woman," he said.

She shook her head. "Please look more closely."

"Why? What—"

"Please. Just look. It's a picture of the bomber, taken seconds before the explosion."

The Sheikh pushed his spectacles above his hairline, accepted the photograph and brought it close to his nose. "Oh, God," he said.

His eyes had become huge. Danusa felt the hairs rising on the back of her neck.

"You know him then?"

The Sheikh nodded. "I know him."

"Who was he? What was his name?"

"Salem Nabulsi," the Sheikh said, shaking his head as if to negate the thought.

"Salem?" Danusa said. "*Salem?*" She repeated it with more emphasis.

He raised an eyebrow. "You know Arabic?"

"I do," she said. "*Peaceful.* What an irony. A suicide bomber named Peaceful. Was he a member of your congregation?"

The Sheikh sighed. "I am sorry to say he was."

"Did he ever give you any indication he was planning a violent act?"

"He did not. And, if he had, I assure you, I would have informed the authorities."

"Any idea how Salem might have become associated with the Chehabs?"

The Sheikh ran a hand through his beard. "I fear I was responsible for that."

"How so?"

"Salem had heard, somewhere, that Carlotta had been a teacher. He spoke good Spanish, and had the rudiments of Arabic, mostly *suras* he'd learned by rote, but his Portuguese was very poor."

"Wait. You mean to tell me that Salem Nabulsi wasn't Brazilian?"

"You didn't know?"

She shook her head. "Until now, I knew nothing about him, not even his name. Only that he detonated the bomb."

"He was from Paraguay."

"Paraguay? Where in Paraguay? Asunción?"

"Ciudad del Este. I've never been there. I've heard it's a dreadful place."

Danusa nodded. "You've heard correctly."

"He's been . . . was in São Paulo no more than a few months, but he told me he intended to stay and wanted help to improve his language skills. Someone told him Carlotta had been a teacher. He asked me to approach her, encourage her to give him lessons, said he'd pay her."

"And she agreed?"

"Not because of the money. They didn't need it, she said. She was a good-hearted person, always willing to help others."

"He'd go to her apartment for his lessons?"

The Sheikh seemed shocked that she'd even asked. "That wouldn't have been at all appropriate. No, she'd meet him here, leave the baby in our crèche and instruct him in a corner of the library."

"How long had this been going on?"

"A month. No more."

"Do you think it was a ploy, this business of the language? That he used it to approach Carlotta and her baby?"

"It must have been, don't you think? If he was planning to blow himself up, why would he put any effort into learning Portuguese?"

"Why indeed. What else can you tell me about Salem?"

"Very little. He was devout. His parents immigrated to Paraguay before he was born. He was not unintelligent, but he was poorly educated. Other than that. . . ." The cleric's words trailed off. He made a gesture of helplessness.

"Nothing else? Nothing more you can remember?"

The Sheikh shook his head. "He was a private person. When he spoke to me at all, which was seldom, he spoke of God, and the Holy Qur'an, and of almost nothing else. He had some strange interpretations, more based upon hate than love. He referred once, with reverence, to a certain Mullah Asim. He asked me if I knew the man."

"And do you?"

"No."

"How did he react when you told him that?"

"He seemed disappointed."

Chapter Eight

LEO'S BAR HAD SEEN better days, and so had that stretch of the Rua Aurora on which it was located. Beyond the open front door, the street was packed with panhandlers. They'd be joined by a horde of whores as soon as the sun went down.

The Colonel recognized Muniz from his newspaper photographs and raised a hand. The wealthy landowner spotted the gesture and made a beeline toward him.

"Colonel?"

"That's me."

"Colonel what?"

"That's unimportant. Make yourself comfortable, Senhor Muniz. I took the liberty of ordering you a beer." He pointed to a brimming glass. "It's what one drinks in here."

Muniz took the proffered seat, but didn't pick up the glass. Instead, he sat studying the beverage, as if he thought the Colonel might be about to poison him.

Meantime, the Colonel studied Muniz.

He hadn't much liked what he'd seen in the photographs. In the flesh, the man pleased him even less. Muniz had a more-or-less permanent scowl, the kind that turned a smile into an evil grin.

"So you're the guy," the Colonel said, "who killed that priest."

"It was self-defense," Muniz said, as he'd said a hundred times before.

"The way I heard it, the old guy was unarmed."

"I was set up. They told me he had a gun. And, besides, he

was a leftist, a liberation theology fanatic, no better than a Communist. He got what was coming to him."

"We share a sentiment," the Colonel said. "I, too, have little use for Communists."

In fact, the Colonel had a visceral dislike for anyone whose politics were even slightly to the left of those of Attila the Hun. During the dictatorship he'd been a young lieutenant, later a captain. His assigned task, one he'd performed with relish, had been apprehending leftists. He'd done it for almost seven years, and it was a matter-of-record that none he'd apprehended had ever been found.

His activities, in those days, had given rise to his reputation for discretion and secrecy; qualities that, in more recent times, had resulted in people like Muniz seeking him out.

"You don't have to keep looking around," he said, smiling slightly at the way Muniz's head was swiveling back and forth on his neck. "No one in this place pays attention to anyone else. It's one of the things I like about it."

"Assuming you're right," Muniz said, grumpily, "what else is there to like?"

"It has the best draft beer in the city," the Colonel said. "Everyone from São Paulo knows that."

"*I* don't know that," Muniz said.

"Ah, but then you're not from São Paulo, are you?"

"Rio," Muniz snapped, "and draft beer is draft beer. Only the brands are different. It doesn't matter where they tap the kegs."

"No, my friend, that's where you're wrong. Leo's draft beer is definitely a cut above the rest. I'm told it has something to do with the metal used to make the tubing between the kegs and the taps. And the fact that they flush the system every day."

The Colonel picked up his glass, took a long swallow and

wiped the foam from his mustache. The mustache was trim, as was everything about the Colonel. He was almost the same height as Muniz, but there the resemblance ended. Whereas Muniz had a roll of fat hanging over his belt, a double-chin and flabby biceps, the Colonel was all muscle. His bearing was erect, and he radiated an air of command. He wasn't wearing a uniform, hadn't worn one for almost five years now, but no discerning observer would have taken him for anything other than a military man.

"Delicious," he said, and saluted Muniz with his glass. "Go ahead. Try it."

Muniz grabbed his, took a sip, grunted, and took a swallow. Then he took two more.

"See?" the Colonel said.

"I'm not here to drink beer," Muniz said. "I'm here to do business."

"And I'm here to do both," the Colonel said. "So how can I be of assistance?"

Muniz put down his glass, shoved it aside, leaned across the table and lowered his voice.

"I think we should go somewhere else to discuss this."

The Colonel's grin belittled Muniz's concern. "As I've already told you once before," he said, "people in Leo's Bar don't listen to each other's conversations. It isn't polite. And it could be dangerous."

Muniz continued to hesitate, still averse to airing his business in public.

"If you've got a problem with someone," the Colonel pressed him, "I'm your man. It's my business, and there's nobody better at it. Speak up. Or finish your beer and leave. It's all the same to me."

It was. These days, people were queuing up for his services.

Caution might have dictated that Muniz get up and leave,

but time was short, and he was an impatient and impulsive man. He took the plunge.

"I want some people taken care of," he said, his voice just above a whisper.

The Colonel took another sip of his beer. He'd learned to react lukewarmly when a client made a proposal. A show of indifference tended to inflate the value of the contract.

"From what I've read about you," he said, "you've got some pretty big estates up north."

Muniz frowned. "What of it?"

"They say labor is hard to find up there. They say land-owners like you bring in workers with all sorts of promises, promises that are never kept. And the next thing those labor-ers know, they're as good as slaves. Too much work, too little money, and not a chance of being allowed to leave."

Muniz sniffed. "People say all sorts of things. You shouldn't believe everything you hear."

The Colonel went on, as if the landowner hadn't spoken. "Slaves have to be kept in line. I'll bet you have *capangas* for that, men with guns and whips who aren't reluctant to use them. I'll bet they have to kill a man, every now and then, *pour encourager les autres*, as the French say."

"Colonel, I didn't come here to—"

The Colonel cut him off in mid-sentence. "What I'm asking myself, Senhor Muniz, is why you don't use your own people? You obviously have them. So what do you need me for?"

"They're ruffians, just a cut above animals. They're useful in their way, but there's not one good brain among them. They're not disciplined, they're not trained—"

"And my men are. I understand that part. But why should you even need trained men? Why not just turn your *capangas* loose on the people you want to attend to, and if it doesn't work the first time, send more. Eventually, they'll pull it off.

And if you're far, far away when it happens, you'll have complete deniability."

"That's just the point, Colonel."

"*What* is just the point, Senhor Muniz?"

"The point is, I don't *want* to be far, far away. I want to be there. I want to do it myself, and I want the people concerned to be looking into my eyes when I do. I want the smile on my face to be the last thing they see on this earth. That's what I want, Colonel, and that's what I want you to help me with."

"That's quite an indulgence, Senhor Muniz."

"I'm a rich man, Colonel. I can afford my indulgences."

"And the role of my men would be?"

"To protect me during the process. And to cover my tracks when I'm done."

"By eliminating witnesses?"

"If need be, yes. Are you interested?"

The Colonel drained the beer in his glass and signaled the waiter for another.

"I, too," he said, "am a rich man. I'm not adverse to a challenge, but I tend to avoid excessive risk. I'd have to know a bit more about this job before I can answer that question."

"Picky, aren't you?"

"Yes, Senhor Muniz, I am."

The waiter arrived with the Colonel's beer, saw Muniz's glass was less than half-full and looked at him expectantly. Muniz waved him away.

"It's like this, you see," the Colonel went on when the waiter was gone, "my employees are all ex-soldiers, highly trained and dedicated. In that sense, it's a bit like a private army of which I'm the commanding officer. And, like any good officer, I take care of my men. They know that. They expect it of me. And they respond with loyalty. That loyalty, more than anything else, has been the foundation of my success."

"I don't give a good goddamn about your success, Colonel. Or how you run your business either. I'm only interested in two things."

The Colonel disliked being interrupted while patting himself on the back. *The price*, he thought to himself, *has just gone up*.

"Very well, Senhor Muniz," he said dryly. "And those two things are?"

The Colonel's evident displeasure pleased his potential client, who was getting tired of being talked down to.

"Whether you're willing to take on the assignment," Muniz said, "and how much it's going to cost me if you do."

The Colonel stroked his lower lip with a forefinger, then said, "Let us, then, get to the crux of the matter. How many people are we talking about?"

"Two."

"Together or separately?"

"Separately."

The Colonel quaffed some beer. "Business rivals?"

Muniz shook his head.

"One is a public prosecutor. The other is a Chief Inspector of the Federal Police. Does that shock you?"

"Very little shocks me, Senhor Muniz, but you've just defined two *hard targets*, as we in the military refer to them. The price of my collaboration will be high."

"How much?"

"Two hundred thousand American dollars. Each."

Muniz blinked, but said nothing at all.

"For that," the Colonel went on, "you'll get the services of three of my men for as long as it takes. They'll provide the weapons. You absorb the expenses for everything else, including transportation, hotels and per-diems, which I will stipulate at five hundred dollars per man, per day."

"Agreed."

"Agreed? Just like that?"

"Are you willing to take less?"

The Colonel grinned. "No. But I'm beginning to think I should have asked for more."

Muniz met the grin with a scowl. "But you didn't. So it's two hundred thousand each, and it's agreed."

"Half in advance. Transferred to a numbered account in Riga. I no longer trust Swiss banks."

Muniz reached for the notepad and pen he always carried with him. "Give me the account information. I'll make the transfer this very day."

The Colonel had come prepared. He reached into his pocket, took out a piece of paper and handed it across the table.

"The routing number is at the top," he said. "The long number below it is the account number. The name of the bank, and the address, are at the bottom."

Muniz snatched the paper and scanned what was written there. "When can I meet your men?"

The Colonel drank more beer before he answered. "I have contact with my banker on a daily basis. I'll get in touch with you as soon as I've received the money."

"Excellent."

"And, now, Senhor Muniz, you may tell me the names of those soon-to-be deceased."

"The public prosecutor is Zanon Parma. The Chief Inspector is Mario Silva."

"Silva I've heard of. He lives in Brasilia."

"Normally, yes. But I've been told he's currently in Curitiba, working on a case."

"Duly noted. And where does Parma reside?"

"Here in São Paulo."

"Do you have a priority?"

"Parma first. Killing Silva is something I want to savor."

"Good. That's all I need to know at the moment."

The Colonel reached into the breast pocket of his black leather jacket and removed a notebook. "Give me a number where I can reach you."

Muniz rattled one off, and the Colonel made a note with a gold-plated pen.

"I believe that concludes our business. Please, have another beer. And can I interest you in lunch? Today is Friday, and, on Fridays, this place serves excellent *bacalhau*."

Chapter Nine

THREE DAYS AFTER SALEM Nabulsi's bid for martyrdom, there was another explosion, this time during Shabbat services in Argentina's oldest synagogue, the *Congregacion Israelita* on the Calle Libertad in Buenos Aires.

The death toll, according to Sunday's *Jornal da Cidade*, was "even greater than that of this week's bombing of the American Consulate in São Paulo." Among the dead were the Israeli ambassador to Argentina, Daniel Grundman, his wife, Devorah, and his two children, Miriam, eleven, and Aaron, thirteen.

Hector took the newspaper into the kitchen, where his fiancée was washing breakfast dishes. "Listen to this," he said.

He sat down and read the article aloud.

"You're thinking," Gilda said, when he'd finished, "that the remainder of that plastic explosive might no longer be totally unaccounted for?"

"I am," he said. "What puzzles me is why they'd cross over into Argentina to do this one. God knows, there are plenty of targets here at home."

"Maybe this isn't home for them," she said. "You told me the stuff was purchased in Paraguay, right? And that bomber you've identified was also from Paraguay. Maybe the terrorists live there, not here."

"Good point," Hector said.

"Any pictures?"

"One."

"Show me."

Gilda dried her hands and Hector handed her the newspaper.

"You know what this reminds me of?" she said, after studying the photograph.

"What?"

"The explosion that killed Isaac Marcus."

Hector took the paper back and studied the picture. "Yes," he said. "It does. He was Danusa's father, you know."

"I didn't."

"Most people don't. She doesn't like to talk about it."

Rabbi Isaac Marcus had been a Brazilian religious superstar. During his lifetime, Isaac's progressive attitudes had earned him the admiration of most of the younger and more progressive members of his congregation—and a good deal of criticism from the older and more conservative ones.

But it was outside of São Paulo's small Jewish community, and in matters not directly related to his faith, where Isaac had made the biggest impact. In the time of the dictatorship, he'd been courageous in his criticism of the regime—and had come close to paying the ultimate price for his outspokenness. When democracy returned, he'd become a media darling, a pundit whose opinions were sought-after on every issue, from sex to the politics of the Middle East.

He was an articulate speaker, a man with charisma, fluent in Spanish and English as well as Hebrew and Portuguese. He was often called upon to speak at commencements, fundraisers, even political gatherings. Businessmen, politicians, clergy of other faiths all knew and respected Isaac Marcus. It sent shockwaves throughout Brazil when his synagogue was bombed, and Isaac was killed in the explosion.

"She was his only child," Hector said, "and very young. She didn't attend the funeral."

"Why not?"

"She was living abroad. Is there any more coffee in that pot?"

Gilda took one of the demitasse cups from the drainer, filled it and set it down in front of him. No milk, no sugar, the way he liked it.

"Abroad where?" she said.

"Israel. Her parents sent her to visit a kibbutz the summer she was twelve. She went back the following year, went back *every* year until she finished university."

He drained the coffee and handed her the cup. She rinsed it and put it back in the drainer.

"And?"

"And returned to Israel to live after she'd completed her studies."

"And then?"

"And then she met this guy—"

"*Cherchez l'homme*," Gilda said.

"It's *cherchez la femme*, Gilda."

"Not in this case."

"Nobody says *cherchez l'homme*."

"I just did. Finish the story."

"They fell in love. They were going to get married."

"Sweet!"

"For a while. Then he was killed."

"Aw." She pulled a face, took off her apron, and took a seat facing him. "Killed? How?"

"I get the impression it was some kind of undercover work. I also get the impression she did some undercover work herself."

"Why no more than an impression? Don't you people investigate the hell out of anyone you're going to hire?"

"We do. Her records say she served honorably in the Israeli Defense Forces. According to them, it was in the areas of logistics and supply."

"But you think she might have been doing something else?"

"She's fluent in Farsi and Arabic. She can quote the Qur'an like a mullah, and she's a mine of information about both Sunnis and Shiites."

Gilda raised an eyebrow. "Unusual in someone who specialized in logistics and supply, don't you think?

"I do, but we didn't think it mattered. She was eminently qualified, and languages are always a plus for us, so we were happy to get her."

"You think she joined up with you lot because she thought it would help her find the people who killed her dad?"

"That would be my guess."

"And did she? Find them, I mean."

Hector shook his head. "No. We ran every lead into the ground. They all just . . . petered out."

"She's attractive, isn't she?"

Hector wasn't about to fall for that one. "I hadn't much noticed," he said.

"Oh, really?" she said, folding her arms and making a study of his face. "Well, maybe you can tell me this: Does she have a new boyfriend?"

"Not that I know of. You do love gossip, don't you?"

"Don't try to change the subject. You think she'll go back to Israel?"

"She might. She talks about it sometimes."

"If she does, will you be sorry to lose her?"

"Well, in a purely professional sense, I suppose I would."

"Are you suggesting there's another side to your relationship with Danusa Marcus? Other than purely professional, I mean."

"Of course not. How about making some more coffee?"

"How about you make it yourself? In case you never noticed, this is an equal opportunity kitchen."

ON MONDAY morning, when Hector arrived, Lefkowitz, Danusa and Mara Carta were waiting in his office.

"I've spoken to the *Federales* in Buenos Aires," Mara said. "The taggants match. The explosive came from the same batch."

Hector turned to Lefkowitz. "You have an estimate on how many kilograms they might have used?"

"Judging by the photos we got, and Mara's conversation with our Argentinean friends, somewhere around ten, maybe a little more. But it was a confined space, so the loss-of-life was higher."

"What's the current total?"

"One hundred and two killed, eighty-seven injured," Mara said, "of which twenty-three seriously."

"Jesus. Another suicide bomber?"

"Apparently not. The device had a timer. It was under a seat, set to go off during the service."

"Ten kilograms," Hector said. "So they'd have somewhere between thirty and forty left."

"At the moment," Lefkowitz said, "but what's to prevent them from buying more? The death merchants in Paraguay are still sitting on seventy-five kilograms short of sixteen metric tons of the stuff."

"Not a comforting thought," Hector said. He turned back to Mara. "Speaking of our friends in Paraguay, did you feed them that name Danusa came up with? Salem Nabulsi?"

"I did. I'm waiting for them to get back to me."

"Anything you can do to speed them up?"

"Sure," Mara said. "I can pay them. How high are you willing to go?"

"That's probably not as much of a joke as you might think," Lefkowitz put in.

"Who's joking?" Mara said.

"Did you manage to extract DNA from that washer?" Hector asked Lefkowitz.

"I did. And we're running the comparison with Carlotta Chehab's blood. The washer, by the way, was soaked in rat poison. The nuts and bolts were as well."

"Nasty."

"But not uncommon."

"And the reason," Mara said, "that we're expecting the number of fatalities to go up."

Hector looked around the table. "Where's Babyface?"

"I was just getting to that," Mara said. "It seems Salem had a cell phone, and I'm not talking about one of those prepaid and untraceable things we would have expected him to have. I'm talking about a cell phone for which he had a conventional account."

"Careless of him," Hector said.

"Contemptuous, I'd call it," Danusa said. "He didn't give a damn if we traced him after his bomb went off."

"And assumed we wouldn't be doing it before it did. Did you ping it?"

"I did," Mara said. "It's either switched off or it's been destroyed."

"What do the account records tell us? Many incoming calls?"

"Not a single one."

"Outgoing?"

"Two numbers: one that he called many times, always on the same day of the week, always at the same time, another that he called only once."

"Let me guess," Danusa said. "Just before he blew himself up?"

"Correct."

"Saying good-bye would be my guess. It's not uncommon for them to do that. Both numbers in Paraguay?"

Mara nodded. "Ciudad del Este. We've requested a trace. Don't get your hopes up, though. The same day of the week, at the same time would suggest he was calling a public telephone, talking to someone who was waiting for him to call."

"How about the billing address?"

"A *pensão* on the Rua Leite de Morais in Santana."

"Likely just a mail drop."

"Maybe. But you asked about Babyface. And that's where he is right now."

THE *HOSPEDARIA* Rio Paraguay was a small and cheap establishment situated in a neighborhood abounding with other establishments equally small and cheap. The owner was Oscar Benitez, a rotund little man with a gold incisor and a thick accent.

Gonçalves flashed his badge.

"You're kidding," Oscar said.

"Kidding about what, Senhor Benitez?"

"You look too young to be a federal agent."

"Nevertheless," Gonçalves said, with a touch of frost in his voice, "I *am* a federal agent."

"Hey, no need to get your hackles up. Not my fault you look like a kid, is it? What can I do for you?"

"Did you have a man staying here by the name of Salem Nabulsi?" Gonçalves said, dropping the temperature another ten degrees.

"He's paid up until the end of the week. So what?"

"Is this him?"

He showed Oscar the photo.

"Of course not," Oscar said. "That's a woman you've got there."

"Look again."

Oscar did and, as recognition hit him, his eyebrows rose almost to his hairline, a neat trick for someone whose hairline was as receded as his was.

"*Dios mio*," he said.

Gonçalves opened his mouth to say something more, closed it when he felt a tap on his shoulder.

"Did I hear you asking about Salem Nabulsi?" a voice behind him said.

"You did."

Gonçalves turned around. The woman who'd done the tapping looked to be in her forties, maybe early fifties, was running to fat, and was dressed in a green tracksuit.

"Let me see that photograph," she said.

Gonçalves showed it to her.

"*Dios mio*."

Same words, same accent, same eyebrow action as Benitez. Gonçalves took them both for Paraguayans.

"It's him then?" he said. "Salem Nabulsi?"

"It's him," she said. "Why is he dressed like a woman? What's he done? Was he the one who set off that bomb in front of the American Consulate?"

Gonçalves saw no reason to deny it.

"Yes," he said, "he was."

"*Gracias*, Malu," Benitez exploded. "*Gracias* for bringing that *hijo de la gran puta* into my establishment."

Malu responded in kind. "*Ponga sus gracias en el culo*, Oscar. You think I knew?"

Gonçalves forestalled the rebuttal from Oscar: "Is what he's saying correct? Are you the one who brought him here?"

"Yes! Yes!" Oscar said. "She's the one. She befriended the bomber, not me."

Malu lifted her purse to hit him with it, but Gonçalves grabbed her arm before she could.

"How about you tell me about it?" he said.

She stammered. "I didn't . . . I was. . . ."

"She's a *sacoleira*," Benitez said.

Sacoleiras were women who rode the buses to Paraguay, bought everything from electronics to perfume (all duty free) and brought it back to Brazil. There was nothing illegal about it, unless the women exceeded their duty-free allowances, or unless they bought it for resale, both of which they usually did. And, because they did, they generally had stockpiles of goods difficult to explain. A search of her room would likely result in her being taken away in handcuffs—all because of Oscar's big mouth.

"*Cabron!*" she said, and tried to free the arm holding the purse.

"Stop it right now," Gonçalves said. "Or I'll arrest the both of you."

She stopped struggling. Oscar looked at his feet.

"What's your name?" Gonçalves said to the woman.

"Malu Caceres," she said, "but I didn't—"

"Hold it right there, Malu. Listen to me. I don't care about how you earn your living."

Her eyes rounded in surprise. "You don't?"

"I don't. All I care about is hearing everything you know about Salem Nabulsi."

"I don't know much," she said.

At which point, Oscar, once again, stuck in his oar. "Me? I know nothing. I gave him his mail, I collected the money for his room, and we exchanged greetings. That was it. We never had a conversation of any—"

"Shut up, Oscar," Gonçalves said.

Oscar shut up.

"Now," he said to Malu, "start at the beginning, and tell me everything you remember."

"I never saw him before he sat down next to me on the bus," she said.

"Which bus? When?"

"A bus from Foz do Iguaçu to São Paulo. Maybe three months ago. I . . . um . . . go back and forth quite a bit, so it's kind of hard to. . ."

"Yes, yes, I understand. Go on."

"He was polite," she said, regaining her equilibrium and anxious, now, to please him, "but he wasn't talkative."

"What did you discuss?"

She took a while to think about it, finally said, "I can't remember us really *discussing* anything. It was more like me asking questions and him giving me one and two-word answers. Except, once, he asked me where I lived in São Paulo, and I told him about this place. He said he needed somewhere to stay, and asked if there were any free rooms. I knew about one, where the lady had moved out the week before, and I wasn't sure if Oscar had rented it, so I suggested he come with me and ask."

"*Muchisimas gracias, Doña Malu,*" Oscar said.

She looked at him. "Didn't you hear the policeman, Oscar? He told you to shut up!"

"Did he say why he was coming to São Paulo?" Gonçalves asked.

"The same reason we all do, to look for work. All of us, that is, except for a few rich bastards who have the money to buy hospedarias and suck the blood of poor working people by charging too goddamned much for their rooms."

"Hey," Oscar said.

* * *

"You search his room?" Hector asked.

Gonçalves shook his head. He was back at the office, reporting on what he'd learned. "I didn't want to run a risk of contaminating the scene, so I called Lefkowitz."

"And he just called me," Mara interjected, crossing the threshold. "He found prints that match the three partials from the crime scene."

Hector rapped his knuckles on his desk. "Good."

"It gets better." She held up the file she'd been carrying. "We received Salem's identity records. There were prints on those as well. They all match."

"That's it then. Salem Nabulsi is our bomber. How about those calls from his cell phone?"

"The number he called regularly was, as we suspected, a pay phone."

"As *you* suspected. Located where?"

"On San Blas, right in the heart of Ciudad del Este's main shopping district. It's one of the busiest streets in the city."

"Damn," Hector said. "Well, that's no help. How about the other one?"

"Registered to a guy by the name of Barir Nabulsi."

"Salem's father?"

"That would be my guess. He lives at the same address Salem used when he applied for his identity card."

"I wonder," Gonçalves said, "if Barir was in on it."

"Only one way to find out," Hector said.

Chapter Ten

"WE'LL BE ABLE TO cover more ground," Silva said as they were finishing breakfast, "if we split up."

"Anything you like," Arnaldo said, "as long as you take the widows. I hate doing the widows."

"Who doesn't?"

"But we have a deal?"

"We have a deal. You can leave Bruna and Senhora Cataldo to me. I'll see them first off."

"Bless you."

"But I'll want you with me when I speak to Stella Saldana."

"Damn. Why?"

"Because she's likely to be elected, and the Director will expect us to give her the full gubernatorial treatment. I'll do the talking. Your role will be to bow, scrape and look subservient."

"None of which I'm very good at."

"Just try your best. I'll tackle Bruna first thing this morning. While I'm there, why don't you go talk to that witness, Nora Tasca?"

"Okay. And afterwards?"

"The Saldanas. You speak to Plínio's brother. I'll take his father."

"Didn't Serpa advise us to stay away from those two?"

"He did," Silva said with a smile. "And since when do we take advice from Braulio Serpa?"

WHEN HER mother ushered Silva in to see her, Bruna was seated on a couch, legs tucked under her, staring at a wall.

It hadn't been six months since last they'd met, but she looked ten years older.

"Bruna," he said.

"Mario."

She uncurled herself and stood up. He came forward and embraced her.

"I am so, so sorry," he said.

They held each other for a moment.

"Please," she said. "Sit."

She pointed him to a chair and sat down. Her mother asked if they wanted coffee, and when both refused, excused herself and left the room.

"They told me you were there," Bruna said.

"In the hospital?"

She nodded.

"Yes," he said. "Arnaldo and I."

"Arnaldo Nunes? He's here? In Curitiba?"

"He'll be coming to see you by and by."

"He always acts so big and tough," she said, "but he's really a pussycat. Tell him to come. Tell him I won't make it too hard on him."

"I'll tell him."

There was a box of tissues on the armrest. She took one and blew her nose.

"You saw?" she said. "You saw what they did to my Nestor's head?"

"I did."

"I made them take the bandage off and show me the wound."

"They only hit him once, Bruna."

"So he didn't suffer? Is that what you're saying?"

"It's true, Bruna. Just one blow, one that would surely have rendered him unconscious. After that . . . it would have been quick. He wouldn't have felt a thing."

She took another tissue and used it to wipe her eyes.

"Get them, Mario," she said. "Whoever did it, get them for me."

"I'll get them, Bruna."

"Promise?"

"I promise."

"Good." She sniffed and raised her chin. "How can I help?"

"You feel up to talking?"

"If it helps you to find who did it, there's nothing I'd rather do. You think it was connected to Plínio's murder?"

"What do *you* think?"

She shook her head. "I don't think anything at this point. I'm numb. What have you done since you got here?"

"Spoken to Braulio Serpa and made an attempt to speak to Nestor. Nothing more."

"Serpa? Why did you start with him?"

"Because I was told to."

"Oh. So it was like that, was it?"

"It was like that. We were sent to investigate the Saldana assassination. Serpa claims he was the one responsible for calling us in. He also claims that neither the governor, nor any of his people, would have involved themselves in the plot."

"Braulio Serpa is a mendacious, despicable human being. He hasn't got an honest bone in his body, and he's Governor Abbas's man to his fingertips. Under normal circumstances, I wouldn't give credence to anything he said."

"But?"

"He's probably right. Anyone with half a brain would have been able to predict Stella would step in if anything happened to her husband. And also predict that, if she did, she'd win by a landslide. I can't believe this, Mario. Ten days ago, Plínio, Stella, Nestor and I were all on top of the world, having the time of our lives. Now Plínio and Nestor are dead, and Stella and I are widows. I just can't get my head around it. It's a nightmare."

"I can't imagine how painful it must be."

"Keep talking, Mario. It helps."

"Did Nestor tell you about our previous visit? The last time Arnaldo and I were here in Curitiba?"

"Last summer? When you came to investigate those bank robberies?"

"Yes."

She nodded.

"And did he tell you we had suspicions about Serpa being involved in the crimes?"

She nodded again. "That too."

"Serpa obstructed our investigation at every turn. He made no secret of the fact that he wanted to see us gone. And, when we finally caught up with the bank robbers, his men killed them. Resisting arrest, they said."

"Nestor told me. He also said Serpa couldn't get you and Arnaldo out of Paraná fast enough."

"True. But this time, he claims, it's different. This time, he's offering complete cooperation."

"All he's doing is taking care of number one. He knows he'll be out on his ear as soon as Stella takes office, and that there won't be a decent job for him in this country if he's fired with Plínio's unsolved murder still hanging over his head."

"He admitted as much."

"Not that he has to worry about getting another job any-time soon. He's probably taken enough in bribes to set him up for the next twenty years. Still, if he's willing to help. . . ."

"I don't want his help, Bruna."

"Why not? Why not accept any help you can get—no matter who it comes from?"

"We have differing agendas, he and I. My concern is to find out who's behind the murders."

"And his isn't?"

"Not if Governor Abbas had anything to do with it."

"And you think he did?"

"I'm not excluding anyone at the moment."

"So you're going to keep Braulio out of the loop?"

"I am."

"He won't like it."

"I don't care whether he likes it or not."

Bruna smiled. It was a wan smile, but it was a smile nonetheless, the first since he'd arrived. "You never change, do you?" she said. "Have you formed any impressions up to now?"

"It's pretty obvious that Plínio's was a contract killing. From what I've seen, it appears as if Nestor's being wounded was . . . collateral damage, the killer trying to protect himself."

"That's what the people who've seen the videos tell me: a contract killing and Cataldo shooting Nestor because Nestor shot him first."

"You didn't watch any of the recordings?"

"No. I couldn't bear to. How about . . . what happened to Nestor in the hospital. Who could have done that? And why?"

"I'm still clueless, I'm afraid."

"Any idea, as yet, about who might have given Cataldo the contract?"

"No. But Serpa suggested someone."

"Who?"

"Lúcio Saldana."

"Lúcio?" She looked surprised. "Plínio's brother? Serpa can't be serious."

"You don't buy it?"

"Lúcio is a nasty piece of work, just like his father, but he's no killer. Forget Lúcio."

"All right. Let's say we forget Lúcio and we forget Abbas—"

She held up a hand. "Unless. . . ."

"Unless what?"

"How about if Plínio had the goods on Abbas? How about if he'd discovered something so bad it would destroy Abbas's political career forever, not just set it back four or eight years? How about if it would send him to prison? Now, *that* would have been a reason for Abbas to kill him, no matter what the backlash might have been."

"A possibility. Here's another one: a motive rooted in the past, maybe even in the distant past."

"Like what?"

"I don't know. An old grudge maybe?"

Bruna thought for a moment and said, "There's a man you could talk to, a man who knew them all back then."

"Before you did?"

"Before. And, down through the years, he's stayed in close touch with all of them."

"Who?"

"Diogo Mariano. A professor they had in law school. Wait."

She stood up and left the room. While she was gone, her mother stuck her head in the door and repeated her offer of coffee. Again, Silva refused. She smiled and disappeared. A moment later, Bruna came back, carrying a piece of paper.

"Diogo's contact numbers," she said. "He still works at the law school."

Silva put the paper in his pocket. "Thanks. Anything else that occurs to you?"

She hesitated. "I'm not sure it's relevant."

"Nevertheless, I'd like to hear it."

"Something was worrying him."

"Nestor? He never struck me as a worrier."

"That's just the point. He wasn't. He was, if anything, a fatalist. If something was going to happen, he'd say, it's going to happen, and it doesn't make sense to worry about it."

Silva nodded. "I can hear him saying it."

"Add to that the fact that Nestor never kept secrets. Not from me."

"Never?"

"I take that back. There was one other time. But I wheedled the truth out of him. I would have done the same this time, if they hadn't killed him."

"What was it the last time?"

"You remember when we were living in Foz do Iguaçu, just before he resigned from the Federal Police?"

"I do."

"He was threatened by a man in Paraguay, a smuggler who told him he was going to kill him if he didn't play ball and take a bribe."

"I had no idea."

"It scared the hell out of me."

"I'm sure it did."

"I can't tell you how relieved I was when Plínio offered him the job, and we packed up and moved out of there."

"Who was the fellow in Paraguay? Do you remember his name?"

"Remember it? I'll never forget it."

Silva took out his notebook and a pen. "Give it to me," he said.

"Al-Fulan. His name was Jamil Al-Fulan."

Chapter Eleven

CURITIBA'S MUNICIPAL MARKET WAS a noisy place, so noisy that Arnaldo would surely have missed Silva's call if his phone hadn't been set to vibrate.

"You talk to the Tasca woman?" the Chief Inspector wanted to know.

"Not yet. This place is a madhouse. I'm still trying to find her. What's up?"

Silva told him about Diogo Mariano, the law school professor, and assigned him the interview.

Arnaldo found what passed for a quiet corner, called Mariano and made an appointment. Then he resumed his search for the woman whose face he remembered from the videos.

He found her unloading boxes of broccoli from a truck.

"It's gonna cost you," she said when Arnaldo explained who he was and what he wanted.

"Wait a minute," Arnaldo said. "Are you suggesting I *pay* you?"

Nora's biceps rippled as she shifted another box. The boxes were made of wood, and they were heavy, but she was moving them from truck bed to hand trolley as if they were feather pillows.

"I'm not *suggesting* anything," she said. "I'm telling it like it is. I get paid by the box, not by the hour. If I take time off to talk to you, it costs me money."

"How about you do what you're doing right now? Talk while you work?"

She topped off the stack with a final box. "How about you go question somebody who hasn't got a living to earn?"

She tilted her trolley and hurried off.

"Hang on a minute, Senhora Tasca—"

"Senhorita," she said over her shoulder.

"Senhorita," he echoed, taking off after her. "After Plínio was shot you gave interviews to every TV station in Curitiba. How come you had time to talk to them, but you haven't got time to talk to me?"

"I didn't have time, I *made* time. And I made it because they paid me. Same thing applies to you."

Three meters away by now, she was approaching shouting distance. Arnaldo was forced to raise his voice. "They were journalists, for Christ's sake. I'm a cop."

"I don't care if you're the President of the Republic."

He was moving fast, but so was she. The distance wasn't closing. "You supported Plínio. You wanted to see him elected. Don't you want to see justice done?"

Above the din, he heard her contemptuous snort. "Justice *has* been done. The guy who killed Plínio is dead. You want to waste your time on conspiracy theories, you go right ahead, but there's no way you're going to waste mine. You want it; you pay for it, just like everybody else."

"I could arrest you for this."

He delivered the line at a volume that caused a couple of people to turn and look at him, but the threat didn't faze her in the slightest.

"Try it, and see how much information you get."

At a near run by now, he tried to come up beside her, but she frustrated his attempt by deftly maneuvering her trolley through a gap between two crates of cauliflowers. He was forced to drop back.

"How much?" he called out as the distance between them began to widen again.

"Twenty Reais for twenty minutes."

That, too, was delivered over her shoulder.

"That's robbery. You don't earn a Real a minute."

She sensed surrender, stopped and turned to face him. "And I don't witness an assassination every day either," she said. "That's the price. Take it or leave it."

He took it.

She unloaded the broccoli, received a chit, and they adjourned to a café up in the eaves overlooking the stalls.

Below, throngs of purposeful housewives were elbowing their way through tightly-packed corridors. Many were trailed by kids from the local *favelas*, there to earn a few coins by carrying their shopping bags, and all were being beset by merchants competing for their attention.

Over here, Senhora, over here! Mangos. Ripe, juicy mangoes, three for two Reais!

Look Dona! Sirloin, just seven a kilo! Seven a kilo!

Sardines! Sardines! Get your fresh sardines! Fresh from the sea!

The place she'd chosen was almost as noisy as the floor below, but Nora Tasca's booming voice cut right through the racket.

"Coffee first," she said, enthroning herself at the head of a long table. "Milk with three sugars."

When Arnaldo got back with their coffee, she rubbed her thumb against her index and middle fingers. "And now," she said, "the money."

He put down his plastic cup, opened his wallet and fished out two ten-Real notes. She put them into a leather pouch suspended from her waist and pointed at a four-sided clock atop a tall column.

"At eight minutes after the hour," she said, "your time is up. It was like this: Plínio had just climbed down from the stage, and—"

"I saw the whole thing on video," Arnaldo said. "And since I've only got twenty minutes—"

She glanced at the clock. "Right now," she said, "you've got about nineteen, but if you want to pay for another twenty, I'll give you a discount. Fifteen Reais."

"Maybe, if we need it, but for now, just let me ask some questions, okay?"

"Okay. But, if you don't want me to tell you what I saw, what do you—"

"What I want you to do," Arnaldo said, "is to shut up and listen."

"Be careful about how you talk to me, Senhor Cop. You don't want to get me mad."

"Look, Senhora Tasca—"

"Senhorita."

"*Senhorita* Tasca, all I want you to do is to answer my questions. Don't offer anything unless I ask you about it. Can we agree on that?"

She took a slug of her coffee. "Sure. It's your money."

"Thank you. Now, was there anything you saw, or heard, that wasn't in the television coverage?"

"How about smelled?" she said.

"Smelled?"

"That killer, Cataldo? He was sweating like a pig, stunk to high heaven, must have been nervous as hell. He came barging in, all elbows, hit me right here." She put a hand on her ribs. "But the little prick had no idea who he was dealing with. I gave him as good as I got and then some. Too bad I didn't look his way just a little bit earlier. If I had, I woulda seen him pointing that gun. And I would have broken his arm, and shoved the gun up his ass. Fucking traitor!"

"Traitor?"

She drank more coffee and nodded.

"You heard me. Didn't you read what they said about him in the newspapers? They said he made a big deal out of supporting Plínio, said he even went out and campaigned for him. And then he turned around and killed him. So was he a traitor, or wasn't he?"

"Yeah," Arnaldo said. "I suppose he was. Why do you think he did it?"

She shook her head and cast her eyes skyward, as if asking God for patience. "*Duh!* What kind of a cop are you?"

"A federal cop. And I'll thank you to keep a civil tongue in your mouth. Just answer the question."

A sigh. "Money, of course. He did it for money."

"And who do you think paid him?"

"You're really dense, aren't you?"

"Senhora Tasca—"

"How many times do I have to tell you? It's *Senhorita* Tasca. Talk about dumb cops."

"*Senhorita* Tasca, then. And I already told *you* to keep a civil—"

"Come on. Was that a stupid question, or wasn't it? Who paid him? Abbas, of course. Who else?"

"Abbas says no, says he didn't do it."

"Of course he does! Would you expect him to? But he was behind it all right. You can be sure of that."

"Let's assume, for a moment, he was."

"No *assume* about it. He was. Full stop."

She rapped her knuckles on the wooden table. They came down within a few centimeters of Arnaldo's as-yet-untouched cup, causing some of the contents to spill over the rim. She didn't apologize, and he chose to ignore it.

"My question remains," he said. "Was there anything you saw, or heard, that wasn't in the television coverage?"

"Are you kidding? Do you know how many cameras there

were? They covered it from every angle. What you saw is what I saw. Cataldo put a bullet into Plínio right here"—she put a forefinger on her forehead—"and it blew out the back of his head. Plínio hadn't hit the ground before his bodyguard had his gun out. I was scared to death. I thought he was pointing it at me. *Bang*, he fired a shot. I heard Cataldo grunt. And then Cataldo shot a second time and blood spurted out of the bodyguard. And the bodyguard fired again, and Cataldo's blood spurted all over me. That was it. End of story."

"How about the others? Did anyone say anything? How about Plínio?"

"With a bullet right through the middle of his forehead? You're kidding, right?"

"Nestor?"

"The bodyguard? He cursed. At least, I think it was a curse. People were screaming. There was a lot of noise."

"And Cataldo? Did you hear him say anything?"

She thought about it. "Well," she said, "there was one thing."

"What?"

"Just after he shot Plínio, he said, 'Noooooo!'"

"He said no?"

She shook her head. "Not like that. It was more like a moan, more drawn out. 'Nooooo!' Like that."

"What do you suppose that was about?"

She shrugged. "How should I know? You're the cop. You figure it out."

Chapter Twelve

JESSICA CATALDO'S KITCHEN WAS a homey space, filled with the comforting smells of spices and coffee, bathed in bright sunlight shining through chintz curtains—and furnished with a table she could use to distance herself from unwelcome visitors. She sat on one side and motioned Silva to a seat on the other. A coffee service, already in place, served as an additional barrier between them.

"Sugar?" she said. "Sweetener?"

"Just black, thanks," he said.

Her hand trembled when she poured. The cup rattled in the saucer.

"I'm afraid you've wasted your time by coming here," she said. "I've already told your colleagues everything I know."

Her reproachful look put him in mind of a puppy someone had kicked.

"They're not my colleagues, Senhora Cataldo. They work for the State of Paraná. I work for the federal government."

She shrugged, as if to say she made no distinction.

After a moment of silence, he went on. "Where did your husband get the pistol? There's no record of him owning a firearm."

"He never did, and he never would. Julio hated guns. He supported the legislation to ban them. Where he got that one from is a mystery to me."

"Where were you when you heard the news?"

Without taking her eyes off him, she gestured toward the counter in front of the window. "There, at the sink, washing dishes. The children were in the living room, watching cartoons. They interrupted the program to show Julio being shot. The children saw it and began to scream."

"My God!" Silva said. "That's horrible."

"I ran into the living room," she said. "I don't know how many times the children saw his neck gushing blood before I got there. They were playing the scene over and over in rapid succession. They said, later, that some of the material was too violent to show on television. But that, apparently, just applied to Plínio. They didn't seem to have any compunction at all about showing what happened to my husband."

Silva visualized the scene. It turned his stomach.

"Where are your children now?" he asked.

"With my sister in Florianopolis."

"Has she sought counseling for them?"

"They're seeing a psychologist."

"A psychologist will help, but what they need most is their mother."

"There's nowhere I'd rather be, but the police won't let me leave Curitiba, and I couldn't keep them here. The other children at school, the people on the street, the telephone calls. . . ." She threw up her hands.

Silva took out his notepad. "Give me the contact information for your sister in Florianopolis."

She did, spelling out the street address, looking at his hand as he wrote.

"You can leave as soon as we're finished," Silva said. "Should further questions arise, I'll contact you there."

She leaned forward. Silva thought she was going to grasp his hand, but she grasped the coffee pot instead. Her nails, he noticed, were bitten to the quick.

"Thank you," she said. "Are you a father yourself?"

"I was, Senhora. My son died of leukemia a number of years ago."

"I'm sorry."

She hadn't been expecting either sympathy, or confidences, from a policeman. It seemed to shake her equilibrium even more than it had been shaken already. She bit her lip and said, "More coffee?"

He shook his head.

She leaned back, not taking coffee for herself either.

"It's my understanding," Silva said, "that your husband was a supporter of Senhor Saldana's."

"You see? That's another thing that doesn't make any sense. Julio used to call Plínio the *only honest politician in the State*. An exaggeration, I know, but that's what he used to say."

As she warmed to him, the tendons in her neck, steel wires under her pale skin, began to relax. Silva took his time phrasing the next question.

"Did he know Plínio personally?"

She nodded. "He did. Not well, but he'd met him."

"Did Julio often support political candidates?"

"No, but he was a great one for causes. I mentioned the abolition of firearms. He also fought for the preservation of the rainforest, recycling, the rights of our native peoples, transparency in government, saving the whales, all sorts of things."

"Some people," Silva suggested, "turn to violence in defense of their beliefs."

She shook her head. "Not him. Never him. Ask anyone who knew him. I know you're going to find this hard to believe after what he's done, but he was a peaceful man. Before this, I never saw him raise a hand against anyone."

"It's also my understanding you were in need of money. I don't mean to pry, but I have to ask."

"We *were* in need of money. I still am. Julio had life insurance, but the insurance company has no intention of paying me anything. They're making a case it was suicide. They don't pay out in cases of suicide."

"Suicide?"

"That's what they're calling it. They're saying that Julio couldn't have possibly believed he'd be able to commit murder in the presence of an armed bodyguard and come out of it alive, that his intention was to die in the attempt. I can't fight it. I don't have any money in the bank, and no lawyer will take the case without money up front."

Silva had once intended to be a lawyer, but being a cop had brought about a shift in his values. These days, with a few noteworthy exceptions, he couldn't stomach people who'd chosen the legal profession. His expression showed it.

"If you don't mind my asking," he said, "how did you get into difficulty in the first place?"

She shook her head. "I don't mind," she said. "In fact, I'm glad you asked."

He gave her a quizzical look. "Why?"

"Because I'm trying to explain to you what Julio was all about, and there's no better illustration of the kind of man he was."

"Go on."

"He quit his job almost a year ago because he disagreed with the way his company was cheating the government out of taxes. Can you imagine? At least half of the companies in this country cheat the government out of taxes, but my husband, the crusader, thought it was wrong. So he resigned because of it. He even blew the whistle to the authorities."

Silva shook his head at the naïveté of the man. He was quite sure he knew the answer to his next question, but he asked it anyway.

"What happened then?"

"The company paid off the tax officials, and a judge, and that was the end of it. For the company, that is, not for us. Julio made no secret of what he'd done. After that, what kind of a chance do you think he had of getting a new job?"

"Not a good one."

"How about none at all? We went through all of our savings, we took another mortgage on the house, and I even borrowed money from my parents. But you know what?"

"What?"

"Right up until the last, Julio remained convinced he'd done the right thing. He kept saying he'd only want to work for a company that would respect what he did."

She snorted.

"I sense," Silva said, "that you found his attitude . . . how shall I put this . . . excessively idealistic."

"That, Chief Inspector, is an understatement. We had . . . words about it. I told him to think of his children."

"And he said?"

"That he *was* thinking of his children. That he wanted them to inherit a better Brazil. And to get there, we'd have to make sacrifices, we'd have to put egotism aside and work for the common good."

Silva was beginning to form the image of a prissy, better-than-thou do-gooder. He didn't think he would have liked Julio Cataldo. But his wife was right about one thing: her late husband didn't fit the profile of a killer.

"Can you see a man like that picking up a gun and shooting someone?" she said, echoing his thought. "Particularly someone he respected and wanted to see elected?"

Silva rubbed his chin. "No," he said, "I can't. And yet it's incontestable that he did."

"Yes," she said. "It is. But *why*? That's what I want to know."

Jessica looked, for a moment, as if she was about to burst into tears. But then she took a deep breath—and the moment passed.

"During those last days of his life," Silva said, "how was his state of mind?"

She took a pensive sip of her coffee. "That's another curious thing," she said, after replacing the cup in its saucer. "For about a month he'd been brooding, having dark thoughts, sometimes sleeping too much, other times not at all. Then, a week or so before the mortgage payment was due, he came home radiant. He'd been out all day, looking for work, and I thought he'd found a job, that's how happy he was. But he said no. It was just that he'd dropped by Plínio's campaign headquarters on the way home. And he'd been able to talk to the candidate himself."

"And that, in itself, caused him to become . . . radiant."

"It did."

"And you?"

"I told him he should be worrying less about elections and more about feeding his family. He said he never ceased to think about feeding his family, and I should show more faith. He quoted the twenty-third Psalm."

"'*The Lord is my shepherd, I shall not want.*' That one?"

"Yes, that one. I told him I'd love to believe it, but that the Lord hadn't done much for us recently. Then he said something strange."

"What did he say, Senhora?"

"He said, 'Just wait.'"

Silva raised an eyebrow. "*Just wait?*"

"That was it. Just wait. It was all I could get out of him. And then, at breakfast, on the day he died, he said something even more enigmatic."

"Which was?"

"He reached across the table, took my hand and said, 'Jessica, this is going to be a tough day, but don't let it shake your faith.'"

"What did he mean by *a tough day?*"

"I don't know."

"Didn't you ask him?"

"Of course I did. He wouldn't say."

"How long was this after his visit to Plínio's campaign headquarters?"

"About a week. I remember because the mortgage was due the next day."

"So he made this reference to a tough day. And what happened next?"

"He went out, shot Plínio Saldana and got himself killed."

Chapter Thirteen

DIOGO MARIANO LOOKED TO be in his mid-to-late forties. Arnaldo had been expecting someone older—and said so.

"I was the youngest professor they had," Mariano explained, "twelve years older than the men, only nine years older than Stella."

Arnaldo was surprised. "Stella was the eldest?"

Mariano smiled. "She doesn't look it, does she?"

Arnaldo shrugged. "I couldn't say. I never met the lady myself, only seen her in photographs."

"Well, take my word for it, she doesn't." Mariano leaned back in his chair, getting comfortable. "Plínio, now, he was the opposite. He always looked older. I think it had something to do with his demeanor. A serious guy, he was, even back then. Not Stella. It was rare to see her without a smile. She used to light up my classroom every time she came in." He smiled a rueful smile. "I wasn't married then, and I had a crush on her. But we've got strict policies here. We're not allowed to date our students."

Arnaldo smiled back. "Odds are, you would have had a better chance than he did."

Mariano shook his head. "Not likely."

"No? Being their professor and all? Besides, three years can seem like another generation when a woman is that young."

"True. But it never seemed to make a difference to Stella. She was crazy about him."

"Different graduating classes?"

Again, Mariano shook his head. "Stella came late to law school. First, she tried nursing."

A wind jostled the leaves outside the window. Shadows danced across the professor's desk. He frowned, as if he found it distracting, and stood to adjust the blinds.

"The key to understanding them," he said, resuming his seat, "is to get a grip on what made them tick. They cared about people. They wanted to *make a difference*. They used that phrase all the time. *Make a difference*."

"As *lawyers*? They wanted to *make a difference* as lawyers? No offense, but. . ."

Mariano raised an eyebrow. "What?"

Arnaldo backpedalled. "Wouldn't Stella have had a better shot at helping people if she'd remained a nurse?"

"If she'd been suited for it, I daresay she would have. But human suffering was something she couldn't deal with on a one-on-one basis. She hated seeing people in pain. She hated seeing people die."

"From nursing to law is still one hell of a jump. It's not . . . uh . . . a profession I associate with altruism. Would it be fair to say most of your students are in it for the money?"

"Yes. But those three were different. They concluded, early on, that the host of problems this country faces could be distilled into three major areas of concern." The professor counted them off on his fingers: "Public health, public education, and public safety."

"And they thought the best way to tackle those problems was through the law?"

"They did. And if money came into their calculations at all, which I really don't think it did, there would have been only one reason for it: a conviction they could use money to do good."

"So it's not a fairy tale. Kids like that actually exist in law schools?"

Mariano took the question seriously. "They're not as rare

as you might think. But kids as talented and intelligent as those three *are* rare. Unfortunately, few are able to keep their early values intact."

"They sell out?"

"Your question, Agent Nunes, betrays your age. We no longer live in idealistic times. Kids don't use that phrase anymore."

"So maybe they call it something different, but it's what they do? They sell out?"

Mariano sighed. "The best and the brightest, the ones that started out with an ideal of service, fall, all too often, into a trap. It's like this, you see: because they *are* the best and the brightest, they get the best offers. And they often wind up taking jobs at the big corporate firms, the ones that pay big salaries. They tell each other that they're only going to do it for a little while, long enough to put a bit of money in the bank."

"But?"

"They generally get derailed."

Outside, in the corridor, someone knocked.

"Come," Mariano said.

A pretty brunette in her early twenties opened his office door and paused on the threshold.

"Sorry," she said, looking back-and-forth between the professor and Arnaldo. "Am I early?"

Mariano glanced at his watch.

"A little," he said. "Give me another ten minutes."

"Sure," she said.

She was juggling an armful of books, and it took her a couple of seconds to back out and close the door again.

"Where were we?" Mariano said when she was gone.

"The best and the brightest generally get derailed," Arnaldo prompted. "By what?"

Mariano shrugged. "Fancy cars, a summer house, a taste for the things money can buy."

"But not those three? They didn't get derailed?"

"No. They continued to view success as being defined by service to the community, not the accumulation of wealth."

"Good for them."

"You and I agree about that, but not everyone does. One day, about halfway through Plínio's third semester, I got a visit from his father."

"Orestes Saldana?"

"Yes. He sat there, where you're sitting right now, and called his son a—and this is a direct quote—'*bleeding heart liberal with his head up his ass.*' He went on to accuse me of being—and, again, this is a quote—'*responsible for letting the damned fool lose his way.*'"

"Whoa! And how did you answer that?"

"I suggested he should have been proud of his son, not angry at him."

"But he wouldn't have it?"

"No, and I wasn't surprised. I'd heard all about Orestes Saldana long before he appeared in my office. He and Plínio were polar opposites. Orestes is a man of no compassion, a man who, forgive the vulgarity, doesn't give a shit about other human beings. He doesn't like, or respect, anyone who isn't as stinking rich as he is. There wasn't a chance in hell I could make him understand, so I didn't even try. I just sat there, staring at him, until he ran out of steam."

"And then?"

"He concluded by saying he was going to teach us both a lesson—and stormed out."

"Did he follow up on the threat?"

"He did. He tried to get me fired."

"Which, obviously, didn't work."

"Not even when he tried to bribe the board by offering them a grant. And then he cut his son off from the paternal money flow."

"So how did Plínio manage to finish his education?"

"His grandmother stepped in."

"Maternal grandmother?"

Mariano waved a finger of dissent. "Paternal, Ariana Saldana. Ariana hates her son as much as she loved her grandson, which was a lot. She gave Plínio the money he needed."

"It must have pissed the old man off."

"Oh, it did. And Orestes Saldana is the wrong man to piss off. He hired a flock of lawyers, paid off a judge, had his mother declared mentally incompetent and institutionalized her."

"Not nice."

"No, Agent Nunes. Not nice. And a complete and total fabrication. The old lady was as sharp as a tack, still is. Fortunately for her, and for Plínio, she'd already given him the money he needed in one lump sum. By the time the judgment came down, and Orestes assumed control of her bank accounts, Plínio's education was assured."

"I'd like to talk to the old lady. Have you got a number for her?"

"Sure."

The telephone on Mariano's desk rang, but he ignored it while he looked up the number and made a note of it. After a while, the telephone stopped ringing, but then, just before he handed Arnaldo the paper, it started up again.

"You want to take that?" Arnaldo asked.

The professor shook his head. "It'll go to voice mail. So, where were we?"

"You were saying Plínio's education was assured."

"Right," Mariano gathered his thoughts and continued, "As soon as Plínio had his diploma, and was admitted to the bar, he managed to have Ariana released into his custody. Then he appealed the judgment."

"Did he win?"

"He won. The case came up in front of an honest judge. Ariana got most of her money back, and Plínio went on to marry Stella."

"Who, by that time, had graduated as well?"

"Yes. Her sister, Joana, was a teacher, and she told her their union needed a lawyer, so Stella volunteered."

"And Nestor became a cop."

"Exactly. First with the Civil Police here in Paraná, then, later, with you fellows."

"And Plínio?"

"He was the one with the most charisma. They chose him to be the guy they'd put up as their political face. While still in law school, he ran for the presidency of the student body— and won. As soon as they graduated, they started working to get him elected to the State legislature. And he won there as well."

"That quickly?"

"It wasn't quick. It took four years. I skipped a few details for the sake of brevity. From that time on, they never wavered. In the course of the next ten years, they always kept their eyes on their three goals, the three ways they wanted to *make a difference*. Remember them?"

Once again, Mariano's telephone started to ring. Once again, he ignored it.

"Public health, public education and public safety," Arnaldo said. And then, pointing at the telephone, "You're a popular guy."

"Goes with the job," Mariano said. "That's right, health,

education and safety. Plínio's battle to get his grandmother released wound up teaching him a good deal about the health care system. Over the next decade, he became a recognized expert on it. Towards the end, he was the guy they always turned to when they were looking for a chairman to head-up a committee on the subject. Stella, working as a lawyer for the teacher's union, became their specialist on education, and Nestor, working with the police, made it his business to learn everything there was to know on the subject of law-enforcement."

"So they turned themselves into a kind of self-contained panel of experts."

"Uh-huh. And on the day Plínio won the nomination, Stella and Nestor quit their jobs and signed on to help elect him governor. Stella was to have been State Secretary of Education and Nestor was going to be the State Secretary of Public Safety."

"So what happens now? Now that Plínio and Nestor are dead?"

"Stella will win. Odds are, her sister will become State Secretary of Education. With Nestor dead, I have no idea who'll become the State Secretary for Public Safety, but of one thing I can assure you: Braulio Serpa will be out on his ear the day Stella takes office."

"I think he knows that already."

"I'm sure he does, the venal bastard."

"Any other appointments you know of?"

"Just one: the governor's Chief of Staff."

"Who's that going to be?"

"*That*," the Professor smiled, "is going to be me."

Chapter Fourteen

"So you're Mario Silva, are you?" Orestes Saldana said. The wiry little man with the sour face was looking at Silva like a housewife might look at a cockroach she'd found in her sugar bowl. "I've heard all about you."

"Really?" Silva said. "From whom?"

"Orlando Muniz."

Two peas in a pod, Silva thought, *arrogant, rich bastards who think they're above the law.* Whatever Muniz had told Saldana, one thing was certain: it wasn't flattering.

"I'm a busy man," Saldana snapped, confirming Silva's conviction, "What do you want?"

"I'm investigating the murder of your son."

"What about it?"

"Forgive me, Senhor Saldana, but you sound. . ."

"What?"

"How shall I put this? Dismissive? Uninterested?"

"I *am* uninterested."

Silva's life as a cop had brought him into contact with a lot of callous people, but this was too much, even for him.

"This is your *son* we're talking about."

"Only in a biological sense," Saldana said. "In every other respect, he was no son of mine. We didn't have a single cordial conversation in the last thirteen years of his life."

"Thirteen years?"

"You heard me. So, as far as I'm concerned, he's no deader today than he was back in law school."

"But—"

"If you're about to start spouting sentimental crap," Saldana said, "save your breath. What do you expect from me? Crocodile tears? I'm not that kind of man. If a son isn't loyal, he's no damned good. Plínio wasn't loyal. In my book, that's worse than having no son at all."

Silva, who missed his dead son every day of his life, was appalled. "Is loyalty the sole criterion? Doesn't love come into the equation?"

Saldana moved a hand in front of his face, as if he was waving away a pesky mosquito.

"Not into *my* equation, it doesn't. This business is my life's work. When Plínio was a kid, it put a roof over his head, food on his plate, clothes on his back. But what did he do as soon as he got into the state legislature? He tried to bite the hand that fed him, that's what!"

"I don't understand what you mean by—"

"Seventy-one percent of my construction company's billings," Saldana cut in, "derive from contracts with the State of Paraná. Seventy-one percent. And a good deal of the rest comes to me *because* my company works for the state. First thing Plínio did when he got elected was to propose a system of sealed bids. Sealed bids! No room to maneuver! Lowest bid gets the job! It was all I could do to stave it off."

"But you did?"

"I did, but it wasn't cheap. And now his whore of a widow is telling everyone she's going to introduce sealed bids by gubernatorial decree as soon as she gets elected. Bitch!"

"Business concerns aside—"

"Business concerns aside? *Business concerns aside?* Jesus Christ, would you say that if it was *your* business?"

"There is a question of justice—"

"Justice? Justice has been done. The guy who shot Plínio is dead."

"The man who pulled the trigger is dead, but the person who enlisted him—"

"Who's to say anyone enlisted him? Who's to say Cataldo wasn't just a fanatic with an axe to grind?"

"He might have been, but—"

"But you prefer to cook up a conspiracy theory? Cataldo as Oswald and Plínio as Kennedy, is that it?"

"In this case, a conspiracy is possible, even likely."

"I. Don't. Care." Saldana leaned forward and punched his desk with his forefinger as he enunciated each word. "I don't care about Plínio, and I don't care who killed him, and I don't care why he was killed. I'm not interested in any of it."

Silva's patience with the man was exhausted. He switched to provocation. "You're not interested" he asked, "even if the person who had him murdered was your surviving son?"

"What?"

"Not even if the man who paid to have Plínio killed was Lúcio?"

Saldana snorted. "That's absolute crap!"

"Is it? The law precluded you from disinheriting either one of your sons. Plínio would have come into a great deal of money upon your death. Now, all that money is going to Lúcio. That's a pretty good motive for murder, don't you think?"

"What I think," Orestes Saldana said, narrowing his eyes, "is it's high time you left. This interview is over."

BEFORE HE could flag down a taxi, Silva's cell phone rang.

"I told you to stay away from Orestes Saldana." Braulio Serpa squawked.

"Ah, yes, now that you mention it, I do recall you saying something of that nature."

In the face of Silva's equanimity, Serpa lowered his voice—but didn't moderate his tone.

"You do, do you? Well, let me tell you this. The old bastard didn't like your attitude one damned bit. He called my boss to bitch about you."

"Governor Abbas?"

"Who else? Those two guys are as thick as thieves."

Silva saw a taxi approaching and raised a hand to flag it down.

"Some would say that's an apt comparison, Braulio."

"What?"

"Thieves."

"Goddamn it, Silva, you know what I mean. You gotta stop this shit. You're doing the same goddamned thing this time that you did the last time."

The taxi pulled over and stopped.

"Which is?"

"Sticking your nose into places where it doesn't belong. This isn't Brasilia. This is Paraná. Around here, you gotta be more circumspect."

Silva got into the back seat of the cab and slammed the door.

"Circumspect?"

"Cooperate with people, not antagonize them."

Silva signaled to continue driving in the same direction. The man behind the wheel responded with a thumbs-up and pulled away from the curb.

"Is that the reason for your call?" Silva asked. "To advise me to be more circumspect?"

"No," Serpa said, "it isn't. The reason is because he wants to talk to you."

"Who?"

"Abbas."

"Why?"

"He wants a progress report."

"I don't report to the governor of Paraná, Braulio. I report to the Director of the Federal Police."

"Not in this case, you don't. In this case, you're gonna have to make an exception."

"And why would I do that?"

"Because you're going to be told to do it. Abbas called Pontes, and Pontes will be calling Sampaio."

Sergio Pontes, the Minister of Justice, was Sampaio's boss—and Sampaio was Silva's.

Silva cursed under his breath, but Serpa must have heard him. His tone turned cheerful.

"Your appointment is for nine sharp tomorrow morning. Don't be late."

Chapter Fifteen

"AT MY AGE," ORESTES Saldana's mother said, "one retires at night with the awareness that one may not wake up in the morning. One accepts there not being anyone left, who remembers the world one lived in as a little girl. One accustoms oneself to one's infirmities. But one can never quite get used to being stabbed in the back by one's own son."

Ariana Saldana and Arnaldo were seated on the terrace of her penthouse, an extensive affair with a distant view of the Oscar Niemeyer Museum. Her maid had served them coffee and then parked herself on a sofa beyond the sliding glass doors leading to the living room. Ostensibly occupied with her knitting, it was likely the maid had chosen the spot because it was an ideal position from which to keep an attentive eye on her ninety-three-year-old mistress.

"Yes, Senhora," Arnaldo said, "I can imagine."

"Permit me to differ with you, young man," she said, "but I doubt you can."

It had been a long time since anyone had called Arnaldo Nunes a young man.

"Children," she said, "are supposed to be a solace, but the truth of the matter is my two boys never caused me anything but grief."

Arnaldo arrested the movement of his cup. "*Two?* It was my understanding Orestes was your only child."

"He wasn't. His twin brother, whom we never named, was stillborn, strangled by his umbilical cord. I used to joke with Plínio that his father had put it there so he could absorb all my attention. My son is a despicable human being. Diogo was the one who put you in touch with me. Did he tell you the story?"

Arnaldo returned his willow-patterned cup, an exquisite piece in delicate porcelain, to its matching saucer.

"Not in detail, Senhora, but he touched on the essentials."

"If it hadn't been for Plínio," she said, "I'd still be sitting in that institution—or dead. Probably dead. I didn't thrive behind bars. I felt like a caged bird."

The comparison, Arnaldo thought, was apt. Like a bird, her bones were frail, her movements swift and constant.

"Before Orestes committed me," she continued, "I owned a parrot. I thought of that creature as a member of our family, thought of him as being happy in his cage. But my time under lock and key changed that. After I was released, I took him into the rainforest and let him go. I'll never own a bird again."

"In all the time you were locked up," Arnaldo said, "the only help you got was from Plínio?"

"From Stella too. Stella's a dear girl."

"Did you appeal to your other grandson, Lúcio?"

"I did, but the pusillanimous little weasel wouldn't lift a finger. Not a finger. He was afraid of offending his father, and in one sense, he's just like him."

"What sense?"

"The only thing he's capable of loving is money. But at least Orestes has balls. Lúcio, that emasculated little turd, has none."

The foul language came as a surprise. She saw his reaction, and a smile creased her lips.

"Sometimes," she said, "in striving for what Flaubert called *le mot juste*, one cannot escape vulgarity."

"And why would one want to?" Arnaldo said.

"A bit of a vulgarian yourself, are you?"

"More than a bit," he admitted.

"Mind you," she said, "Lúcio, for all his faults, is still my grandson. The last thing I want to do is hurt him."

"Last thing, maybe, but it's still on your list, right?"

She gave a delighted laugh. "I like you, Agent Nunes. Thank you for coming to see me. I appreciate your efforts."

"*De nada*, Senhora."

"I mean it. My grandson was one of the finest human beings I've ever known. I don't say that because he was my grandson, or even because he was so good to me. I say it because he *was*. Julio Cataldo, may he rot in hell, did more than hurt me, and Stella, and a number of other people who knew and loved Plínio. He also did Paraná a tremendous disservice. In fact, he did all of Brazil a disservice. Plínio had everything it would have taken to go all the way, to go beyond the governorship, to become President of the Republic. And, if he'd succeeded, he would have made the best President of the Republic of all those I've experienced in my long lifetime."

She sat back in her chair and took a deep breath. "My grandson's death, Agent Nunes, has tired me of life. I'd like to see Stella take office before I go. And then I'm done. I have no other reason for living."

"Not even to see the person or persons responsible for Plínio's murder brought to justice?"

"That person was Julio Cataldo. And Julio Cataldo is dead."

"He's dead. But suppose he didn't act alone. Suppose someone recruited him."

"You think that's what happened?"

"I think it's possible. And so does my boss."

"What evidence, if any, do you have to support that theory?"

"No hard evidence at all. But. . . ."

"But what?"

"You know about Nestor?"

"Nestor Cambria? Plínio's friend? The one who shot Cataldo, the one who's in the hospital?"

"He's not there anymore, Senhora. Someone went into his room and murdered him."

"*Murdered* him?"

"Rendered him unconscious by striking him with something heavy, and smothered him to death with a pillow."

Her pale skin turned even paler, and she put a hand over her mouth, as if she was about to be sick. "Oh, my God," she said. "The poor, poor man. And such a nice man, too!"

"He *was* a nice man, Senhora, and a good friend of mine."

"How's his wife taking it?"

"Badly, I expect. I haven't seen her yet, but they were crazy about each other."

"You'll get the man who did it, won't you?"

"Man or woman, Senhora."

"Do you have any reason to suspect a woman?"

Stella Saldana was on their list of possibles, but Arnaldo didn't feel it was the time to mention it—or the person to mention it to. "No," he said, "no particular reason."

"Do you think the two murders might be linked? Plínio's and Nestor's?"

"It's conceivable."

"In what way?"

A clear possibility existed that Nestor was involved in a conspiracy to kill Plínio, and that someone had killed him to keep it quiet, but Arnaldo wasn't about to talk about that either.

"Sorry," he said. "It wouldn't be right for me to speculate about that."

"I understand. You're supposed to keep an open mind, so you don't want to talk to me about any suspicions you might have. But I've probably heard the same rumor you have."

"Which rumor is that, *Senhora?*"

"That Abbas had something to do with my grandson's murder. I give no credence to it. I don't think Abbas would be that stupid. Wouldn't he have foreseen that Stella would step-up in Plínio's place? Surely, he would. And then, wouldn't he have killed her as well? No, I think you can exclude Abbas from your list of suspects."

Ariana Saldana wasn't only bright, she also didn't mince words.

Arnaldo took the decision not to mince his either: "This is a stretch, Senhora, but I'm going to ask it anyway: Do you think we should be looking at your son?"

"You're suggesting Orestes killed my grandson to forestall a threat to his business?"

"Not suggesting, Senhora. Just asking if you think it might be possible."

"I think not. Orestes has assets that go far beyond his construction company. The bankruptcy of that company would hurt him, but it would hardly ruin him, no matter what he says."

"How about your other grandson, Lúcio? With Plínio dead, he stands to inherit it all."

She shook her head.

"Not Lúcio. He wouldn't have the courage."

Arnaldo rubbed his chin. "Not even to commission the job?"

"If he managed to convince himself it couldn't be traced back to him . . . well, yes, he *might* do it. Certainly, he'd have no moral reservations. He hasn't *got* any morals, that one."

"Any other ideas?"

Her answer was a long time in coming. "No," she finally said.

Chapter Sixteen

LÚCIO SALDANA'S OFFICE WAS in a modern high-rise sheathed in mirrored glass. The spacious lobby soared for two stories. The ceiling was peppered with tiny spotlights, and the floor was of a creamy, white marble. Upstairs, the elevator opened to reveal carpets of thick burgundy.

Arnaldo's initial impression was of success, luxury, expense, but that impression shifted the minute he entered Lúcio's suite.

The waiting room was empty. A two-tone chime, rather than a receptionist, greeted his arrival. The coffee table was strewn with magazines, but none were recent, all had seen hard use, and some were even lacking covers.

On a desk, next to a computer, was an appointment book. He flipped through the pages and discovered that most of them were blank. When he moved the mouse, the computer came to life—on a game of solitaire.

Two doors opened off the waiting room. Arnaldo heard footsteps approaching the closest one and moved away from the desk, just before it opened

"Whatever you're selling," the woman said, taking in his cheap suit and scuffed shoes, "we don't want any."

She was a blonde, and a pretty one, but with a minor flaw in her well-groomed façade: she'd neglected to completely close the zipper on the side of her skirt. Arnaldo had the distinct impression he'd interrupted something—and she wasn't pleased about it.

"Please, don't turn me away," he said. "I need the business. I've got a wife and fourteen children to support."

"Fourteen?" she said. "How come I don't believe you?"

"Then how about this," he said. "I'm a federal cop, and I want to see your boss."

She didn't believe that either. "Maybe," she said, "you might want to think about getting out of here before I call security."

"And maybe you might want to look at this," he said, holding up his warrant card.

She came closer and squinted at it. "Oh," she said.

"But I admit," he said, "I lied about the fourteen children. Is your boss in there?" He pointed at the door behind her.

Her response was oblique. "I don't care if you *are* a federal cop," she said. "You can't just barge in here without an appointment and disrupt our schedule."

"I just did. Call him right now, or I'll get out my brass knuckles."

She heaved a sigh, went back through the door, and slammed it behind her.

Two minutes later she was back. This time, her zipper was properly closed, She saw Arnaldo looking at it, avoided his eyes, and stepped aside.

"Down there," she said. "The door at the end."

Two other doors, one to the left, and one to the right, were closed. The corridor she'd ushered him into was no more than four meters long. *A toilet and a small storage closet,* Arnaldo thought.

There was nothing small, though, about Lúcio Saldana's office. There were windows on two sides, and the view from both was impressive: in one direction, urban sprawl backed up by distant mountains, in the other, the river. Off to one side was an informal seating area with a couple of armchairs and a couch.

Saldana was standing behind his desk with his necktie askew. He was a weasel of a man with distrustful eyes and a sunken chest that even his expensive suit couldn't conceal. He looked nothing at all like his handsome sibling.

"Saldana," he said, forcing a smile, and belatedly extending a hand.

Arnaldo took it. It was moist, and Saldana's grip was weak. "The name's Nunes," he said, "I'm an agent with the Federal Police. But your receptionist has probably told you that already."

"She has," Saldana said. "What's this all about?"

He indicated one of the chairs in front of his desk.

"Your brother's death."

Arnaldo sat down and crossed his legs. Lúcio resumed his seat. "I was told," he said, "that we wouldn't be bothered about that anymore."

"We?"

"My father and I."

"Told by whom?"

"Governor Abbas. Why are you here?"

"I'm here, Senhor Saldana, because the Minister of Justice told the Director of the Federal Police to send my boss and me to Curitiba to investigate your brother's death."

"So investigate. But that's no reason to come and bother me with it. Governor Abbas told my father specifically—"

"We wouldn't be here at all if it wasn't for your friend Governor Abbas. He's the one who called the Minister of Justice in the first place."

Lúcio made a dismissive gesture. "The governor isn't *my* friend; he's my father's friend."

"Despite the fact your brother accused him of being a crook? Despite the fact your sister-in-law is running against him?"

"The governor knows what my father thought about my brother, and he knows what he thinks about Stella."

"Which is?"

"He hated Plínio, and he's got no use for her."

"Hated his own son?"

"That's what I said."

"Enough to kill him?"

"Certainly not."

"And how about you?"

"What about me?"

"Did you hate your brother?"

"What kind of a question is that?"

"A simple one. Did you hate your brother?"

"No, I didn't hate my brother. We had our differences, I admit, but hate is too strong a word. I didn't hate him, I didn't even dislike him."

"Did you associate with him? Visit him? Talk to him?"

"No."

"Why not? If you didn't dislike him?"

Lúcio gave an exasperated sigh. "Plínio and my father were . . . estranged. I couldn't have it both ways. I had to choose between them. I chose my father."

"Are you telling me that neither one would have accepted you having a relationship with the other?"

"That's what I'm telling you."

"Why not?"

"My father thought Plínio was an ingrate who'd bitten the hand that fed him. Plínio thought my father had no social conscience, that he'd mistreated my grandmother and that he was supporting a crook."

"Governor Abbas?"

"Yes, Governor Abbas."

"And what did *you* think?"

"I told you. I supported my father."

"Out of conviction? Or because you're dependent upon him?"

Lúcio frowned. "I find your question offensive in the extreme."

"Too bad. How about you put your offense aside and answer it?"

"My father prizes loyalty above all things. I feel it's my duty to please him. Venality plays no part in our relationship."

"And you had no part whatsoever in having your brother killed?"

Lúcio placed three fingers on his breast. "I? You must be joking."

"No, Senhor Saldana, I'm not joking. The first thing we do when we set out to solve any case is to look for a motive. And you had one: with Plínio's death, you became your father's sole heir."

"What you're suggesting is outrageous."

"Is it?"

"It is! Now, I suggest you leave."

Arnaldo had said his piece, received the denial he expected and didn't think he was about to get anything more out of the interview.

So he took Saldana's suggestion. And left.

Chapter Seventeen

THERE WAS A TIME when people called Lebanon the Switzerland of the Mediterranean, so peaceful and prosperous was the country.

But peace and prosperity were short-lived.

In 1957, just fourteen years after winning independence from the French, Lebanon was invaded by the US Marines.

Ten years later, 300,000 Palestinians, fleeing the Arab-Israeli conflict, surged across the border and established camps, many of which remain until this day.

Nine years after that, the Syrian military moved in (they stayed for more than thirty years) and twice, in 1976 and 1982, Lebanese territory was invaded by the Israelis.

Each new outbreak of violence plunged the country deeper into chaos and caused more of her children to seek new homes abroad.

Many chose Brazil.

By the beginning of the 1990s, there were, it was said with some justification, more Lebanese in São Paulo than in Beirut.

But, before the refugees, before the great torrent of immigration began, there were a few young Lebanese upon whom Brazil exerted its attraction, not as a refuge, but as a land of limitless opportunity.

Two such adventurous spirits were Farid Nassib, newly graduated from the American University of Beirut with a degree in medicine, and his wife, Shada.

They arrived in São Paulo in the spring of 1950. Two years

later, their son was born. They named him Jaco, after Farid's father, and fate decreed that he should enter the world at the same hospital, and on the same day, as Mario Silva.

Placed in adjoining rooms, and shuffling around a common hallway, it wasn't long before the new mothers struck up a conversation—and discovered they had much in common. It was the first child for each. Their husbands practiced the same profession. Both mothers had lost their own mothers, so both were lacking in that support so important to a woman about to bring home a baby for the first time. A friendship arose, first between the wives, later between their husbands.

When their sons were five, a house became available on the Rua Bela Cintra, the street where the Silvas lived. Doctor Nassib bought it and became the Silvas' neighbor.

The two boys, Mario and Jaco, were friends from earliest childhood. They maintained their friendship after Jaco married and moved to Curitiba, his new wife's hometown. The marriage was of short duration, less than three years, but Jaco's relationship with Curitiba became permanent.

Even as a boy, Silva's friend had been an inveterate gossip, so it was quite natural he'd be drawn to journalism as a profession. He'd been a reporter for as many years as Silva had been a cop and, during the last twenty-five of those years, had drawn his pay from the *Gazeta do Povo*, the most important newspaper in the State.

Jaco had begun his career as a reporter, covering the long, mostly boring, meetings of Curitiba's City Council and the public and private lives of its members. Fifteen years later he'd been given his own column, and in the course of the last decade he'd become universally recognized as one of the country's leading authorities on the complicated world of Brazilian politics.

Jaco and the two federal cops met for dinner at a little

place on the Rua Amintas Barros. Jaco had told them it was the best Lebanese restaurant in the city, and Silva believed him. Jaco had always been somewhat of a gourmet.

There was none of the faux atmosphere that often permeates such places, no middle-eastern fabrics decorating the walls, no hookahs, no photos of the Bekaa Valley, no *mijwiz* playing in the background, but it was exotic all the same. The scents that perfumed the air were of spices uncommon to Brazilian cuisine and at least half the clientele were conversing in languages other than Portuguese.

Jaco, as he was accustomed to doing with non-Lebanese, ordered for them all. The *hummus*, *baba ghanouj*, *esfihas* and *kibbeh* that preceded the main course were all more than good, but the beef *chawarma* that followed was extraordinary. Silva pronounced it the best he'd ever eaten and Arnaldo agreed with him.

Meals in Brazil, as in Lebanon, are made to be enjoyed—and business is never discussed in the course of them, but after the dishes had been cleared away and the owner, solicitous to a fault, had left them to their coffee, Jaco leaned forward, lowered his voice and began talking about Plínio and Stella Saldana.

The story he told stood in sharp contrast to everything they'd heard before.

"Plínio was a politician," Jaco said, "not as bad as some, maybe even better than most, but no saint. He started off as an idealist, I'll give him that, but he fell in love with the power of office."

"And his idealism didn't last?"

"No. It didn't last."

"How about his wife's?" Arnaldo asked.

"She retained hers. She's a stronger person than he was, and smarter, but. . . ." Jaco toyed with his cup.

"What?" Silva said.

"This is going to sound weird."

"Say it."

"I think there's something dangerous about her."

Arnaldo frowned. "Dangerous?"

"Maybe dangerous is too strong a word. Immoderate might be a better one." He looked at his old friend. "Do you recall, Mario, how we thought, how we acted, back in 1968?"

Silva smiled at the memory. "Our foolish youth, Jaco. I look back on that time, and I think, was that me? How could I ever have been that naïve? That idealistic?"

"Foolish, yes. Naïve, maybe. Idealistic, certainly, but here's the thing: we weren't out to kill people. For us, and for most of our fellow students, it was all just riot and rhetoric."

"Your point?"

"Excessive zeal, even when it's rooted in a desire to do good, can have terrible consequences. The worldwide student riots in '68 led to the founding of organizations like the *Aliança Libertadora Nacional*, the *Brigata Rossa*, the *Rote Armee Fraktion* and the *Weather Underground*, all of which viewed the killing of innocents as morally justified as long as it led to the achievement of their goals."

"What has all this got to do with Stella Saldana?"

"She's a zealot, Mario, committed to her ideals, maybe even fanatically so."

"To the extent of being a physical threat to someone who might get in the way of her programs?"

"Potentially, yes."

"Including her husband?"

"Anyone."

"Come on, Jaco. Even from you, that's pretty far-fetched."

Jaco smiled. "Hey, if I can't share my thoughts with you, who can I share them with? I sure as hell can't print them in my column. The last thing the *Gazeta* needs these days is another lawsuit."

"Does anyone, other than you, see these tendencies in Stella? Is anyone else saying the sort of things about her that you're saying to me right now?"

Jaco shrugged. "Not as far as I know. Maybe you want to take everything I'm telling you with a grain of salt. I've been so close to so many politicians for so long I don't trust any of them anymore."

"Plus the fact," Silva said, with a smile, "that you have a tendency to exaggerate."

Jaco returned the smile. "It's my Levantine character. Some people think we Lebanese live on *chawarma* and *esfihas*. In fact, we live on intrigue. Now, about Nestor Cambria. . . ."

"What about him?"

"You know about him and Stella?"

"Him and Stella? What about him and Stella?"

"They were an item once. About that, there's no doubt. It's a fact."

"After she married Plínio?"

Jaco shook his head. "Before. Long before. Before she met Plínio, before they were all in law school together."

"Ancient history."

"Perhaps. But there was a rumor, not long before Plínio was killed, that they'd gotten back together."

"Any proof it's true?"

"If I had proof, I wouldn't have called it a rumor."

"You believe it?"

"I'm of two minds. But here's the thing: if, and I say if, it's true, it might just have been Stella getting her own back on Plínio."

"Getting her own back? What do you mean?"

"So you don't know about Eva Telles?"

"Who's Eva Telles?"

"Plínio's girlfriend."

"He had a girlfriend?"

"He did. And Stella might have known about her, because Stella isn't stupid, and Eva isn't discreet. Senhorita Telles was running around telling people Plínio was going to ditch Stella and marry her."

"You think Governor Abbas knows about this woman?"

"Without a doubt. Abbas has Madalena Torres working for him, and Madalena is a lady who makes it her business to know everything about everybody. She even has a dossier on me. She told me so herself. Fair enough. I've got one on her. She's had so many lovers she—"

"Let's stick with Abbas. If he knew Plínio had a mistress, why didn't he use it against him in the campaign?"

"The talk on the street is because Abbas has his own little affair going on, and Plínio found out about it."

"Ha. So it was a standoff?"

"Uh-huh. Plínio agreed to keep his mouth shut if Abbas did the same. That kind of stuff happens more than you might imagine in politics."

"It could never be more than we might imagine," Arnaldo said. "We live in Brasilia, remember?"

Jaco grinned at him. "Of course we do. I stand corrected."

"So what's your best guess?" Silva said. "If he'd been elected governor, would Plínio have ditched Stella for Eva?"

"No way. Eva is pretty, but she's not . . . um . . . intellectually gifted. She wouldn't have been of any help to him, and in many ways she'd have been a hindrance. I'm more inclined to put credence in the other rumor."

"Which is?"

"That Plínio had tired of Eva and was about to break it off."

"So there's another damned suspect," Arnaldo said.

"Two," Jaco said. "Don't exclude Stella."

"We're not," Silva said. "About this Telles woman, can you get me contact information?"

"Sure. I'll send it to you in a text message, first thing in the morning. How about some more coffee?"

Silva and Arnaldo both nodded. Jaco raised a hand. The waiter came to their table and took their order.

"Have you spoken to Plínio's old man, Orestes?" Jaco asked when the waiter was gone.

"I have," Silva said. "He's a nasty piece of work."

"He is. But the world won't have to put up with him for much longer. He's sick. Cancer. He's got a year, at most."

"How do you find out these things?"

"A quarter of a century of cultivating contacts," Jaco said. "If the politicians in this town knew how well-informed I am, I'd fear for my life."

He treated it as a joke, but Silva knew he was serious.

"Braulio Serpa," Arnaldo said, "thinks Plínio's brother might have been behind his murder."

"So he could inherit all the loot when the old man kicks off?"

"Exactly."

"A possibility," Jaco said. "Lúcio's a greedy bastard. But Orestes is another possibility. The old man's capacity for hatred is boundless, and he hated Plínio. The thought of Plínio getting his hands on any of his money would have been intolerable to him."

"Lovely family," Arnaldo said.

"If I agreed with you," Jaco said, "we'd both be wrong."

"How about Orestes's mother?" Silva said. "What do you think of her?"

"Ariana? She's the exception. A splendid old bird; the last of her kind. How she could have produced that son of hers is a mystery to me."

The waiter brought their coffee. Jaco waited until they'd been served before he spoke again.

"I've been saving the best for last," he said.

"There's more?"

"Oh, yes, Mario, there's more. And it's a bombshell. Have you ever heard me mention Ismail Khouri?"

"No. Who is he?"

"Ismail is an old friend. Not as old as you, but an old friend nonetheless. Most Lebanese in this country are Christians. Only a few of us are Muslims. I'm one. Ismail is another. Back in São Paulo, we used to spend quite a bit of time together, attended the same mosque. I thought you might have met him. Short little fellow? Beard? Walks with a limp?"

"Not that I recall."

"Okay, it doesn't matter. Here's the story: a number of years ago Ismail moved to Foz do Iguaçu and opened a business."

"What kind of business?"

"A shop specialized in electronics, cell phones, digital cameras, televisions, video disk players, that sort of thing. He lives in Foz, but his business is in Paraguay."

"Ciudad del Este?"

"Indeed. He wouldn't live there on a bet, but he makes good money, so he goes across the bridge every day to work. "

"And?"

"And Ismail tells me there's a rumor floating around that Plínio was involved in an illegal business venture in that benighted country."

"Benighted?" Arnaldo said. "Where do you get a word like that?"

"I write for a living, remember?"

"What kind of business venture?" Silva asked.

"Luxury automobiles, stolen in Brazil, smuggled across the river and reregistered and resold in Paraguay."

Silva held up a hand. "Wait. You're telling me Plínio Saldana, Senhor Morality, the guy who was running on a platform of sweeping Paraná clean, was a *crook?*"

Jaco nodded. "That's the rumor. Unsubstantiated, I hasten to add. I haven't heard it from anyone but Ismail."

Silva looked dubious. "The car smuggling business has been going on for years, Jaco. Saldana, if the rumor is true, would have been the new guy on the block, and the Paraguayans wouldn't have looked favorably on him trying to cut himself in."

"Ah, but what if his partner was a Paraguayan, already established in the business?"

"That, of course, would be different. Who was it?"

"A gentleman of Syrian extraction who has an automobile dealership in Ciudad del Este. He's said to be involved in the smuggling of arms and drugs as well. Moreover, he's a hate-monger, a fanatic, maybe even a terrorist."

"And what is this nasty character's name?"

"Al-Fulan," Jaco said. "Jamil Al-Fulan."

Chapter Eighteen

ORLANDO MUNIZ, WHEN HE wasn't visiting one of his far-flung *fazendas*, lived in an apartment facing the sea on Avenida Vieira Souto in Rio de Janeiro. But he also kept a small place on Rua Pamplona in São Paulo, and it was there that he met the Colonel's men.

Aldo—none of them gave Muniz a surname—was an enigma: a Mediterranean type, perhaps of Italian or Greek heritage, possibly of Portuguese, or Spanish,—but with a thick Slavic accent.

Reiner, blond-haired and blue-eyed, might have stepped out of a Nazi propaganda poster, but the way he spoke was suggestive of Rio Grande do Sul, a place where German immigrants had been settling ever since the nineteenth century.

Careca, the leader, was a huge man with a shaved head, tattooed arms and an incongruously high voice. He looked like a thug, but expressed himself like an officer—and a *Paulista*.

Muniz placed them side-by-side on a large couch, took an armchair facing them and posed his first question: "How much has the Colonel told you?"

"That we're going to kill two men, Senhor," Careca said. "The first is to be Public Prosecutor Zanon Parma, the second Chief Inspector Mario Silva of the Federal Police."

"Then let me begin by clearing up a misconception. *We* are not going to kill anyone. *I* am going to kill them. Your assignment is to assist. I want you to help me to set it up, protect me while I'm doing it, and cover my tracks after I'm done. You are *not*, repeat *not*, to kill either Parma, or Silva, not unless there's an imminent danger of one of them killing me. Killing them is my privilege and mine alone. Do you understand?"

"Understood, Senhor."

"Good. Now, our first problem will be getting at Parma."

"Yes, Senhor. Aldo, here, is our intelligence expert. Would you like to hear what he's learned?"

"What? Already?"

"After your conversation, the Colonel instructed Aldo to get a head start with his inquiries."

"I applaud the initiative."

"Thank you, Senhor. I will tell the Colonel."

Muniz turned to Aldo. "What have you learned?"

Aldo reached into his breast pocket and retrieved a small, leather-bound notebook.

"Senhor Parma," he said, "lives in an apartment on Avenida Higienópolis in the *bairro* of the same name. Security in the building is excellent. There is an armed man situated in a guardhouse in the front garden and another armed man behind the front door. The front door is the sole pedestrian entrance to the premises. The windows of the guardhouse and the glass of the front door are resistant to weapons of all but the heaviest caliber."

Muniz grunted.

Aldo wet a finger and turned a page.

"Entry to the garage," he said, "is via an arrangement with two gates. One gate opens. The vehicle enters, and the gate shuts before the other gate opens. This precludes any attempt to make a successful frontal assault. In addition, there is a third armed guard who patrols the garage area."

Muniz started scratching his chin.

Aldo turned another page.

"Guards are on duty twenty-four-seven. There are security cameras throughout the building, not only at the pedestrian entrance, and at the entrance to the garage, but also on each of the floors."

"How did you discover all this?" Muniz said.

"I posed as a rare gems dealer, much preoccupied with security, and in search of a new home. I spoke, by telephone, to a real-estate agent selling an apartment in the building. May I continue, Senhor?"

"Go ahead."

"The cameras feed into a room where all the images are displayed at once, not in rotation. Two men are on duty in the room at all times, and they take turns, each observing the monitors for one hour at a stretch. That way, it's said, they're always alert. The room is protected by a steel door, and linked, by both landline and radio, to a security service."

"Which one?"

"*Watchdogs*, Senhor."

"I've heard of them."

"They're the best in the business, Senhor. They pay well and pride themselves on a response time of five minutes or less."

"And they're all ex-military, drawn from elite units."

"That, too, is true, Senhor."

"We don't want to tangle with those guys."

"No, Senhor, we do not," Careca said.

"Senhor Parma's car," Aldo went on, "is armored. A rocket-propelled grenade could take it out, but nothing short of one is likely to be effective."

"All right, we can't get Parma in his home, and we can't get him in his car. How about his office?"

Aldo shook his head. "Too public. We'd be seen."

"We could wear hoods."

"In which case, Senhor, we'd never get in. There is a security check at the front door."

"We could put them on after we're inside."

"By which time, Senhor, images of our faces would already have been captured by the security cameras. In addition, all visitors are required to sign a book."

"So his office is also out?"

"Correct, Senhor."

"So how *do* we get at him?"

Aldo turned another page, glanced at what he'd written there and met Muniz's eyes. Now he was coming to it. Muniz could sense it.

"Are you familiar, Senhor, with Ilhabela?"

"I am. What about it?"

"Senhor Parma has a home there. He often goes on weekends, and he *always* goes there on long weekends."

"Like *this* weekend?"

"Just so, Senhor. He's already left São Paulo." Aldo looked at his watch. "He might even be there by now."

"What are you proposing?"

"I propose to investigate Senhor Parma's security arrangements on the island. I would not be surprised if he has none."

"All this security here in São Paulo? And none on Ilhabela? How likely is that?"

"That remains to be seen. But the choice of an apartment might well have been motivated by reasons other than security. His wife's mother lives in the same building, and her residence predates that of Senhor Parma."

"Is that a fact?"

"That's a fact, Senhor. In addition, his office is at the *Promotoria de Justiça* in Barra Funda."

"So?"

"That place, Senhor, has criminals coming and going at all hours of the day, and has, therefore, heavy security dictated by the State."

"How about that armored car? What about that?"

"Provided to public prosecutors as a matter of course. He didn't have to ask for it. There is, therefore, a good chance he didn't. And there's one thing more."

"Which is?"

"He won't feel threatened in an out-of-the-way place like Ilhabela. He'll be in holiday mode, less likely to be on his guard when we approach him."

Muniz was pleased. "Good," he said. "Very good."

"All speculation at the moment, Senhor."

"So what's the next step?"

"I'll depart for the island immediately after this meeting. I'll confirm my assumptions by tomorrow morning at the latest."

Muniz turned to Careca. "So, if Aldo is right, that's where I'll kill him?"

"Yes, Senhor," Careca said. "That's where you'll kill him."

Chapter Nineteen

"THE GOVERNOR WILL SEE you now."

Both men rose.

"Not you, Agent Nunes," the secretary said, "just him." She pointed at Silva and opened the door to Abbas's inner office.

Silva entered to find two men awaiting him.

The one with the silver-gray hair and moustache circled the desk, intercepted Silva, and gave him the firm handshake of a practiced politician.

"Chief Inspector Silva," he said, as if they were old friends. "What a pleasure."

"Governor," Silva said.

He recognized the man from the election posters plastered all over the city.

"And this," Abbas said with a flourish of his arm, "is my Chief of Staff, Rodrigo Fabiano."

Fabiano was at least a decade younger. He had protruding incisors that reminded Silva of a rabbit, or maybe a beaver. His eyes, however, were those of a jackal, or maybe a hyena.

"My associate Agent Nunes is outside," Silva said. "He—"

"We won't keep you long," the governor interrupted smoothly. "Let's sit over there."

He led his guest to an oblong table, indicated a chair, and sat down facing him. Fabiano, sliding a silver tray within reach, took the seat to the governor's left.

On the tray were a pot, a milk pitcher and a sugar bowl, all in matching porcelain.

"Coffee?" Abbas asked, picking up a cup.

"No, thank you," Silva said.

Abbas and Fabiano exchanged a glance, as if Silva's refusal had some deeper significance. Fabiano put down the cup. Both leaned backward in their chairs.

"So," the governor said, "what have you to report?"

"I'm sorry, Governor," Silva said. "Our investigation has barely begun."

"But, surely, there must be something you can tell us."

Silva shook his head. "We're still interviewing, still gathering information."

"Well," Fabiano said, "let me ask you this. Do you have any theories?"

"Perhaps one theory," Silva said.

Abbas leaned forward. "And what might that be?"

"The murder of Nestor Cambria might be linked to that of Plínio Saldana."

"Yes, yes," the governor said. "The same thought occurred to us. Perhaps to keep him quiet. You policemen have a clever expression for such things, but I can't—"

"*Queimando o arquivo?*" Fabiano suggested.

"That's it," Abbas said, snapping his fingers, "*queimando o arquivo.*"

The literal meaning of the phrase was *burning the files*, but it had come to mean the destruction of any kind of evidence, including the murder of witnesses.

Abbas opened an inlaid wooden box sharing table space with the coffee tray. "Cigar?"

Again, Silva refused.

Abbas blinked. "You're sure? They're Cuban."

"I'm sure."

"Go ahead, take one. Take two. You can bring them with you, smoke them later."

Silva shook his head. "I no longer smoke," he said.

Abbas closed the humidor without taking one himself and without offering one to Fabiano. After a short pause, he went on. "Braulio Serpa told us you're thorough."

"I try to be," Silva said.

"I'm sure you do."

And there Abbas stopped, as if uncertain about what to say next. He looked at Fabiano.

"We all have our secrets," Fabiano said. "I know I do. I'm sure you do. I suspect even the governor does."

"We're all men of the world here," Abbas said, "so I'll give it to you straight. If you should uncover anything damaging. . ."

"Come to us with it," Fabiano finished for him.

"Mind you," Abbas continued. "I wouldn't think of interfering with your investigation. You've been sent here to discover who might be behind the murder of Plínio Saldana—"

"If, indeed, anyone was behind it," Fabiano said.

Abbas looked at him and smiled. "Come, come, Rodrigo. There's no need to be coy with the Chief Inspector. We all know Cataldo was unlikely to have been acting on his own." He turned back to Silva. "But, right now, we're talking about something else."

Silva nodded. "We're talking about information I might come across in the course of my investigation, information unrelated to the murders, but damaging to you or your campaign. And we're talking about you rewarding me for suppressing it."

The governor smiled, like a teacher proud of his pupil. "I can see we're on the same wavelength," he said. "Rodrigo, give the Chief Inspector your card."

Fabiano had the card ready. He handed it to Silva.

"Feel free to call Rodrigo anytime," Abbas said, "day or night." He rose to his feet and extended a hand. "It was a pleasure meeting you, Chief Inspector."

* * *

WHEN THEY were outside on the street, searching for a cab and not finding one, Arnaldo said, "That was quick. What did he want?"

Silva told him.

Arnaldo rubbed his hands. "You gonna cut me in for half?"

"Half of nothing is nothing," Silva said.

"That's what I like about you, Mario. You're as honest as my bank account is thin."

"Is that another of your aphorisms?"

"I doubt it. Mainly because I don't even know what an aphorism is. By the way, there's news on another front."

"What?"

"While you were in there getting bribed, I placed a call to Raul Sintra, that security guy over at the hospital."

"And?"

"And Sintra was just about to call us. He reviewed all the videos and spoke to half the world. He managed to attach a name, and a reason for being there, to every person but one."

"And?"

"And I gave him Mara's email address. By now, she's got a freeze-frame of the mystery man."

Chapter Twenty

THEIR NEXT APPOINTMENT WAS with Stella Saldana.

She, like her husband before her, was running her campaign from the topmost floor of the Mabu Palace Hotel. The corridor was still decorated with posters bearing the late candidate's image.

"She's terribly busy, Chief Inspector," one of her two secretaries said, "but she instructed me to give you as much time as you needed."

"I'm grateful," Silva said.

"And how much time might that be?" the secretary asked, a ballpoint poised over her steno pad.

"Not long," Silva said. "Fifteen minutes?"

"Excellent." She seemed pleased, as if Silva had just solved one of her problems. "She told me to bring you right in."

In one of the bedrooms, Stella Saldana was using a banquet table as a desk. A couch and four chairs completed her office ensemble. Even with the bed removed, there was little room for anything else.

Slim in frame, and boyish in appearance, she was wearing jeans and a faded T-shirt bearing Plínio's picture.

"Which of you is Chief Inspector Silva?" she said.

"I am. This is Agent Arnaldo Nunes."

She smiled. "I'm pleased to meet you both. Please take the couch. Those chairs will destroy your back."

"Fifteen minutes," her secretary said.

"Thanks, Alice," she said.

The secretary nodded and went out, closing the door behind her.

"Fifteen minutes?" Stella said, with a glance at the clock on her desk. "That's all you need?"

"At the moment," Silva said. "Let me start by expressing our condolences for your loss."

"Thank you," she said.

"I don't want to rake up unpleasant memories but. . . ."

"But you have to. It's your job. I understand that. Please, ask away."

She was totally in control of her emotions, not at all the bereaved widow Arnaldo, and to a certain extent Silva, had feared being confronted with. Was it simply because she was good at keeping her feelings in check?

"You weren't an actual witness to your husband's death?"

She shook her head. "I forced myself to watch the television coverage. I wish I hadn't."

"Had you ever met Julio Cataldo?"

"No."

"Do you recall your husband mentioning his name?"

"No."

"If someone put him up to it, do you think that person might have been governor Abbas?"

"I doubt it."

"Why?"

"Because Abbas isn't stupid. If things had run their course, Plínio might have lost. But as soon as he was gone, Abbas didn't stand a chance. The simpler people, the people who swing elections in this state, are convinced he was behind my husband's murder. The backlash has been tremendous—and entirely predictable. All the polls agree. I'm going to win this one by a landslide."

"And you're certain the Governor would have foreseen that?"

"If he hadn't, Chief Inspector, Madalena Torres would have. You've heard about Madalena?"

"We have. And we'll be having a chat with her. Can you think of anyone else we should be talking to? Looking at?"

She shook her head. "It would be a cliché to say my husband had no enemies. Nor would it be true. But I can't think of a single one who hated him enough to kill him. I'm sorry. I'm not being of much help."

"You have nothing to apologize for, Senhora Saldana. We appreciate your taking the time to talk to us. I'd like to ask you about another killing, if I may, that of Nestor Cambria."

"Poor Nestor," she said.

Silva sensed a subtle shift in her demeanor, a sadness that hadn't been there a second before. He looked at her closely. She met his gaze without flinching.

"Have you any reason to doubt Nestor's loyalty to your husband?"

She shook her head.

"None. There was no one more loyal, no closer friend. Nestor would have done anything for Plínio."

"It's my understanding you visited Nestor in the hospital shortly before his death."

"That's correct."

"And, at a given point, you asked the other members of your entourage to leave, so you could spend time with him alone."

"Yes," she said. "You're well-informed, Chief Inspector."

Not quite a compliment, he thought, *more of a cautious observation.*

"Can you tell us why you did that? Tell us what you discussed?"

"No," she said.

He frowned. "No?"

"Nestor and I were friends, close friends, for a long time. We shared many things that are no one else's business. Our conversation was a confidential one. I'm not going to talk to you about it."

Silva let the silence stretch out, but to no avail. She seemed comfortable with it.

So he changed tack. "Nestor's wife, Bruna, told us that, in the days before his death, her husband seemed deeply concerned about something."

Stella's face remained expressionless, but he spotted a slight tic at the corner of her right eye. There was something she wasn't telling him.

"Concerned?" she said. "About what?"

"He wouldn't talk to her about it."

"So it's a mystery."

"It's a mystery. But I have to ask myself if his concern might have had something to do with your conversation."

"Ask yourself, Chief Inspector, but don't ask me. I've already told you our conversation was confidential. Stop probing. I'm not going to talk about it."

"When I spoke with Senhora Cataldo, she also told me something was preoccupying her husband."

Stella gave a ladylike little snort. "The man was planning a murder. That's enough to preoccupy anyone, don't you think?"

"I do. But I still found it curious that both women were going through the same experience at the same time. How about your husband?"

"What about him?"

"In the days before his death, did you note any change in his mood?"

"No."

"Did you sense what Bruna sensed about Nestor? That something might have been preoccupying him?"

"No."

Her answer to both questions was quick and definitive. Too quick. Too definitive.

Silva didn't believe her.

Chapter Twenty-One

AFTER THEIR INTERVIEWS WITH the governor and the probable governor-to-be were concluded, the two federal cops reverted to working separately.

"He loved me," Eva Telles said, when she and Silva were seated in her living room. "I could never have afforded this place if he didn't."

The quantum leap from the emotional to the material seemed to reinforce Jaco's opinion that the woman was no intellectual powerhouse.

Her physical attributes, however, were another story. Eva was in her mid-twenties, with huge brown eyes and thick, lustrous hair. She wore it loose, some spilling over her ample bosom, more cascading down her back.

They were in her apartment on the fifteenth floor of the St. Moritz, an establishment with more marble in the foyer than in many a Greek temple and with elevators gleaming with varnished wood and polished brass.

There were, however, no doormen, nor any of the other amenities the wealthier families of Curitiba took for granted.

But, then, the St. Moritz had no pretension of being a *family* building. It had been designed as, and was, a stack of love nests in which wealthy gentlemen could lodge their mistresses.

Doormen could gossip, and concierges as well. The St. Moritz didn't have them, because discretion was prized over convenience. Common social areas were eschewed, because they might lead to embarrassing encounters with

other gentlemen. And recreational facilities were super-
fluous, because the recreational activities taking place in
the St. Moritz were confined to the building's bedrooms—
and, occasionally, its dining room tables and living room
floors.

Eva began their conversation by establishing her
credentials.

First, she brought Silva to the window to admire the view
that "Plínio used to love," an impressive vista of park and
river.

Then she crossed the room to show him "Plínio's favorite
picture of the two of us together." It was a color photograph
that had been blown up, almost to the size of a poster, and it
occupied a place of honor on the wall above the couch.

Finally, she invited him to sit down in "Plínio's favorite
chair," a throne-like affair that looked, and felt, as if it had
been upholstered in genuine chamois leather.

"Plínio was going to tell Stella about us just after the election," she said as she took a seat opposite him. "With the new
law, you can get a divorce in forty-eight hours."

"Yes," Silva said, "I read about that. So you two were
intending to marry?"

She sniffed, nodded, and delicately dabbed at the corner
of one eye with her lace handkerchief (black to match her
dress). The absence of tears was, perhaps, the reason she was
able to do so without smudging her mascara.

"I was going to have my own office," she said, "right there
in the governor's mansion. Plínio said I could decorate it
however I liked. And he'd give me a social secretary, and a
car, with a driver. The governor's wife has a lot of duties, you
know."

"I know."

"But we were going to Europe first. On a honeymoon.

No one knew Plínio over there. We'd be able to wander the streets all by ourselves, without that Nestor always tagging along and invading our privacy. We were going to London, and to Rome, and to Venice, and . . . and then it all turned to shit. I hate her!"

The outburst gave Silva a glimpse of the real woman behind the innocent eyes. "Stella?" he said.

"Of course, Stella," she said. "Stella the Bitch. You're trying to find out who's behind Plínio's murder? Well, look no further. It's Stella the Bitch. She's the one. She's the one for sure."

"That's a serious charge, Senhorita Telles."

He might as well not have spoken. She was intent on having her say.

"Things were going so well," she said. "So well. But she must have found out about us. So she had him killed, and now she's going to be the governor, and she has everything, and I've got nothing. It's so . . . so *unfair*."

A tear appeared at last. And her mascara *did* smear when she dabbed at it.

"Do you have any facts to support your allegation?" Silva asked.

"What?"

"Do you have any proof that what you say is true?"

"No, I don't have any *proof*. I just know it. Anyway, that's what you cops are supposed be doing, isn't it? Finding proof?"

She blew her nose. Silva waited her out. It wasn't long before she began to speak again.

"Scratch his eyes out, okay, I could understand that. Or go after his money? Any wife would do that. But have him killed? That was just so . . . over the top."

"How about Plínio?"

"What about him?"

"How did he think Stella would react if she found out?"

"*When* she found out, you mean."

"I beg your pardon. *When* she found out."

"He used to joke about it, tell me not to worry, tell me he was bigger and stronger than she was, and, besides, he had Nestor to protect him."

"Did you know," Silva said, "that there was a rumor going about that Plínio was about to end his affair with you?"

"Affair? *Affair?* Where do you get off calling it an affair!"

"Sorry, I meant to say relationship."

"And you heard he was planning on ending it?" She leaned forward in her chair. If she'd had claws, they would have been out. "Who's filling your head with that shit? Stella the Bitch?"

"No," he said.

"Who then?"

"I'm sorry. I can't tell you."

"Why not?"

The way she said it brought the word wheedling to mind.

"We keep our sources confidential," Silva said.

She pouted. "Can't you at least tell me if it was a man or a woman?"

Silva saw no harm in that—and he wanted her cooperation. "A male," he said.

"Well," she said, "whoever he is, he's full of it!"

"He also said you made no secret of your relationship with Plínio."

"You think I should have kept my mouth shut? As if it was something to be ashamed of? As if it was some kind of dirty little secret? As if I was just some slut he was fucking? I *loved* him. And he loved me. And that's the truth."

The truth? Silva didn't think so. No governor, no matter how besotted, would have wanted a woman like Eva Telles as his first lady. Not if he didn't want to become a laughing stock, not if he wanted to be reelected.

The question confronting him now was whether Eva knew Plínio had lied to her.

And what she might be capable of doing to him if she did.

Chapter Twenty-Two

ARNALDO CAST HIS EYES around Madalena Torres's living room. It was strewn with boxes and suitcases.

"Packing?" he said.

"How can you tell?" she said.

"I'm a detective."

"And flippant."

"That too. Leaving town?"

"Wow, amazing powers of detection!"

"True. And, at the moment, I detect sarcasm."

"Like I said, amazing powers. What can I do for you, Agent Nunes?"

"Do I get coffee before we start?"

"No, you don't. As of today, my sojourn in Curitiba is at an end. I'm a meticulous planner, and I used up the last bit of coffee this morning. But I erred with the guaraná. I've still got four cans."

"*Errare humanum est,*" Arnaldo said.

"Literate, too," she said. "You want the guaraná or not?"

"I want."

"Self service. Ice in the freezer, glasses in the cupboard to the right of the sink, cans in the fridge. Help yourself and bring one for me."

"Where do you want me?" he said when he got back.

"On the couch," she said.

"Am I to take that as innuendo?"

She looked him up and down. "Not yet," she said, after a short pause. "We've hardly met."

"There's a suitcase on the couch."

"And I've finished packing it. Close it, please, and put it next to the front door before you sit down."

"Right."

"But, before you do, get a couple of coasters to put under those glasses."

"And the coasters are where?"

She pointed. "Over there, on the shelf."

When he was seated, and sipping from his guaraná, Arnaldo looked around him and said, "I take it this place was rented furnished?"

"You take it correctly. And they're holding back a fat deposit against damages, which I'm personally responsible for, so don't you dare put that glass down anywhere else but on that coaster."

She picked up her own glass and took a tiny sip.

"When are you leaving?" he asked.

"Seven o'clock flight," she said, "so we've got plenty of time." She perched on the arm of a chair and crossed her legs to display several kilometers of thigh. "You married? Or is the wedding ring just for show?"

"Not for show. Two kids."

"Me too," she said, looking at him over the rim of her glass. "They're in São Paulo with my mother."

"Two kids," he said, "but no ring."

"It's all over," she said, "but the shouting."

"Shouting?"

"Uh-huh. He shouts a lot. I've got the money. The lazy bastard wants half of it, but he's not gonna get it."

"São Paulo's home?"

She nodded. "When I'm not working somewhere else."

"Home for me too," Arnaldo said, "although I'm currently in durance vile."

"Brasilia?" she asked.

"Brasilia," he confirmed.

"Doesn't get much viler than that," she said. "All those damned politicians."

"Wait a minute," he said. "You work with politicians."

"Familiarity breeds contempt," she said. "But it's a living."

"A good living, from what I hear."

"For people who're good at it. I'm good at it."

"I trust your departure has something to do with the fact that your job with the Governor just dried up?"

"Wow! Staggering insight! In the tradition of the great Sherlock Holmes."

"I confess," Arnaldo said, with false modesty, "to being the envy of many of the less gifted in my profession. So what's next for Madalena Torres?"

She took another tiny sip and put down her glass. The level hadn't lowered significantly since he'd given it to her.

"I've got a couple of irons in the fire," she said. "I won't starve. Meantime, I'm going to spend some time in Ilhabela with my kids."

Arnaldo put down his own glass. He'd drained it.

"Nice place, Ilhabela. How did you get into this business?"

She shrugged. "I used to work in advertising as an account planner, developed communication strategies for soap, and toothpaste, and margarine. We got the account of a politician running for senator. He lost, but I got a good inside look, and I thought I could do better than my agency had done. I started with small-town municipal elections. I built up a track record of getting people elected. Word got around." She held out both hands, palms upward. "And here I am."

"Is Abbas's defeat going to be a major setback for you?"

"Nope. Every politician in this country knows God himself couldn't win an election against Stella. Against Plínio, we had a chance, but from the time Cataldo put that bullet in his head, the election became a foregone conclusion."

"You really think Abbas could have won against Plínio?"

"I really do. And I daresay I know more about it than you do."

"So you still had some moves up your sleeve?"

"Maybe."

"And you were just waiting for the right time to spring them?"

"Maybe."

"And one had to do with a young lady by the name of Eva Telles?"

"Did it?"

"The way I hear it, there was some kind of a deal between Abbas and Saldana. If Saldana didn't talk about Abbas's mistress, Abbas wouldn't talk about Saldana's mistress."

"And, at your age, you still believe in fairy tales?"

"What's that supposed to mean?"

"It means politicians' promises mean nothing. Whether it's true or not, the consensus has always been that Abbas is a crook."

"Are you telling me it's *not* true?"

"No, I'm not telling you that. You're not listening. Pay attention and you might learn something."

"Okay. Go on."

"The electorate in this country is convinced *all* politicians steal. It's expected. But not all politicians deliver on their campaign promises—and Abbas always delivered. That fact, bolstered by the fact he spread around a lot of what he was said to have stolen, made him a viable candidate for re-election."

"Ah. I see."

"You get it?"

"I'm beginning to. But wasn't the girlfriend issue a standoff?

If Abbas divulged the existence of Eva, wouldn't Saldana have turned right around and started talking about Abbas's mistress?"

"Of course. But Abbas wasn't selling righteousness. The people who supported him knew what they were getting, or at least, they thought they did."

"Which was?"

"A crook whose campaign promises they could believe."

"And Plínio?"

"The people who supported him *didn't* know what they were getting. Many would have been disillusioned, even pissed off, to discover their golden idol had feet of clay. And they'd start asking themselves to what degree his campaign promises could be believed. So, in the balance, if the mistress issue came up—"

"And you planned to make sure it did."

"Plínio would have lost many more votes than Abbas."

"Jesus Christ! What a dirty business."

"Isn't it? And don't tell me it comes as a complete surprise. You're a master detective, aren't you? You live in Brasilia, don't you?"

"Point taken. Did you have anything else up your sleeve?"

"Maybe."

"What?"

"I have no intention of telling you. You're the detective. Detect."

"Come on, Senhora Torres, you told me about Eva."

"No, Agent Nunes, I didn't tell you about Eva. You told *me* about Eva. And, when you did, I elected to set you straight on a few issues. But I did *not* divulge anything of a confidential nature about my client's campaign. Nor do I intend to."

"Let me ask you this: Was it predictable that, if something happened to Plínio, his wife would step in to replace him?"

"Entirely."

"And was it predictable that, if she did, she'd be elected?"

"Entirely."

"And you made that clear to Abbas?"

"I didn't have to. He knew it already. He's not a brilliant man, Agent Nunes, but he's not stupid."

"Might someone have been trying to do him a favor by eliminating Plínio?"

"It's possible, of course. But of one thing I can assure you: if Governor Abbas had been made aware of any such plan, he would have scotched it."

"So who do *you* think was behind the death of Plínio Saldana?"

"What's that Latin expression, the one that means *who benefits?*"

"*Cui bono?*"

"That's it. *Cui bono.*"

"People make that mistake all the time. It doesn't mean *who benefits*. The correct translation is *as a benefit to whom.* It's a double dative construction."

"Double dative, eh? Agent Nunes, I'm impressed. How come you're so good with Latin?"

"I went to a Catholic school. My Latin teacher was a Jesuit with a grudge against kids. He beat it into me. So tell me: As a benefit to whom?"

"At least two people I can think of. Lúcio Saldana, for one."

"Because of the money."

"Of course, because of the money. He's going to inherit a bundle."

"Braulio Serpa said the same thing, and he probably got it from his boss. And I wouldn't be at all surprised if his boss got it from you."

She smiled. "Does it matter?"

"No, I suppose it doesn't. You said two people. Who's the other one?"

"Stella Saldana."

"You really think that's possible?"

"I really do."

"The playback we're getting on Stella is she's honest."

"I think she probably is. And not only honest, but concerned about people as well."

"So. . ."

"So how about this? How about Stella saw a real opportunity to make a change for the better in this state? And how about she'd lost faith in her husband's ability to do it? And how about she'd recently discovered he'd taken a mistress? And it made her jealous and furiously angry? How about that? Motive enough for you?"

"Put that way," Arnaldo said, "yes."

"Uh-huh," she said. "I think so too. Want another guaraná before you start helping me lug this stuff downstairs?"

Chapter Twenty-Three

Marca Zero, THE BRASS-TOPPED monument from which distances to all corners of the State of São Paulo are measured, stands on the Praça da Sé, in the heart of the capital.

From there to the ferry dock on the island of Ilhabela is a mere 197 kilometers, but getting from one to other can be an ordeal.

The city is famous for its gridlocks. Kilometer-long congestion arises for no apparent reason. The roads leading to the coast are potholed, narrow, hairpinned and steep. The descent from the highland plateau to sea level often involves passing through low-lying clouds that can reduce visibility to a few meters. And there's often a long wait for the boat. The journey, three hours on a good day, can stretch to eight on a bad one. Yet even on holiday weekends, when the traffic is heaviest, many *Paulistas* think the time it takes is time well spent.

Six times the size of Manhattan, and seven kilometers from the mainland, the island is ringed by 41 beaches. Inland the terrain rises, through rainforest lush with vegetation, to a granite peak topping-out at 1,400 meters. Ilhabela abounds with freshwater streams and waterfalls, and the encircling ocean teems with fish.

None of which mattered a damn to Orlando Muniz.

There was only one thing about the island that attracted him: the opportunity it offered to kill Zanon Parma.

The operation against the public prosecutor began with a call from the Colonel's intelligence expert.

"He's here," Aldo reported. "Conditions are perfect. I suggest we do it tonight."

Muniz felt his pulse quicken. "Excellent," he said. "What's the next step?"

"Drive to São Sebastião, Senhor, and wait for a call. Expect it shortly after sunset. Everything you need will be provided."

"A gun as well?"

They were speaking over an unsecured line. Aldo expressed his disapproval of the question with a long pause, and said, "It's my understanding, Senhor, that the Colonel already informed you about that part of the arrangements."

Muniz didn't like being chastised by the help, but he swallowed his irritation. "Yes," he said. "Yes, you're right. He did."

"Cell phone reception in the region can be spotty. Please be sure to choose a location where you have a signal."

"Understood," Muniz said. "I'll leave now."

He dressed himself in island gear—a T-shirt, shorts and sandals—grabbed his wallet and sunglasses, and took the elevator down to the garage.

Most of the holiday traffic had left the day before. His progress was rapid. He stopped at a *churrascaria* between the Via Dutra and Caraguatatuba, ate a leisurely lunch, drank two *caipirinhas*, and still managed to arrive well before dark. He checked his cell phone, confirmed he had a signal, and waited.

The call came ten minutes after sunset.

"Where are you, Senhor?" The high, squeaky voice was unmistakable. It was Careca.

"Parked on the road," Muniz said, "between the ferry dock and the tanker port."

"Turn around and go back. Less than a kilometer beyond

the entry to the port you'll see a path to the beach. Walk down to the water. It's unlikely you'll meet anyone. The area is generally deserted after sundown."

"Then what?"

"Wait for a ride."

THE RIDE came in the form of a Zodiac tender about five meters long. The bow met the sand with a soft *shush*, hardly louder than a whisper. There was no moon, and not a breath of wind. The sea was a black mirror.

"Hop in, Senhor," Careca said.

Muniz wasn't pleased. "We're going to cross over in *that?*"

"Sim, Senhor."

"Why can't we just take the ferry?"

"You're too well-known, Senhor. You might be recognized."

"I've got a hat in the car. Dark glasses."

"It would still be a risk, Senhor. Do you have a problem with boats?"

"No. No, of course not."

It was a lie. Muniz hated boats of any size, but he had an absolute loathing for the little ones, a loathing rooted in fear. His palms began to sweat if he came anywhere near a small boat, and his heartbeat went wild whenever he got into one. He even had nightmares about them. One time, he dreamed that an inflatable, not unlike this one, sank under him after being holed by a swordfish. That time he'd been attacked by sharks. In another dream, he was aboard a small boat that sank in heavy weather amid waves as high as houses. Then there was the time he'd been run down by a supertanker and was being drawn toward the ship's huge propeller when he awoke in a sweat.

He'd never experienced real danger in a small boat, but he'd feared them since earliest childhood. And when his grandmother, who'd practiced spiritualism, told him he'd meet his death in one, the nightmares got worse.

But, if he wanted the satisfaction of killing Zanon Parma, he'd have to climb aboard, and he deeply, deeply wanted that satisfaction, so he steeled his resolve and stepped over the gunwale.

Careca picked up an oar, pushed the boat free of the land and dropped the prop to the vertical position. "Hold on, Senhor."

And they were off, streaking toward the island.

"How long is this going to take?" Muniz shouted over the sound of the engine.

"Not long, Senhor," Careca shouted back. "About twenty minutes."

"*Twenty minutes?* The ferryboat takes fifteen. And this thing is a lot faster."

"The ferryboat docks at the closest point to the mainland, Senhor, and it's a long way from our destination. This way, we land less than a hundred meters from Senhor Parma's house."

Crossing in front, red and green running lights glowed from small vessels navigating the channel. Beyond them, the white lights of the island sparkled.

"That's the Ilhabela Yacht Club," Careca said, pointing to a cluster somewhat yellower than the rest. "The Parma house is several kilometers that way."

He gestured off into the darkness. That part of the island was no more than a towering, black lump.

Muniz looked up. There was no moon. A veil of mist dimmed the stars. He looked down. The water, too, was black—and God only knew how deep. The thought of immersing himself in it terrified him. He took it out in impatience and anger.

"Where's my goddamned gun? You were supposed to provide me with a gun?"

"And we have, Senhor. You'll be using a Taurus PT 92."

Muniz's anger escalated.

"I've never fired a Taurus PT 92."

"We'll be happy to show you the weapon's features, Senhor. And, since you specified you wanted to be close—"

Muniz cut him off. "Is that the only weapon you've got?"

"No, Senhor. Reiner has a Smith and Wesson .44 Magnum, I have a Glock .40, and Aldo has a Sig Sauer P290. But I suggest you use the PT 92."

"I don't give a good goddamn about your suggestion. I'm going to use that .44 magnum of Reiner's. I have one of those myself."

"It doesn't have a noise suppressor, Senhor. None of them do. Only the PT 92. That's why we provided it."

Muniz wiped his sweating palms on his shorts. The trip was taking too damned long. But he recognized that a note of hysteria had come into his voice, and he didn't want to give his terror away to Careca, so he fell into a petulant silence.

After ten minutes of it, more or less, Careca pointed to a plastic crate in the bow of the boat. "Can you see a flashlight in there, Senhor?"

Muniz leaned forward to look. "Yes," he said. They were much closer to the shoreline now, and he felt he might be able to trust his voice once again, so he swallowed and said, "How are we going to do this thing?"

"Aldo visited the house, Senhor, while the family was at the beach. He made a sketch of the interior and discovered where everyone sleeps."

He sounded relieved that Muniz had backed off on his anger. But Muniz hadn't. He was simply suppressing it.

"Who's *everyone?*" he snapped.

"Parma's wife and two daughters are with him. The wife shares his bed; the two children are in a separate bedroom. What I propose, Senhor, is that Aldo, Reiner and I enter the house wearing hoods. We'll herd the children into their parents' bedroom. Reiner will hold them, and the wife, at gunpoint. Aldo and I will bring Parma out to you."

"The hell you will. Let me tell you how it's really going to work. I'll go into the house with you. You hold Parma at bay while I kill his wife and kids in front of him."

Careca looked at him aghast. "His wife, Senhor? And his children?"

"Yes. That will be much worse for him. The bastard will suffer even more. That's it! That's what I want to do. And we won't have to worry about witnesses, because there won't be anyone left to—"

"No," Careca said, dropping the *Senhor*.

Muniz was outraged. "What the hell do you mean, *no*? How dare you say no to me? I'm paying the bills. I call the shots."

Careca shook his head, calm, but firm. "The Colonel," he said, "would not approve of the extermination of Parma's entire family."

"Oh, for Christ's sake! Do you think I'm stupid? I know what you're doing, and you know what? I won't even quibble. How much more do you want?"

"It's not a question of the money, Senhor."

"What?"

For Muniz, *everything* was a question of money. His astonishment at learning that a thug like Careca was capable of thinking differently almost banished his fear of the boat from his head. Almost.

"It's not a question of the money," Careca repeated.

"That's the stupidest damned thing I've ever heard. Let's call the Colonel."

"The Colonel instructed me, Senhor, not to call him from the region of Ilhabela. He doesn't want any record of telephone calls that might tie him to this incident. I'm the operational commander, the decision is mine, and the decision is no. We will *not* help you kill Parma's wife and children."

Muniz still didn't quite believe him.

"A hundred thousand," he said. "An additional hundred thousand American dollars for the wife and kids."

"No, Senhor."

"Two-hundred, then. Two-hundred thousand to split any way you like. None of it has to go the Colonel."

Again, Careca shook his head. "For all the money in the world, Senhor, the answer would still be no."

"You may be some kind of a goddamned moralist, but I doubt your friends Reiner and Aldo will think the same way."

Muniz couldn't see Careca's features in the darkness, but he felt his eyes upon him.

"I know them better than you, Senhor, and I assure you they will. We are not in the business of killing children or innocent women."

"Don't give me that holier-than-thou shit. You're hired killers, for Christ's sake. It's what you do."

"We may be hired killers, Senhor, but we are not psychopaths."

"Are you calling me a psychopath?"

"No, Senhor, I'm not calling you a psychopath."

He wasn't. But he was thinking it. Muniz was sure of that.

Again, a silence fell between them. And it went on long enough for Muniz's anger to surge up again. He was a maelstrom of emotions now, fear, anger and, the closer they got to the shore, anticipation.

About fifty meters out, Careca turned the bow 90 degrees to port and said, "Please pick up the flashlight, Senhor, and point it straight ahead."

Muniz didn't reply; he just did it.

"Yes, Senhor," Careca said, speaking as if he had, "like that. Now turn it on, count to three, and extinguish it."

Muniz did—and was answered by a flash of light off the starboard bow. Careca changed course and steered toward it.

Emerging out of the darkness, Muniz saw a sandy beach and the dim outlines of two men. Careca cut the engine and raised the prop. Just as the boat lost headway, one of the figures stepped into the water, seized the mooring line coiled in the bow and dragged the vessel onto the sand.

It was Reiner.

Careca climbed out of the boat and signaled his passenger to do likewise. Muniz, with great relief, and still trembling slightly, set his feet onto dry land. The four conspirators gathered together just short of the road.

"Almost no traffic," Aldo reported. "The last car was ten minutes ago, the previous one about thirteen minutes before that. We go with the plan?"

"We go with the plan," Careca confirmed.

"If last night is any indication, they'll retire early, about ten."

Careca looked at his watch. Muniz could see his lips moving as he made the calculation. "About two and a half hours to go," he said. "I'm going to have a little nap behind that big rock over there. Aldo, you take the first hour, Reiner, the second. Then wake me. And Reiner. . ."

"Sim, Senhor?"

"Give Senhor Muniz his PT 92—and show him how to use it."

Chapter Twenty-Four

SOMEONE TURNED ON THE overhead light. Zanon Parma blinked in the sudden glare.

"Wake up," a high, squeaky voice said.

The prosecutor raised his head, caught sight of two hooded figures in his bedroom and shot bolt upright.

"Cooperate, Parma," the man said, "and your wife and daughters won't get hurt."

Beside him, Iara trembled in fear and clutched at his hand. As best he could, he leaned over to shelter her with his body.

The man who'd spoken was the larger of the two, taller and wider at the shoulders. The short sleeves on his black T-shirt exposed tattoos on his arms. On the right, above the hand holding the pistol, the design was of a bird of prey. On the left was a lynx, or maybe a cougar, baring its fangs.

The other hooded figure also held a pistol, but he had no tattoos, had not spoken, offered nothing to remember him by.

There was a commotion in the hallway. A third hooded figure entered the room, herding Doxy and Lili. Lili had tears streaming down her cheeks. Iara whimpered in his arms.

"If you don't want your family hurt," the spokesman said to Zanon, "you'll do exactly as I say."

Zanon remembered the advice his cop friends had given him: *If you're ever the victim of armed assailants, never provoke them. Never react. Never resist. Always obey.*

"We won't give you any trouble," he said. "Will we, darling? Will we, girls?"

"No," Iara said. "Take anything you want."

Doxy took her thumb out of her mouth and shook her head. Lili sniffled and looked at her lap.

"She's only six," Zanon said, "but she's a very good girl. Aren't you, Lili?"

Lili, still sniffling, nodded.

"You see?" Zanon said. "She'll do exactly what you tell her to do. And so will I."

"Get up," the man said.

"Where—"

"Shut up. Do it!"

Zanon threw the covers aside. "You want me to get dressed?"

"I told you to shut up. Stand up, take three steps toward me and face the bed."

As soon as he'd turned his back, one of them, he couldn't see which, grabbed his wrists and shackled them.

"Now turn around and start walking."

Not a robbery then, Zanon thought. *A kidnapping.*

At the door of the bedroom, he looked back and gave his wife and children a reassuring nod.

"It will be all right," he said, "you'll see."

He badly wanted to believe it. But he couldn't—not quite.

Iara made a valiant attempt to smile at him—and failed.

They marched him out the front door, across the road and onto the beach.

Out of the darkness, a figure emerged, a man without a hood.

It was Orlando Muniz.

And it was only then that Zanon Parma realized what fate awaited him.

MUNIZ WAS ecstatic, but cautious. The prosecutor was a much bigger man—and, no doubt, desperate. "Is he cuffed?" he asked Careca.

"He is, Senhor."

"Make him kneel."

Careca pressed a heavy hand on Zanon's shoulder. The prosecutor lost his balance and fell to one side. Aldo bent over and righted him.

"*Boa noite*, Senhor Public Prosecutor," Muniz said gleefully. "How does it feel, eh? How does it feel now the roles are reversed?"

"What do you want, Muniz?" Zanon's voice was dull. Muniz was sure he already knew exactly what he wanted, but he told him anyway.

"Your life," he replied with a grin.

Parma nodded, as if he'd known the answer before he'd asked the question.

"And you want me to beg for it? So you can refuse? Forget it! I know what kind of a man you are, Muniz. You're going to kill me whatever I say. So fuck you."

Muniz frowned in disappointment. This was wrong, not at all as he'd imagined it. Whenever he'd played out this scene in his head, Parma had been begging for his life, not treating him as if he was something the prosecutor had picked up on the sole of his shoe. Where was his two-hundred thousand dollars worth of satisfaction?

But then he had a thought.

"Call Reiner on the radio," he ordered. "Tell him to bring the bastard's wife and children."

And that did the trick.

"Leave my wife and children out of this," Parma said. "You want me to beg? I'll beg. I'll do any goddamned thing you want, as long as you leave them alone."

Muniz leaned in close, studied Parma's eyes in the dim light.

Yes! The man was starting to cry. This, now, was more like it!

"Your wife is going to get bullets in both of her kneecaps," he said, slowly and distinctly, relishing every word for the exquisite pain he knew he was causing, "and I'm going to bring your daughters up close so they can see it happen. They'll get the same treatment before I kill them. Then, and only then, it's going to be your turn."

Parma pitched forward on the sand, laying his head at Muniz's feet. If the prosecutor hadn't been cuffed, he would have been gripping his tormenter by the ankles.

"For God's sake, Muniz, they're innocent! They never did anything to you."

Muniz's smile became an outright laugh.

"Innocent?" he said. "I don't give a damn about innocent. All I care about is making you suffer." He turned to Careca. "Call Reiner."

"No," Careca said.

Muniz's good humor vanished. He turned on the bigger man.

"What? What did you say?"

"We had this conversation once before, Senhor. My position is still the same."

"Three-hundred thousand," Muniz said. "Three-hundred thousand United States dollars."

Three-hundred thousand dollars was a trifle, a bagatelle, a miniscule part of his vast fortune. But it was a considerable sum for a man like Careca, and Muniz, accustomed to buying men the way he bought objects, was certain the killer would be unable to resist.

But he was wrong.

"Not for four," Careca said, "not for six, not for any amount. I'm not negotiating with you. I'm telling you no."

Muniz was more than humiliated, he was flabbergasted. Everyone had their price. Everyone. But he was in a hurry, and he didn't want to argue with the idiot, so he appealed to Aldo.

"How about you, eh? Three-hundred thousand American dollars?"

"No," Aldo said.

Parma, with an effort, raised his head and looked first at Aldo, then at Careca.

"Thank you," he said, with relief. "Thank you both."

Muniz kicked sand at him.

"You keep the fuck out of it! Don't you get it, you stupid bastard? They're helping me *kill* you."

Parma blinked the sand away and met Muniz's eyes. "But they're *not* helping you kill my wife and daughters. And that, you degenerate, sadistic bastard, merits my thanks."

Muniz saw red. Frustration overpowered reason. He struck the prosecutor in the face with the barrel of his pistol, then reversed it, and using the grip like the head of a club, hit him again and again, taking out his anger not just with Parma, but with the whole damned lot of them.

He might well have finished the job right there, by beating Parma's head to a bloody pulp, if Careca hadn't reached out and grabbed his wrist.

"What the hell are you doing?" Muniz said. "Take your hands off me."

"We didn't sign on, Senhor, to watch you beat him, or to harm his wife, or his children. We signed on to help you kill him. And that's all. Shoot him now and end it."

"No."

"Yes," Careca said. "Do it now. Or I will."

"The hell you will," Muniz said. "I paid for him. He's mine, and I'm going to get my money's worth. He worked the slide on his pistol and chambered a round. "Every last centavo's worth."

He brought the muzzle of his silencer within a few centimeters of Parma's knee and fired, then destroyed the other kneecap in the same fashion, then shot him in the genitals. He was smiling while he did it, but when there was no reaction from his victim, the smile faded.

"He didn't feel a thing, Senhor," Careca said. "You knocked him unconscious before you shot him."

Muniz stared at the pistol in his hand, as if he was surprised to find it there. He looked down at Parma. It was true. The prosecutor had suffered no pain.

"We'll wait," he said. "We'll wait until he wakes up."

"No, Senhor, we will not," Careca said. "We'll leave now. It's finished."

"It's not. He's not dead."

Careca pointed his pistol at Parma's forehead and fired a single shot.

"He is now," he said.

Careca's weapon had no noise suppressor. Up at the house, Reiner must have heard the report. The radio on Careca's belt burst into life.

"That's it?" came Reiner's voice.

Careca pushed the talk button. "That's it," he said.

"I'm on my way," Reiner said.

Careca turned to Muniz. "We're leaving now, Senhor Muniz," he said, "so take your disgusting psychotic ass over to the goddamned boat and get on board."

Chapter Twenty-Five

"THAT WAITRESS," ARNALDO SAID, as she sashayed away from their table to fill their order for a third round of after-dinner drinks, "has the soul of a china cabinet."

After his second post-prandial whiskey Arnaldo was apt to turn philosophical. But this time, although he'd obviously designed the remark to be intriguingly enigmatic, it didn't engender the desired response.

Silva's mind was occupied with their next move, so instead of asking his sidekick why he thought the waitress had the soul of a china cabinet, he said, "I think we should question Jamil Al-Fulan."

Arnaldo willingly switched gears.

"Jamil Al-Fulan? That guy Jaco called a hatemonger? The one Bruna was afraid of?"

"Him."

"We know, for sure, that he threatened to kill Nestor. You think he might also be connected to the bombing case?"

"Maybe."

Arnaldo stirred the ice in his glass with a forefinger. "So you want to go to Ciudad del Este?"

Silva nodded. "We've pretty much run out of people to question here in Curitiba."

"Plus the fact," Arnaldo said, "that Hector told you he's going there, and you want to get back into that bombing case."

"It makes sense, doesn't it? Team up, so we can cover more ground."

"You're the boss. You want me to get the concierge to book us a flight?"

Silva nodded. "For tomorrow morning. They'll be staying on the Brazilian side of the river, at the Hotel das Cataratas. Book us into the same place."

"For how long?"

"Three nights. We'll extend it if we have to. Meanwhile, I'll call Jaco and get him to set up a meeting with that friend of his, Ismail Khouri."

"You gonna tell Serpa we're leaving town?"

"I'd better."

"Are you going to tell him why?"

"No. Just that we're going south on a lead—and we'll contact him when we return."

It was almost three in the morning when Orlando Muniz got back to São Paulo, but he was still furious. He tossed his keys on the coffee table, picked up the telephone and called the Colonel to complain.

To his surprise, the Colonel answered immediately. What was more, he sounded alert.

"I don't discuss business by telephone," he said. "Meet me in the same place as last time."

"When?"

"Noon."

"I'll be there," Muniz said.

Once again, the Colonel was sipping beer. He was at the same table, and wearing the same black leather jacket. This time, though, there was but one glass.

Muniz took a seat and opened his mouth to speak, but the Colonel spoke first.

"I'm cancelling our arrangement," he said.

Muniz was taken aback. "You're *what?*"

"You heard me, Senhor Muniz. I won't repeat myself. You got half of what you wanted. You'll have to be content with that."

Muniz leaned across the table. "I didn't get half of what I wanted. I got nowhere near half. I wanted the *filho da puta* to beg for his life—and he didn't. I stipulated I wanted to kill him myself—and I didn't get the chance. Careca fired the kill shot. Did he tell you that?"

The Colonel nodded. "He did."

"Did he also tell you that Parma wouldn't crawl, wouldn't grovel? That it was only when I told your guys to bring his wife and kids down to the beach that I got any reaction out of him at all? And then fucking Careca ruined it by saying he wouldn't do it. Did he tell you that?"

"He did."

"And did he also tell you that Parma thanked him? Actually *thanked him* for leaving his wife and daughters out of it?"

"He told me the whole story. He even told me that Parma told you to *go fuck yourself.* And you know what? I sympathize with that sentiment. You, Senhor Muniz, go too far."

"What the hell do you mean, I go too far?"

"Don't raise your voice to me, Senhor Muniz. I'm not one of your employees, and I don't like it."

Muniz repeated the question, but in a softer voice and without the epithet.

"You don't think trying to bribe my men so you can torture and kill a perfectly innocent woman and her children is going too far?"

"What is it with you? You and your men are all professional killers. Why should you care?"

"I care, Senhor Muniz, because I have principles, which you clearly do not."

The Colonel picked up his glass and took a sip of beer.

Muniz extended a forefinger, would have pointed it at the Colonel's face, then realized whom he was talking to and stabbed it onto the table instead. "You accepted a deal whereby I was supposed to fire the kill shot. Then one of your men did it. And you defend him? Where's the principle in that?"

"Careca was the tactical commander. As such, he had responsibility for the safety of his men. In his judgment, staying on that beach any longer could have led to discovery, which, in turn, could have put those men into jeopardy. He didn't knock Parma unconscious. You did. And to wait for him to recover consciousness would have been foolhardy. He instructed you to fire the kill shot. He even insisted. Isn't that true?"

"Well, yes, but—"

"But nothing. You, Senhor Muniz, are a psychopath with the morals of a feral cat. I want nothing more to do with you. The price we agreed upon was four hundred thousand dollars for both men. You paid half in advance. That will cover my fee for Parma. In addition, we incurred expenses of about five thousand Reais, but that amount of money is trivial, and in the interest of severing our relationship as quickly as possible, I'm going to forget about it."

"Not so fast. I—"

"Senhor Muniz, do you have any idea, any idea at all, who you're dealing with? We do not like you. So stop pushing your luck. Get up from that chair, right now, and get out of my sight."

MUNIZ, FUMING, stormed out of Leo's Bar and returned to his flat. He was in the hallway, fishing for his keys, when he heard the telephone ring. He managed to unlock the door, and pick up the handset before the caller hung up.

"Muniz," he said, treating it like a business call. The vast majority of all his calls could be so classified. Muniz had few friends, but as it turned out, this was one of them.

"Congratulations," Orestes Saldana said.

"You heard?"

"I did. It was on the radio. I look forward to hearing the details sometime."

"It was nowhere as good as I thought it was going to be. Did you call me just for that? To congratulate me?"

"No. I called about the other one. You asked me to keep tabs on him, remember?"

"Of course, I remember."

"He left town this morning."

"Damn!"

"But not for Brasilia."

"Where then?"

"Foz do Iguaçu."

"Foz do Iguaçu? Why that's—"

"Perfect. I know. I thought you'd be pleased."

"How long is he staying?"

"Three days."

"Do you know where?"

"The Hotel das Cataratas."

"Good. Good. You're a real friend. Listen, I'm going to need some . . . people. I've had a . . . misunderstanding with my former associates."

After a short pause, Saldana said, "You'll be flying to your place in Argentina?"

"Tomorrow."

"How many do you need?"

"Three should do it."

"You'll have room on your aircraft?"

"Yes."

"Then stop off in Medianeira. I'll have them waiting for you."

Chapter Twenty-Six

THERE IS A PLACE, on the border between Brazil and Argentina, where the Iguaçu River plunges over a highland plateau.

On the Brazilian side, within a huge national park, stands the Hotel das Cataratas.

Pink with white trim, and built in the Portuguese colonial style, the building is a fifteen-minute stroll from the mightiest of Iguaçu's 275 waterfalls, a U-shaped, 82-meter-high, 700-meter-long chasm called *A Garganta do Diabo*, the Devil's Throat.

Almost half of the river's water tumbles over it; a cloud of mist sometimes rises above it, and the roar that emanates from it can often be heard within the rooms of the hotel.

That day, the river was high from the rains, and the wind was blowing toward them, carrying with it a thunder so constant, and so loud, that Hector's voice was proving difficult to hear.

Arnaldo got up from his seat on the couch to close the window; Danusa gave him a thankful nod, but Silva, sitting closer, and hanging on his nephew's every word, seemed oblivious to the reduction in noise.

". . . what the news reader said was sketchy," Hector was saying, "so I called Mara and asked her to contact the cops on Ilhabela for more details. She wasn't able to get back to me before we took off."

"So you only got the full story when you landed?"

"Correct."

"Who found him?"

"Some kids," Danusa said, "on their way to have an early-morning swim."

"They don't get many murders on the island," Hector continued. "The police chief himself turned out for it. He knew Zanon by sight, saw how it went down, realized he was out of his depth, and called in reinforcements."

"From where?"

"São Paulo. And when Janus Prado heard who the victim was, he assigned himself as lead investigator."

"Good," Silva said. "Nobody better."

"He took a full forensics team. Mara's liaising with him and will call whenever there's anything new to report."

"So what do we know up to now?"

"They shot Zanon four times, once in each knee, once in the groin, once in the head. The wounds to his knees and groin looked to be from one weapon, the wound to his head from another."

"What about Iara? Was she in the house when they took him?"

"Yes."

Silva grimaced. "The children?"

"Also."

"Are they all okay?"

"Physically, yes."

"Thank God. Do they know?"

"There was no keeping it from Iara. She heard the shot."

"Didn't you just say there'd been four shots?"

"Yes, but she only heard one. Another reason why Janus suspects two weapons were used. He figures one had a silencer."

Silva's compassion for Zanon's wife and children was layered with a cold anger. He gave in to the anger. It was more productive.

"What's Iara's story?"

"Two men woke them from a sound sleep. Then a third man brought in their two kids. All three wore hoods."

"So there's no chance she can identify any of them?"

Hector shook his head. "But we're not entirely clueless. Iara's observant. One had some pretty unique tattoos, and she can describe them. He also had a high, squeaky voice that sounded, she said, very strange coming from a guy as big as he was. Another one had blond hair on the back of his hands, so probably ditto on his head."

"Okay. Go on."

"They handcuffed Zanon and led him out. The blond guy stayed with her and the kids. A while later she heard the shot. The man talked to someone on a radio, warned her not to leave the house unless she wanted her children to wind up dead. So, of course, she didn't. She was still there when the cops came knocking."

"And that's all she knows?"

"In essence, yes."

Arnaldo muttered an unintelligible word, just one and delivered just above a whisper. The times when Arnaldo was most subdued were the times when he was most angry.

For a moment, all of them were silent. Then, Silva said: "The scene?"

"On the beach, just a short walk from the house. The killers arrived and escaped by boat. It left an impression on the sand. An inflatable, apparently."

"Can they identify the size and type?"

"They're working on it. Also, there was an additional set of footprints, a man wearing sandals. He stayed near the waterline, pacing back and forth, until they brought him Zanon. Zanon was made to kneel. At a given point, the guy also knelt, probably to get a better look at his handiwork."

"Handiwork?"

"Zanon's head was beaten to a pulp."

"Pistol whipped?"

"Probably."

"Did they take anything from the house?"

"No."

"Was Zanon wearing his watch when they found him?"

"Yes."

"So that rules out robbery."

"It was revenge," Arnaldo said. "The beating and the shots to the knees and groin speak to that. The person behind it not only wanted Zanon dead, he also wanted to see him suffer. He was the guy on the beach."

"I agree," Hector said. "And I'll take it a step further: He was waiting there, because he didn't cover his face. He wanted Zanon to know who was torturing him, who was killing him."

"So who do we know," Silva said, "who not only hated Zanon enough to want to torture and kill him, but also had the means to hire people, professional people, to help him do it?"

"That *filho da puta*, Orlando Muniz," Arnaldo said, slapping the coffee table hard enough to rattle the cups in their saucers.

Silva nodded and turned to Hector. "Tell Mara to call Janus, let him know he should interrogate Muniz."

"Not that it's going to do any good," Arnaldo said, "Muniz is an *escroto*, but he's not stupid. He'll have an ironclad alibi, we can be damned sure of that."

"And damned sure of something else," Hector said.

"Which is?" Silva said.

"If it was him, he's going to go after you next."

Chapter Twenty-Seven

IN THE EARLY SUMMER of 1983, Orlando Muniz went to Buenos Aires.

Most Brazilians, back then, visited the city to enjoy the wine, the food and the nightlife for which the Argentinean capital was justly famous.

Not Muniz. He was there for one reason alone: to make money.

The country was going through another of its periodic crises. Cash was tight. Houses and apartments, estates and businesses, could be had for a song.

In five years, or ten, Orlando figured, they'd be worth three, four, five times more than they were then. And it was highly unlikely they'd ever be worth less.

He was sitting in a restaurant on the Costanera Norte, his knife sliding through an extremely rare *bistec de lomo*, when his real-estate agent, a woman who was helping him to gobble up one property after another, posed a question.

"Did you notice the wall?"

"Wall? What wall?"

"There," she said and hooked a thumb.

He glanced over her shoulder—and froze.

"Are those real?"

She nodded. "Yes, Señor Muniz, all real, every last one of them."

He put down his knife and fork, got up from his chair, and went for a closer look. The wall was papered entirely with banknotes, most of them of one peso, but there were fives and tens as well.

She rose and stood beside him.

"The old currency," she said. "So worthless, now, that it's cheaper per square meter than paint, cheaper, than wallpaper. When we switched from the old to the new, these *pesos antiguos*"—she tapped the wall with a lacquered forefinger— "were exchanged at a rate of ten-thousand to one, ten thousand *antiguos* for a single *Peso Argentino*. And you know what the *Peso Argentino* has come to be worth. Almost nothing! That's hyperinflation for you. You won't see *that* in many places in the world."

Compared to us, she seemed to be saying, *you Brazilians are amateurs. We Argentineans are the real experts at destroying a nation's economy.*

Back then, before they'd been humbled by subsequent events, arrogance had been an Argentinean national characteristic. Muniz had been exposed to a great deal of it in recent days.

"But the owner of this restaurant," the woman went on, as they returned to their table, "didn't put those banknotes there just because they were cheap."

"No?" Muniz picked up his fork, speared a piece of meat and popped it into his mouth.

"No," she said. "He was making a political statement. He is a great landholder in Corrientes Province. He raises the beef you're eating."

Muniz didn't care a damn about the great landholder of Corrientes Province, but he appreciated the quality of the man's beef—and he said so.

"Yes," she said. "It's good, isn't it? That's one of the reasons I brought you here."

"*One* of the reasons?" he said, a trickle of blood escaping from one corner of his mouth.

She waited for him to blot it away with his napkin, and then got down to it: "He has always been rich, and he isn't poor now, but by buying this restaurant, and renovating it, he has overextended himself."

"You mean he needs an influx of cash?"

"Precisely, Señor."

She put down her knife and fork, leaned back in her chair and looked at him expectantly.

Muniz cut another piece of meat and thought while he chewed. Then he swallowed and shook his head.

"I'm not interested," he said. "I don't know anything about the restaurant business, and I wouldn't trust any Argentinean to run one for me."

To her credit, the real estate agent, a nationalist to her fingertips, didn't even raise a plucked eyebrow at the slur. "I'm not talking about this restaurant, Señor Muniz."

"No? What *are* you talking about?"

"In addition to his estates on the pampas, and this restaurant, Señor Nogales—that's his name, Señor Nogales—also owns a *hacienda* in Misiones Province."

"Misiones Province. Where the hell is that?"

"It borders on your country. Also on Paraguay."

"He wants to sell it?"

"He does Señor, and he's been trying to sell it for the last several months. He's had no takers."

"What's the land good for?"

"Agriculture."

"What does he grow?"

"Yerba mate."

"That stuff *gauchos* drink out of gourds?"

"That's right, Señor. A great deal of it is consumed here in Argentina."

"In the south of my country as well. So there's a good market for that stuff, is there?"

"An excellent market, Señor. I even drink it myself."

"I think it tastes like shit."

Her smile didn't falter. "But many, many people do not. And you, Señor, are an agriculturist yourself, are you not? You grow sugar cane? Coffee?"

"What if I do?"

"I'm told the land in Misiones Province is also suitable for the cultivation of other crops."

"Such as?"

"I don't know them all, Señor. Sugar cane is one."

"Now you're talking. How big is the property?"

"Big, Señor. Twelve hundred hectares."

"Big? That's not big."

"For Argentina, Señor, it's quite big."

"And, for us, it's nothing, but that's not to say I'm not interested. Any houses? Outbuildings?"

"A large house, Señor. Various barns. Servants' quarters. Modern agricultural machines of various types. Hookup to the electric and telephone networks and located just off a paved road. There's even an airstrip."

"An airstrip, eh? So I could install a reliable Brazilian manager in the house and fly in and out to check on the staff growing my sugar, or whatever the hell else I choose to grow?"

"There is already a manager, a man who has lived there with his family for many years. I am told he's honest, reliable and—"

"And, if I buy the place, he's out of a job. I'm not about to entrust a property of mine to some Argentinean. If we go any further with this, I'll bring a man down from Brazil."

Her smile was getting brittle, but it was still there. "You're interested, Señor?"

"I might be. Let's try offering half of whatever he's asking." Muniz picked up his empty bottle of Quilmes and waved it under her nose. "Order me another beer."

Thus it was that Orlando Muniz came to own a property separated by little more than a river from the Hotel das Cataratas—which made it an ideal staging point from which to launch an attempt on the life of Mario Silva.

Chapter Twenty-Eight

"When I think of suicide bombers," Luis Chagas said, studying Salem Nabulsi's photograph, "I think of guys with beards, not some kid with pimples."

Chagas headed the Federal Police's Foz do Iguaçu field office. He'd replaced Nestor Cambria when Cambria resigned to work with Plínio Saldana.

The photo had been provided by the Paraguayan authorities. It showed Nabulsi as he'd been at fifteen, when he'd applied for his national identity card.

"You're not alone," Danusa said, "but it's a misconception. Many of them aren't much older than he was back then."

"Really?"

Chagas was in his mid-thirties, but already balding. He scratched the crown of his head where hair had once been.

"Teenagers are just about the most selfish creatures on the face of the earth," he said. "I know. I've got one. How do you go about convincing a teenager to blow himself up?"

The three of them, Danusa, Chagas and Hector were in a high-rise in downtown Foz do Iguaçu. The window of Chagas's office afforded a splendid prospect of the minarets and dome of the Omar Ibn Al-Khattab mosque, the largest in Brazil and the pride of the city's Muslim community. But none of them were in a mood to appreciate the view.

"By convincing him," Danusa said, "that the rewards of Paradise are greater than anything he can expect from this world, and that killing infidels is a quick and easy way to get there."

"You make it sound easy."

"Not at all," she said. "Overcoming self-preservation, which is what it takes, can't be done overnight. It's a question of years. And it can't be done at all if the person being brainwashed is already locked into an adult mindset. That's why the mullahs like to get them young."

"Mullahs? So it's done by clerics?"

"Mullahs aren't always clerics. They're Islamic scholars, respected for their knowledge of the Qur'an, but there are those among them who bend and twist that knowledge. They sell their students on martyrdom, and paradise, and the *houris* waiting for them there, and send them out into the world to maim and kill."

"And they do all that in those madrasas I keep hearing about, right?"

"Generally, yes."

So why don't we just crack down and close them all?"

"Because most are perfectly innocent places run by well-intentioned people."

"So there are good madrasas and bad madrasas?"

"There are. But the only way to find out which is which is by making inquiries in the Islamic community. And many of the people you talk to will tell you good madrasas are bad madrasas, and vice-versa."

This time, instead of scratching his bald spot, Chagas rubbed it. "Depending on their personal convictions?"

"Exactly."

"Which is why," Hector said, finally joining in, "we'd like to know more about the Muslim community around here in general—and about the madrasas in particular."

Chagas kept rubbing, but he moved his hand from his head to his chin.

"I've got just the guy to help you with that. One of my best men. Raised locally. Egyptian parents. Speaks Arabic. His name's Abasi Ragab."

"Sounds perfect," Hector said. "Why don't we get him in here?"

"He's off today. Where are you staying?"

"The Cataratas."

"Nice. Lovely place. I'll arrange for a meet. What else can I help you with?"

"The explosives."

Hector filled him in on what Lefkowitz had learned by tracing the taggants and said, "So we've got to talk to someone within the Paraguayan military."

Chagas shook his head. "The man you want to talk to," he said, "is Matias Chaparro."

"We've already scheduled an appointment with him. But he's police, not military."

"Doesn't matter. He's still the guy to talk to. Matias has his finger on the pulse of everything that happens around here. Everything dishonest, that is."

"If he's dishonest, what makes you think he'd be willing to talk to us?"

"Because I doubt Matias would approve of the stuff having been used in a terrorist attack. If he was involved in the deal, and the odds are he was, it's my guess they told him it was going to a drug gang. He would have found that acceptable."

"But not that the stuff would be used by terrorists?"

"No."

"A moral objection?"

Chagas shook his head. "Matias isn't moral. He's purely practical. Terrorist attacks call down too much heat. They're not good for business. That's what he'd object to."

"I don't think he and my uncle are likely to get along."

Chagas didn't ask who Hector's uncle was, a sure sign he knew it already.

"You might be surprised," he said. "Matias can be quite charming. Comes from a good family, has a university education, is well-read and all that."

"But he's crooked."

"He wouldn't have been appointed if he wasn't."

"Then I guarantee you, my uncle won't like him. Have you heard of a guy named Ismail Khouri?"

Chagas shook his head. "The name doesn't ring any bells. Who's he?"

"A Lebanese Muslim, lives here in Foz, has a business in Ciudad del Este."

"So he's a crook?"

"In his case, we have no reason to think so."

"No?" Chagas looked dubious. "Let's see."

He picked up his phone, gave Khouri's name, and asked to check the files. When he hung up, he said, "Why are you interested in him?"

"He's a possible source of information, a friend of a friend."

"Friend or not, it doesn't mean he'll talk to you," Chagas said. "If he knows anything, and he passes it along, it could get him and his whole family killed. He'll know that. They all know that. It's the reason that getting reliable information out of anybody in this town is like pulling teeth."

The door opened and his secretary came in. She was Chinese, slim and elegant.

"Thanks, Mei," he said.

"*Não há de que*," she said in accent-free Portuguese. "Anything else?"

"Not at the moment," Chagas said.

She nodded to him, smiled at the visitors, and went out. Chagas opened the file, a thin one, and flipped through it.

"Surprise, surprise," he said. "It looks like your man Khouri is honest after all. Or, at least, what passes for honest in this part of the world." He looked up. "But that's not to say he doesn't make payoffs to the Paraguayan authorities. You can't run a business around here if you don't."

"So I've heard. Let's talk a bit about Jamil Al-Fulan."

Chagas's eyes narrowed, and his nose wrinkled. "That bastard?" he said. "We've got a file on him thirty centimeters thick. Want to see it?"

Hector shook his head. "We requested a copy as soon as his name came up. We've already been through it."

"So why are you asking?"

"We want you to speculate."

"About what?"

Hector told Chagas about the conversation with Nestor's wife, and also about the rumor they'd picked up from Jaco Nassib concerning Plínio Saldana.

"I was aware," Chagas said, "that Al-Fulan was behind the threats to Nestor. We couldn't prove it, of course, much less do anything about it. But that one about Saldana being a crook? That's new for me. First time I've heard it."

"And yet you don't seem surprised."

"I'm not. You work here for a while, and you wind up with a low opinion of most politicians. Matter of fact, you wind up with a low opinion of most cops."

"I don't like to say this, but it has to be asked: Nestor worked here, and he left to work for Saldana. You think he might have been crooked too?"

"Nestor? No way! Nestor was as honest as the day is long. If he had an inkling Saldana was involved in anything dishonest, he wouldn't have taken the job."

"I'm glad to hear you say it," Hector said. "I liked Nestor."

"I more than liked him," Chagas said. "He was a close friend."

"So you weren't happy to see him leave? Even though it meant a promotion for you?"

"On the contrary. I was happy to see him go. As long as he remained here his life was in danger. No doubt about it. I went out to the airport to see him and Bruna off—and I breathed a sigh of relief when I saw them going up the stairs onto the plane."

"How about you?" Danusa said.

"What about me?"

"If Nestor was in danger, you must be as well." She pointed at his wedding ring. "How's your wife dealing with it?"

"She dealt with it," Chagas said, "by taking our son and moving back to Porto Alegre. She said she had no intention of hanging around here and seeing me murdered."

"Your wife left, yet you stayed. Does the job mean that much?"

"I asked for a transfer. He wouldn't give me one."

"Who's *he*?"

"Our revered leader."

"Sampaio?"

"Who else? And since he wouldn't, I've decided to give it all up. I'm looking for a job in the private sector, and as soon as I nail down a halfway decent one, I'm out of here."

"Sorry to hear it. You're going to be a difficult man to replace."

"Sorry is a sentiment you can best save for the poor bastard who takes over this job. As long as Al-Fulan is alive, any honest guy who sits in this chair is going to be a target. Sometimes I think I'm crazy. I could be earning a lot of money. I could have my wife and kid living with me. I could stop worrying about having somebody put a bullet in my back. And all I'd have to do is to turn a blind eye to what that man is doing, but. . ."

"You can't."

"No. I can't." Chagas waved a dismissive hand. "But you didn't come to hear me bitch and moan. Let's get back to Al-Fulan."

"Have you got enough on him to arrest him?"

"I do. I have a warrant, and I have a constant watch on the bridge, but the bastard never crosses it."

"And you can't get him extradited?"

"Al-Fulan? Never! Every damned judge and cop in Ciudad del Este is on his payroll."

"Including Matias Chaparro?"

Chagas twisted impatiently in his chair. "*Especially* Matias Chaparro. And Matias doesn't make any bones about it either. I complain, and he just shakes his head and laughs."

"How about Al-Fulan's links to the Muslim community? Does he have any?"

"Big time. He's making a bid to become the sixth pillar of Islam. He supports mosques on both sides of the border, contributes to charities all over the Muslim world and goes on and on about nonviolent support for the Palestinian cause."

"Nonviolent? You buy that?"

Chagas shook his head. "Not for a minute. If the guy has no compunction about having people killed for business reasons, and he doesn't, why wouldn't he have them killed for Allah as well?"

"What turns a crook into a militant religionist?" Danusa said. "Did he undergo some kind of epiphany?"

"Hell, no," Chagas said. "It's not about God, it's about the greater glory of Jamil Al-Fulan. He's richer than Croesus. And, since his ego is bigger than the Sugar Loaf, he's perfectly willing to part with some of that wealth to play the big man."

"Could playing the big man include blowing up innocent people?" Hector said.

"I wouldn't, for a moment, put it past him," Chagas said.

Chapter Twenty-Nine

THE FRIENDSHIP BRIDGE SPANS the Parana River between the Brazilian city of Foz do Iguaçu and the Paraguayan city of Ciudad del Este. It's a single-arch construction, in reinforced concrete, which measures some 550 meters in length and towers, when the river isn't in flood, as much as 60 meters above the surface.

But this was November and Arnaldo and Silva, as they crossed the frontier from one country to the other, found themselves looking down at an eddying, brown, swift-running stream no more than 30 meters below.

Almost half-a-century old, the bridge was no longer adequate for the volume of traffic. From eight in the morning until past nine in the evening, it was always congested.

Their cab crept forward at a snail's pace, surrounded by hordes of Brazilians heading toward, or returning from, the frenzied bazaar on the Paraguayan side.

Two of the four lanes, one in each direction, were given over to buses. And the buses were packed with people who'd traveled, in some cases, as far as a thousand kilometers to make their purchases.

Flanking the vehicular traffic were pedestrians. Those to their right were crossing into Paraguay. They were empty handed. On the other side, people loaded down with boxes and shopping bags were on their way back.

Weaving among the buses and automobiles were hundreds of motorcycles and motorbikes. The noise they made was giving Silva a headache.

"Is it always like this?" Arnaldo asked.

"Always, Senhor," the driver replied. "So what will you be shopping for today? You want electronics? Perfume for your ladies? Whiskey? Or maybe something a little . . . difficult to find, eh?"

"It's a business trip," Silva said.

"It almost always is, Senhor. That's what Ciudad del Este is all about. Business. Most people are buying there so they can sell somewhere else. Since those bastards from the Brazilian Federal Police have been making such nuisances of themselves, and you might not be able to bring everything you want back with you in my taxi, I know people with whom I can make . . . other arrangements. So what do you want? Don't be shy. Come right out with it. Drugs? Young girls? Weapons? How can I help?"

Silva resisted telling him to whom he was talking and showed him the address he'd jotted onto a piece of paper. "Just take us here."

The driver glanced at it. "Ha!" he said.

"What? Is there some problem?"

"That address, Senhor, is in the heart of the busiest part of town. The street will be congested. If I bring you in there, we'll be stuck in the traffic for an hour or more. That's a waste of your time and mine. I'll bring you close-by and give you directions. You walk the rest of the way."

"Fair enough," Silva said.

"Are you going back today? I'd be honored to take you."

"Not necessary."

That meant he wouldn't be earning a return fare, or a commission from any of the shops he touted, or a tip for putting them into contact with a purveyor of illegal merchandise.

"Oh," the driver said, managing to pack all his

disappointment into a single syllable. He didn't smile again during the remainder of the trip.

When he dropped them off, the two federal cops elbowed their way through seething crowds until they reached their destination.

Inside, Ismail Khouri's establishment was almost as crowded as it had been on the street. Boxes containing MP3 players, cellular phones and cameras lined the shelves. TV sets, complete audio systems and computers were stacked in their original boxes on the floor. Around and about the stacks, salesmen and customers dickered in a number of languages.

"We're looking for Ismail Khouri," Arnaldo said to a man with a nametag.

"In the back."

The man waved them toward the rear of the shop.

Silva had to repeat the process several times, moving deeper and deeper into the establishment with each inquiry.

At last, someone indicated a little man engaged in negotiation with two other men. One was speaking in Spanish, the other in what Silva assumed to be Arabic, and Khouri, if it was Khouri, was doing the translating.

When the business was concluded, and the other two had left, the little man turned to Silva and flashed him a smile.

"Español?" he inquired. "Português?"

"Português," Silva said. "Are you Ismail Khouri?"

"I am," Khouri said in an accent that identified him as a native of São Paulo. "How can I be of service?"

"My name is Silva."

The smile vanished. Khouri gripped Silva by the arm and gave an almost imperceptible shake of his head. His meaning was clear: *Not here. Too many ears.*

"Jaco's friend!" he said effusively. "What a pleasure, what a pleasure. I'm delighted to meet you. And this is?"

"My associate, Senhor Nunes."

Khouri shook hands with both of them. "This is no place to do business. Much too noisy. Please, come to my office. We'll drink tea, or coffee, if you like."

He turned to open a door in the wall behind him. Beyond the door was a corridor, and at the end of the corridor, a stairway. They climbed to the second floor, passed through another door, through a storage room heaped with boxes and, at last, through a third door into a windowless room with three chairs and a Formica-topped table with an ashtray full of butts. Silva, an ex-smoker, wrinkled his nose at the smell.

Khouri switched on the light, took one of the chairs and waved them into the other seats.

"Now," he said, when they were all seated, "we can talk. I hope you haven't identified yourselves as policemen to anyone in my shop."

"We have not," Silva said.

The merchant took a pack of American cigarettes out of his breast pocket and stuck one in his mouth before offering the pack to the other two men. Both refused, but he left the pack on the table anyway.

"In case you change your minds," he said. He lit up and shook out the match before going on: "I can't be seen to be speaking with policemen, not Brazilian policemen anyway."

"So Jaco gave me to understand," Silva said.

"He told me," Khouri said, expelling smoke, "that he's known you even longer than he's known me. May I call you Mario?"

"Please do."

"And you must call me Ismail. How can I help?"

"We'd like to know more about that fellow you mentioned to Jaco."

"Jamil Al-Fulan?"

"Yes."

"Where shall I begin?"

"Wherever you like. The more you can tell us about him, the better."

"Well, let me see." Ismail took a pensive puff. "He's a local boy. I don't know if he was born here, but he was certainly raised here. I heard, once, that his parents owned a small landholding some twenty kilometers outside the city, so he was already visiting Ciudad del Este from his earliest youth. And he quickly saw the opportunities. You'd have to be blind not to."

"So he holds a Paraguayan passport?"

"A Paraguayan one for sure. He may hold others as well, but certainly not a Brazilian one. There was a time, however, when he lived across the river. But problems arose, and he moved back here."

"What kind of problems?"

Ismail tipped ash from his glowing cigarette into the overflowing ashtray and said, "Did you know a man by the name of Nestor Cambria?"

"I did."

"Jamil despised him."

"Why?"

"Because Nestor couldn't be bought. Because Nestor was destroying Al-Fulan's business. Because Nestor made it so hot for Jamil on the Brazilian side he was forced to move back here. Which he didn't like one bit."

"Why didn't he return after Nestor left?"

"Nestor's successor has no more use for Al-Fulan than Nestor did. A fact, by the way, which suits me perfectly well. I'd prefer not to have men like Jamil anywhere in this world, but if Allah wills they must exist, I prefer they exist here, in Paraguay, rather than in Brazil, where I live."

"There was a rumor about Al-Fulan being involved in the smuggling of luxury automobiles."

"That's no rumor. Jamil has been doing it for years."

"For years?"

"Yes, Mario, for years. It's like this: rich Paraguayans, and there are many, like to change their cars every year. They also like luxury, the German cars, mostly, but also the fashionable Italian ones like Ferraris and Maseratis. Jamil founded his business by getting a number of them to place orders and pay a deposit. Then he commissioned people in Brazil to locate and steal the cars and bring them here. His vehicles were much cheaper than those imported legally. Word got around. Even rich people aren't averse to economizing. His business grew."

"And the authorities did nothing?"

Ismail shook his head. "Mario, Mario, this is *Paraguay*," he said, extinguishing his cigarette. "Of course the authorities did nothing. The authorities are his partners. Have you met Matias Chaparro? The head of the National Police here in Ciudad del Este?"

"Not yet. But I have an appointment with him."

Ismail pursed his lips and nodded his head. Then he stood up to empty the contents of the ashtray into a wastebasket in the corner of the room.

"Be careful what you say to him. Chaparro is the man who gets the cars registered. He also turns a blind eye to their being brought into Paraguay."

Silva followed him with his eyes. "Wait. Do you mean to tell me, Ismail, that the registrations aren't falsified? They're real?"

Ismail resumed his place at the table. "Correct. Matias has contacts inside the registry office. He has contacts everywhere."

"So there's never any risk to the purchaser?"

"That's right."

Ismail picked up the pack and took out another cigarette.

"What about the Brazilian side?" Silva went on. "Al-Fulan would need people to locate and steal the vehicles, and he'd have to get them across the border."

"Jamil spent years building up a network," Ismail said, contributing more smoke to the room. "He gets cars from half-a-dozen Brazilian cities, and there was never any problem getting them across the border—until Nestor came along."

"Nestor's predecessor was corrupt?"

"Either that, or he didn't properly control his people. Either way, payoffs were happening for sure. But Nestor changed all that, and his successor has kept up the pressure. So can you see why having a relationship with the Governor of the State of Paraná would have been so very useful to Jamil?"

"I can. A governor would be in a position to do the same thing Chaparro does here: arrange documentation for stolen vehicles. Jamil's supply problem would be solved."

"Exactly."

"So you think it unlikely Jamil was involved in Plínio's murder?"

Ismail tipped more ash. "I do. I cannot imagine how killing Plínio would have been advantageous to Jamil. Quite the contrary."

There was little ventilation in the room and the smoke was beginning to sting Silva's eyes. He blinked. "A falling out among thieves perhaps?"

Ismail shrugged. "Always possible, of course, but . . ."

"You don't think so?"

"No. I don't."

Arnaldo coughed, reminding Ismail of his presence. Reminding him, too, of what he was doing to the atmosphere.

"Sorry," Ismail said. "It gets like this because there aren't any windows. You want me to open the door?"

"Not necessary," Silva said, not wanting to interrupt the flow. "What about Jamil's politics?"

"What about them?"

"Does he support the Palestinian cause?"

Ismail took a moment to consider. "Speaking for the Muslim community here in the Tri-Border-Area, almost all of us do. I object to what the State of Israel is doing to my fellow Muslims. That said, I reject violence as an instrument of change, and I abhor the killing of innocent civilians."

"And Jamil?"

"Jamil's politics, and he makes no secret of them, are far more radical. I cannot say whether he has any hand in the recent outrages in São Paulo and Buenos Aires, but I can tell you he supports a madrasa over on the Brazilian side of the river. The mullah who runs it, a man chosen by Jamil personally, is a fanatic. All he teaches is rote memorization of the suras, a twisted interpretation of the Holy Qur'an, and the hatred of non-Muslims."

"Twisted how?"

"Islam is a religion of peace and love, Mario. He presents it to his students as a religion of violence and hatred."

"Why do their parents put up with it? Why don't they take their children out of there?"

"Jamil regards such withdrawals as an affront. Parents were beaten, intimidated. Word got around. Now, they're too frightened to do anything other than to allow the mullah to brainwash their offspring."

"Were you personally affected by this?"

Ismail put up a forefinger and waved it back and forth.

"Fortunately not. My sons were too old to be enrolled.

The madrasa doesn't take girls. Only boys, and the younger, the better."

"Are all of the parents disillusioned?"

"Not all. That's another one of the problems. In some households, the parents actually endorse what the mullah is teaching."

"They endorse hatred?"

Ismail looked pained, but he nodded. "The older and wiser members of our community continue to stand for what we've always stood for: to live in peace with our neighbors. But Al-Fulan, with the help of that mullah, is working to change all that."

"Preaching jihad?"

Ismail held up a hand, the palm facing Silva.

"Be careful with that word, Mario. It is much misused. For Muslims, there has *always* been jihad. Essentially, jihad is an effort to practice Islam in the face of oppression and persecution, or of fighting the evil in your own heart, or even standing up to a dictator. It does *not* mean, and it has never meant, until quite recently, to spread Islam by slaughtering innocents for the cause."

"Have your people thought about going to the police?"

Ismail shook his head. "People who've been abused are afraid to come forward."

"If Jamil could be taken out of the picture," Silva said, "that would solve it, would it not? The money to run the madrasa would dry up."

"It would," Ismail said. "But our law, Brazilian law, cannot touch him. He never goes to Brazil anymore. And here, in Paraguay, he lives under the protection of the National Police."

"Surely," Silva said, "there must be some judge, some prosecutor here in Paraguay—"

"There isn't. Every last one is on his payroll."

"A man like that," Arnaldo said, no longer able to contain himself, "should be put down like a mad dog."

"I am, as I told you, a man of peace," Ismail said. "But, in Al-Fulan's case, I don't disagree."

BEFORE LEAVING the shop, Silva called the number Ismail was able to provide him with, and asked to speak to the owner of the dealership.

Al-Fulan's secretary, a male, inquired as to the nature of his business.

"I'm a Chief Inspector of the Brazilian Federal Police," Silva said. "I'd like to make an appointment to see him about a confidential matter."

"One moment," the secretary said.

The moment stretched to a full five minutes.

After which, the secretary came back on the line and told Silva that his employer had no interest in meeting with any-one from the Brazilian Federal Police.

And that, consequently, his request for an appointment had been denied.

Chapter Thirty

SMALL AIRCRAFT, MUNIZ HAD long ago concluded, were the most practical form of transport for visiting the more remote corners of his far-flung empire. Down through the years he'd owned five.

His latest, a Cessna Corvalis TTX, was a low-wing monoplane with a range of well over 2,000 kilometers. It took him a little over an hour to pilot it from the Campo de Marte Airport in São Paulo to Saldana's fazenda in rural Paraná, where he touched down on the red earth landing strip at quarter to three in the afternoon.

As he rolled to a stop, trailing dust, Orestes drove up in a jeep.

"Saw you circling the house," he said, when his friend opened the cabin door. "Climb down and hop in."

Muniz shook his head. "I appreciate the invitation, but there are no lights on my landing strip. I have to get there before dark. Where are those men you promised me?"

"There's more than enough daylight left. Come on. They're up at the house."

Muniz glanced at the sky and gave a curt nod. Then he clambered to the ground. Saldana took his foot off the brake and swung the vehicle in a half-circle.

"Good flight?" he asked as they picked up speed and he shifted to a higher gear.

"Blue skies all the way," Muniz said. "Who told you where Silva is staying?"

Saldana took his eyes off the road long enough to shoot

him a conspiratorial grin. "Braulio Serpa. He's State Secretary of Security here in Paraná."

"Serpa's on your payroll?"

Saldana's grin got wider. "He's on everybody's payroll. Serpa's a bigger crook than most of the people he's supposed to be protecting us from. I'll be sorry to see him go."

"He's going?"

"Oh, he's going all right. Don't you read the papers?"

"I've no stake in Paraná. This state doesn't interest me."

"Ah," Saldana said. "Well, it's like this: Serpa was appointed by Abbas, the incumbent governor. And Abbas is about to get his ass whipped in an election. When he goes, Serpa goes."

"Inconvenient for you."

Saldana shrugged. "I'll cut a deal with the next one, or his secretary, or his assistant. Everyone has their price."

"Not everyone. Silva doesn't. Parma didn't."

"They're still talking about that one on the radio. You messed him up good."

"Not good enough."

"Tell me."

"I don't want to talk about it."

"Suit yourself," Saldana said, but his tone of voice suggested he was disappointed.

They topped a rise, and the *casa grande* came into view. Three men were standing on the veranda.

"There they are," Saldana said, pointing them out. "I had them working at my place in Acre, but things got hot, so I brought them here. They've been sitting around on their asses, doing nothing, for over a month. Truth to tell, your request was welcome. I've been getting tired of paying them for nothing."

Acre was a state in the far northwest, deep in the Amazon

rainforest, bordering on Bolivia and Peru. When things got 'hot,' it was because the Federal Police were doing a blitz. And, when the Federal Police were doing a blitz, it was generally because some great landowner, or more than one, had been driving indigenous people, or small farmers, or both, from their land. Murder of those who resisted was essential to the process.

"Damned federal cops," Muniz said. "What do they expect us to do? Give the country back to the Indians?"

"Speaking of federal cops," Saldana said, "you're going to have to use a boat to get at him."

Muniz frowned. "The hell I am. I hate boats. I'll use the bridge."

Saldana shook his head. "You can't."

"Why the hell not? What's going on?"

"They're making a record of everyone who crosses in either direction."

Muniz's mouth dropped open and he turned to stare at Saldana. "Since when?"

"The last six months or so. It's all computerized. They make a digital photo of your identity card, and it goes into a database."

"*Merda!* So, if I cross that bridge—"

"It would generate a record, defeat the whole purpose of making Argentina your operational base."

"Goddamned federal cops! I don't know which I hate more. Them, or boats!"

"For Christ's sake, Orlando. It's only a river. It's either that, or wait for another opportunity."

"I can't wait. I'm running out of time."

"So do it."

Muniz sighed. "I don't know," he said. "I've got to think about this."

The news about the new system of controls had thrown his mind into turmoil. His original plan was no longer valid, because the bridge was no longer an option. And he couldn't land his aircraft on the Brazilian side, because that, too, would leave a record. So Saldana was right. The only way to get at Silva, and not leave a trace of his presence, was to use a boat.

But the mere thought of venturing out onto that infernal river in a little boat absolutely terrified him. And, to make matters worse, he didn't know a damned thing about boats, couldn't steer one, wouldn't even know how to start the engine. And he didn't *want* to know.

What to do?

Saldana brought the jeep to a halt. They climbed out and approached the steps. The three *capangas* stepped down to meet them.

"Donato, Virgilio and Roque," Saldana said, pointing at each as he presented them.

All three men were short and wiry, with skin the color of shoe leather. They could have been brothers. Maybe they were. Muniz didn't care, and he didn't bother to ask. He came straight to the point that was troubling him.

"Raise your hand if you know how to handle a boat with an outboard motor," he said.

All three did.

And that decided him.

Chapter Thirty-One

WHEN DANUSA TOLD THE Nabulsis what their son had done, Aqsa, his mother, dissolved into hysteria.

Barir held his wife close until her wails subsided, then helped her to her feet.

"Wait," he said before leading her out of the room.

They heard the couple mounting the stairs and moving along a corridor above their heads. A moment later a door opened and softly closed. The clock on the mantelpiece ticked. Outside, a child squealed and another laughed. The living room, smelling faintly of middle-eastern spices, was small, but immaculately clean. A sofa in red leather stood against one wall. The Nabulsis weren't rich, but they'd forged a comfortable living for themselves in their new country.

"My guess," Danusa said, "is that neither had an inkling of what their son was up to."

"I agree," Hector said. "I'll go out and give our taxi driver a heads up. This is going to take longer than we thought."

He was back within a couple of minutes, but another quarter-of-an-hour passed before Barir Nabulsi returned.

And, when he did, the distraught father didn't sit down.

"Please," he said, "come back tomorrow. Right now, my wife needs all my attention."

Hector shook his head. "Forgive me. I'm truly sorry to intrude on your grief, but we desperately need to ask you some questions."

Nabulsi became irritated at his persistence: "Why? What's

the hurry? Our son is dead. He can't hurt anyone anymore. Can't you see my wife is devastated?"

"After your son's death," Hector said, responding as if he'd been asked a perfectly reasonable question, "a second bombing occurred in Buenos Aires."

Nabulsi, working hard to control his emotions, nodded. "I saw the coverage on television. Terrible, but—"

"The explosives came from the same source."

Nabulsi put a hand over his mouth, as if he was about to be sick. About ten seconds passed, punctuated only by the ticking of the clock on the mantelpiece and the barking of a dog in a nearby yard. Then Salem's father removed his hand and said, "How can you be sure?"

"They contained tiny color-coded pieces of plastic called taggants. Taggants, when they exist, are unique to every batch of explosive, and they aren't damaged by detonation. "

"So there can be no mistake?"

"None," Hector said. "And we have strong indications that your son's associates have still more of the same explosive."

Nabulsi took a step backward, sank onto the sofa and looked at the floor. "Ask your questions," he said.

"You have no sympathy for your son's act?"

Nabulsi lifted his head, stared squarely into Hector's eyes.

"I share none of Salem's insane convictions. I was a lawyer back home. My wife was the daughter of a doctor. Here, I work in a shop. But I thought it would all be worth it if we could just get away from the fanatics, and the bombing, and the killing. And now this! My own son, a suicide bomber! You ask me if I have sympathy for his act? I answer I have none, none whatsoever. I deplore it."

"Then I am sorry to have to tell you this," Danusa said, "but we also believe that your son murdered a woman in cold blood."

He looked at her as if she'd slapped him.

"Salem? My Salem? When?"

"Shortly before the bombing. He cut her throat. And then he kidnapped her baby."

He shook his head in disbelief, massaged his forehead with the tips of his fingers as if in pain.

"Her baby? In God's name, why?"

"The bomb was heavy. He couldn't carry it on his person. He put it in a baby carriage and used the child to help conceal his intentions."

Barir paled. "May Allah forgive him," he said, "and us for having given life to him."

"You shouldn't fault yourselves in any way," Danusa said. "Suicide bombers, Señor Nabulsi, aren't born, they're made. Do you have any idea who might have turned your son into a killer?"

"I know *exactly* who turned him into a killer."

The shift from deep sadness to deep anger took place in a heartbeat. Hector, for all his sympathy for the man, felt a flash of excitement. A breakthrough was coming. He could sense it.

"Who Senhor Nabulsi? Who was it?"

"Asim Massri." Barir spit out the name as if it polluted his mouth. "He was presented to us as a pious, well-educated man. We thought he'd be an excellent influence on our boy, but instead he poisoned his mind."

"That's Massri with two Ss?" Danusa asked, making a note.

He nodded. "In your alphabet, it would be rendered that way. And Asim with one."

"How did your son come into contact with this man?"

"Have you heard of the Escola Al-Imam?"

Both cops shook their heads. "Tell us," Hector said.

"It's a madrasa in Foz do Iguaçu. We thought it important

Salem study the Holy Qur'an, and when the Escola Al-Imam opened, we saw it as a golden opportunity. The mullah, we'd been told, had attended University in Cairo—"

"And that mullah was Asim Massri?"

"It was. And instead of educating Salem, he filled his head with crazy ideas."

"What kind of ideas?"

Barir shook his head.

"So many," he said.

"Please," Danusa said. "Just an example, or two, to help us understand."

"Jews are evil incarnate. That was one."

"What else?"

"The State of Israel must be wiped off the face of the earth. That was another." He began to speak more quickly as he gathered steam. "And the Christians are working to destroy Islam. And America is the Great Satan. And Brazil, Argentina, even Paraguay, are enslaved to the Great Satan. Paraguay! Imagine! Paraguay is a slave to nothing but money. And I, I was a backslider because I didn't pray five times a day. His mother was immodest because she showed more of her body than just the skin of her hands and face."

"I understand," she said. "And what did you do when he started coming home with these . . . ideas?"

"I tried to reason with him, but nothing I said made any impression. We fought all the time. Finally, I got to the point where I couldn't take it anymore."

"So you. . . ?"

Barir heaved a sigh. "Told him to leave the madrasa or leave our home."

"And?"

"He chose to leave our home. Perhaps if I hadn't. . ."

He drifted into silence and hung his head.

Danusa reached out, as if to touch him, but drew back her hand before he noticed.

"You mustn't think that way," she said. "By then, it was almost certainly too late. If he'd stayed here at home, with you, it would have been unlikely to have made any difference."

He looked up, wanting to believe it.

"You think so?"

"I think so," she said. "And, believe me, Señor Nabulsi, I know about these things."

"How long ago was this?" Hector said. "How long since you . . . gave him the option?"

Barir took a moment to consider. "In August, near the beginning of the month."

"A little over three months ago, then?"

Barir nodded.

"When did you next hear from him?"

"Not until. . ."

"Until?"

"Until . . . the day of the explosion in São Paulo. He made a single telephone call. Not to me. To Aqsa. He knew my schedule, knew I leave home at seven to open the shop, knew I would already have left."

"The record of that call," Danusa said, was what brought us here. What did he say to her?"

"He asked her forgiveness for anything he might have said, or done, that had given her needless offense. He told her he loved her. . ."

"And she?" Danusa prompted.

Barir ran a hand through his hair. He was very close to tears. "She thought he was about to tell her he was coming home."

"But?"

Barir took a deep breath. "He cut the conversation short, said goodbye and hung up. She found the call totally mystifying, thought he might have been interrupted in some way, kept expecting him to call again, but he didn't."

"Not one word about what he planned to do?"

"Not a word. You saw how my wife took the news. It came as a complete surprise, a complete and horrible surprise."

"In the three months he's been gone, did he send you a letter, an email?"

"He did not." Barir's jaw set. He'd mastered himself again. "And now he's killed all of those innocent people and broken his mother's heart. I'll never forgive him. Never. And I'll never forgive that mullah."

Chapter Thirty-Two

MUNIZ DIDN'T BELIEVE IN engaging in small talk with social inferiors, and his attitude discouraged those of them in his presence from conversing among themselves, so the flight to his hacienda in Argentina took place in the absence of chitchat.

Upon arrival, he called his manager to arrange accommodation for the *capangas*.

"Not in the main house," he said, "in the servant's quarters. And tell the cook I'll be dining at seven. Alone."

"Sim, Senhor. Anything else?"

"That boat you use for fishing. Where is it?"

"In the milking barn, Senhor."

"Show it to them."

After the evening meal, he summoned the *capangas* to his office.

"Now," he said, "I'll tell you why you're here."

He logged on to the internet, typed Silva's name and title into the search engine and opted for images. A number of photos appeared on the screen: Silva being decorated by the President of the Republic. Silva surrounded by a group of agents wearing body armor. Silva behind a stash of recently apprehended drugs and weapons. Silva giving a speech to a citizens' group. Silva in a publicity portrait. He selected that one and enlarged it.

"This man," he said, tapping the screen with a forefinger, "is the reason we're here. I'm going to kill him."

Virgilio and Roque neither moved, nor spoke, and Donato's only reaction was to shrug and settle back in his chair.

"That's not a problem for us, Senhor," he said with a self-satisfied air. "We have killed—"

Muniz didn't like his attitude, didn't like complacency and hadn't asked for a presentation of the man's credentials. He interrupted with a vengeance.

"Are you about to tell me something I don't know?" he snapped. "Because, if you aren't, keep your damned mouth shut."

He'd dealt with men like Donato before, men born dirt poor, willing to do anything for money, totally ruthless. There were many such in Brazil's North and Northwest, all of them prepared, for pay, to attend to a rich landowner's every whim. Up to now, it had been Saldana who'd been paying the bills, but now the time had come to establish his own authority. And Muniz, from long experience, was a man who knew exactly how to do it.

Donato, staring at him openmouthed, knew the rules of the game as well as Muniz did, but was still taken aback by the sharpness of the reaction.

"I know what you men do," Muniz continued before the man could recover. "I know the services you perform for Senhor Saldana. Do you think they're any surprise to me? Why the hell else would I have brought you here?"

"I'm sorry, Senhor. I don't understand—"

"You don't understand because you're not paying attention. Shut up and listen."

Donato, accustomed to subservience all his life, reacted predictably. He lowered his head and said, "Sim, Senhor."

Muniz paused for a moment and then continued.

"I repeat," he said. "*I'm* going to kill him. I expect you'll be killing some other people, but you're not going to kill him. That's a pleasure I reserve for myself. Got that?"

"Sim, Senhor."

Muniz extracted a nod of acknowledgment from the other two thugs, then turned his attention back to the computer, called up a satellite image and enlarged it.

"This," he said, giving another tap to the screen "is the Hotel das Cataratas. It's over on the Brazilian side. We'll cross the river with that boat you looked at this afternoon, take a passkey to his room from the reception area, kill him and return with the same boat. We'll be going in after midnight, so we shouldn't encounter too many people, but it will be your task to kill any we do. I want no witnesses."

"Understood, Senhor."

"Did you make a close inspection of that boat?"

"Sim, Senhor."

Virgilio and Roque were looking back and forth between Donato and Muniz, like a pair of twin Dobermans expecting a treat.

"And?" Muniz said.

"Your manager asked why you wanted him to show it to us."

"Nosy bastard. What did you tell him?"

"That you wanted us to take you fishing."

"Fishing, eh? And what did he say to that?"

"He was surprised, Senhor. He said you'd never expressed an interest in fishing."

"Anything else?"

"That the fishing is good at this time of the year, but the river is in flood, and the current is strong. We should always keep the motor engaged and the bow pointed upstream. Otherwise, we could drift dangerously close to the falls. The drop to the lower river, he said, is more than eighty meters."

Muniz felt a cold shiver of fear, but suppressed it. "How long will it take to make the crossing?"

"From where to where, Senhor?"

"Let's have a look."

Donato leaned closer to the computer screen while Muniz surveyed the river upstream and down.

Below the falls it would be difficult to launch a boat; more difficult, still, to land it. The image showed white, disturbed water and high banks.

Downstream, conditions were better. The river wasn't as wide, and the water wasn't as rough, but it would be too far from the hotel to make a quick getaway.

Further upstream, the banks on the Brazilian side ran along the ecological reserve. There were no roads at all, only thick jungle. That jungle, Muniz knew, concealed pumas, spotted jaguars and poisonous snakes. To cut their way through it, if they could do it at all, would take hours. So that approach, too, he rejected.

A road ran south and west from the hotel and ended at the river. The scale of the satellite image indicated it was about two kilometers long. And the Iguaçu, at that point, was less than a kilometer from bank to bank.

Muniz centered the image on the point where the road ended and zoomed in. The magnification revealed a little T-shaped dock protruding from the bank.

"That's where we land," he said. "Now, let's find a place to launch the boat."

With his forefinger, he traced the narrow road paralleling the river on the Argentinean side. It ended in a tiny settlement called Puerto Canoas.

Embarking near the beginning of the road would bring them dangerously close to the falls. Embarking near the end would put two islands in their path. The departure point would have to be somewhere in between.

Muniz settled, at last, on a position near the tip of an

unidentified island. After rounding it, they could turn upstream, motor along in what appeared to be calm water, then strike out in a straight line toward the dock on the Brazilian side.

He used his index and middle fingers as a compass and measured the distances: about 300 meters to the tip of the island; another 500 meters along the coast of the island, and an additional 800 meters, no more, to make the major crossing.

"How long," he said to Donato, "with that boat and that motor?"

The *capanga* shrugged. "Depending on the current, less than five minutes."

The trip out to Ilhabela had been four times that. Muniz grunted his approval.

"Tomorrow morning," he said, "you go into Ciudad del Este. I'll give you money and an address. Buy four silenced pistols and plenty of ammunition. Look at what the Brazilian tourists are wearing. Dress yourselves in a similar fashion. Hats, shoes, belts, everything. When we walk into that hotel, I want you to look like you belong there. Oh, and buy scarves we can use to mask ourselves with."

"Understood, Senhor. And after the shopping, we come back here?"

"Two of you do. One goes to the Brazilian side and rents a car. He takes this." He reached into the drawer of his desk, removed a two-way radio, and held it out. "It's already charged."

Roque took it.

"This will put him in touch with the boat, Senhor?" Donato asked.

Somehow, without a word being exchanged on the subject, it had already been decided Roque would drive the car.

"It will. Here, take the other one." He removed another unit from the same drawer. "On and off here. Volume here. Push to talk here. Channel selection here. We'll use channel twenty-two."

Donato accepted the radio and studied the controls.

"Try both units tonight. Make sure you know how to use them. We'll call when we're halfway over, and you"—he pointed to Roque—"will come down to the dock to pick us up. Wait for us in a place where you can see the river. The radios may not work otherwise."

Roque nodded.

"Good. That's it. Ask my manager for a barrel, fill it with water and verify that the motor is running smoothly. Make sure we have fuel. See me tomorrow morning, after breakfast, and I'll give you the cash you'll need to make the purchases. Make sure you get receipts for everything. We'll push off tomorrow an hour after dark."

"*Com licença*, Senhor," Donato said.

"What?"

"There will be no moon tomorrow night. We can set up a light on this side before we leave, and that will give us a point to steer toward on the way back, but we'd best make the crossing to the Brazilian side in daylight. If not, we may get lost."

"We'll go earlier, then. Half an hour before dark. What do we use for a light?"

"In Ciudad del Este, Senhor, I'm sure I can find something appropriate."

"Good. Any other questions?"

Donato looked at his companions. They shook their heads. Then he shook his.

"No, Senhor," he said.

Chapter Thirty-Three

MATIAS CHAPARRO GLANCED AT his wristwatch—the only gold Rolex Silva had ever seen on a cop.

"I'm somewhat pressed for time," he said, "so I hope you'll pardon me for getting right down to business. To what do I owe the pleasure of this visit?"

Silva reached into his pocket, removed a piece of paper and offered it to the chief.

"What's this?" the Paraguayan said, taking it in his carefully manicured fingers.

"It's a batch number," Silva said, "for a shipment of plastic explosive."

Chaparro raised an eyebrow. "Why are you giving it to me?"

"The entire batch was shipped to the Paraguayan army. Three drums, each containing 25 kilos, have been illegally sold."

Chaparro smiled, set the paper aside without looking at it and leaned back in his chair.

"Why should you assume they were sold? They could just as easily have been misplaced. Perhaps they're sitting, right now, in some dark and forgotten corner of an army supply dump."

"No," Silva said, "they're not."

Chaparro studied his nails.

"How can you be sure?"

"Do you know what post-detonation taggants are?"

"Of course." Chaparro brushed a barely-visible bit of lint from his starched khaki shirt. "Why do you ask?"

"The explosive used in two recent terrorist bombings came from the batch on that piece of paper."

Chaparro sat bolt upright. "Surely you're not referring to the bombs recently detonated in São Paulo and Buenos Aires?"

"Surely," Silva said, "I am."

Chaparro frowned, unfolded the paper and stared at it "Who knows about this?"

"At the moment," Silva said, "Just us."

"And by *us* you mean?"

"The Brazilian Federal Police."

"Your director? That fellow Sampaio?"

"No. Just this gentleman here,"—Silva indicated Arnaldo—"myself, and a few other members of my team."

Chaparro looked relieved. "No one else within your government?"

"Not yet."

"Are you going to tell the Americans? The Argentineans?"

"Sooner or later we'll have to. And don't forget the Israelis. Their ambassador, his wife and children were among the victims of the second explosion."

"I would never forget the Israelis," Chaparro said. "It's best not to. They're not a forgiving people." He was still frowning. Now he rubbed his chin. Mario," he went on, his tone friendlier than before, "may I call you Mario?"

"By all means. This is Arnaldo."

Chaparro favored Arnaldo with a nod and an ingratiating smile.

Arnaldo returned the nod.

"And you must call me Matias. You must also believe me when I tell you that I find this very unwelcome news. It causes me a great deal of concern."

"I'm glad it does," Silva said, "because we badly need your help."

"And you shall have it! The last thing poor Paraguay needs is more problems with your government, or with the Argentineans. And we certainly don't need any with the Israelis, or, God forbid, the Americans. What do you propose?"

"A trade-off. You tell us who bought the explosive. We tell the Americans, the Argentineans and the Israelis that the Paraguayan government abhors terrorists as much as the rest of us do"—Chaparro began nodding vigorously—"and that you not only gave us full cooperation, but that we also support your story."

Chaparro's nodding came to an abrupt halt.

"Wait," he said. "What story?"

"The only story you can possibly tell without your country being labeled a pariah by the world community: Rogue elements within your military sold the explosive in the belief that it was going to criminals and totally unaware that the buyers were actually terrorists."

"That's no story. It's the God's honest truth. I have no doubt of it. Count on my complete cooperation."

"Thank you. But now, Matias, we must act quickly, before they have a chance to use more of that explosive and strike again. How long is it going to take you to get back to me?"

"It's too late to do anything today. It could be—"

Silva cut in before he could finish. "Complicated?"

Chaparro shook his head. "No," he said, "that's not the word I was about to use."

"But it's the correct one, isn't it? First, you'll have to determine how high the corruption went. And if someone important, like a general, was involved, he'll have to find someone to take the rap, or expect you to find such a person for him."

Chaparro flashed Silva a sardonic smile. "What a rich imagination you have, Mario. Important people? Generals? I'm sure our investigation will show that the perpetrator, or perpetrators, were people much further down the totem pole than that, people of no significant rank."

"I have no doubt," Silva said dryly, "that your investigation will show precisely that. And you know what Matias? I don't care. I have no interest whatsoever in who gets blamed for the sale. I need information about the buyer, not the seller. The seller is your problem. Do we have a deal?"

"Most certainly. This is an instance where the interests of your government and mine entirely coincide. Where are you staying?"

"The Cataratas. You'll call me?"

"I'll do better. I'll go there to see you. Two o'clock tomorrow. In the bar. Does that suit you?"

"If you can't make it sooner."

Chaparro considered for a moment—and then shook his head. "I think not."

"Thank you. Now, before we leave, there's something else I'd like you to help me with."

"And that is?"

"I want to talk to Jamil Al-Fulan. He's refused to see us, but he's unlikely to reject a friendly request, on our behalf, from the chief of his own National Police."

Chaparro frowned. "You think Jamil might be behind these bombings?"

In truth, Silva had, as yet, no firm indication that Jamil had anything to do with them. But he saw an opportunity to drive a wedge between the two Paraguayans—and he took it.

"I think it's likely," he said.

Chaparro gave Silva a long look.

"How likely?"

"Very likely," Silva said. "A friend of yours, is he?"

"If he ever was," Chaparro said, "and if there is any truth to your allegation, I can assure you, with total sincerity, that he no longer is."

Chapter Thirty-Four

LUIS CHAGAS MET THE other cops at their hotel for dinner. Coffee had just been served when a bellman appeared at Silva's elbow.

"Call for you, Senhor."

"That was Chaparro," he told them when he got back. "Al-Fulan will see me at ten tomorrow morning."

"Do you want my guy, Abasi, to go along?" Chagas asked. "Al-Fulan hates his guts. It might shake him up a bit."

"I think we can make better use of him with that mullah over at the madrasa," Silva said, "but I heartily concur with the shaking-up part." He turned to Danusa. "That little pendant you sometimes wear, the one in the form of a Star of David?"

"Yes?"

"Do you have it with you?"

"Always," she said. "It was a gift from my father."

"I want you to wear it—and come with me."

"A Jew *and* a woman," Luis said. "That will *really* shake him up. He has nothing but contempt for women. All his employees are male."

"I don't want you letting on that you speak Arabic," Silva said to Danusa. "If he does so, look mystified, as if you don't understand."

"And be pushy," Luis suggested. "He'll hate it!"

"Fine," she said. "I can do pushy."

"You sure as hell can," Arnaldo said.

"Watch it, Nunes," she said.

"See?" he said. "Pushy."

"And Arnaldo goes with me to talk to the mullah?" Hector asked.

"He does. Arnaldo is naturally pushy himself."

"Hey," Arnaldo said.

"As far as I know," Luis said, "the mullah doesn't speak Portuguese."

"English? Spanish?"

Luis shook his head. "I don't think so. I've only ever had dealings with him through Abasi. Speaking of Abasi"—he looked at his watch—"it's getting late. I'd better call him. What time do you want him here?"

"Eight A.M.?" Hector suggested.

Silva shook his head. "Too early."

Hector caught on immediately. "You want to coordinate the visits? The mullah and Al-Fulan? Surprise the mullah, so he can't collude?"

"Precisely."

"Then make it nine, Luis," Hector said.

THE FOLLOWING morning, Abasi Ragab showed up promptly at the stipulated hour. They had coffee in the restaurant and went out to his car. Arnaldo, taller and broader in the shoulders than Hector, took the seat in front.

"So what do you want with that damned mullah?" Ragab asked as his passengers were buckling themselves in.

"Sounds like you're not fond of him," Hector said.

"Fond of him? I tried to get his sick ass deported."

"No luck?"

Ragab shook his head. "Turns out, he's got a permanent residence visa."

"How did he get that?"

"The *filho da puta* is a Qur'anic scholar with a doctorate

in Arabic. On paper, that makes him look like a figure who could"—he made quotation marks in the air —"*contribute greatly to our multicultural society.*"

"Who said that?"

"The idiots who administrate immigration and naturalization. They *love* candidates like Massri. Besides which, Al-Fulan put together a committee of Brazilian nationals to give financial guarantees and sign a petition to accompany the paperwork."

"Why do you dislike Massri so much?"

Ragab had been about to start the engine. He took his hand off the key and turned around so he could see Hector's face. "I'm a Muslim," he said.

"And I'm a Catholic," Hector said. "So what?"

"So this: ever since people like Asim started running around preaching a philosophy of *blow up the infidels*, I'm sensing a rising tide of prejudice. Time was, when nobody in this country cared what your religion was, whether you were a Muslim or a Catholic, a Jew or an Evangelical, but not anymore. Now, a lot of folks look at us sideways, like we're all a bunch of goddamned fanatics. And the more Massris there are in the world, the worse it gets."

Ragab shook his head, as if to clear it, started the engine and pulled away from the curb.

"He gets innocent kids into that madrasa of his," he went on, "and teaches them to hate. They come out at odds with their parents and with the rest of society. The only people they get along with are other deluded kids like themselves. He's breaking up families."

"You think he's training terrorists?"

"I can't prove it."

"But you think it?"

"I do."

"I heard some folks in the community tried to withdraw their kids."

"And you probably heard what happened when they did."

"Yes."

"Same thing with parents whose sons are approaching school age. They get a visit from the mullah, who offers them bullshit and carrots. Then, if they don't enroll the kids right away, they get the stick."

"What kind of stick?"

"Threatening phone calls from a thug of Jamil's, a man named Kassim. Not many are able to resist. Those that do suffer . . . accidents."

"You have children?"

"Two, both girls, so they're safe. The mullah doesn't take girls, considers them lesser creatures. How do you want to handle this interrogation?"

"It's not an interrogation. Not yet. Think of it as an interview."

"All right. An interview. What, exactly, do you want me to do?"

"Does the mullah speak Portuguese?"

"If he does," Ragab said, "and I'm not even sure about that, he sure as hell won't speak it with you guys. He'll act like he doesn't understand a goddamned word of what you're saying. Conversing in the languages of the crusaders is beneath him."

"Like that, eh?

"Yes. Like that."

"Then translate, that's all, just translate. Don't editorialize."

"You got it," Ragab said.

Chapter Thirty-Five

AL-FULAN'S AUTO DEALERSHIP OCCUPIED a full block in the heart of downtown Ciudad del Este. Neon signs and logotypes of famous European brands hung in the windows. A fortune in luxury vehicles sparkled on the showroom floor.

But no one was inspecting the cars. The front door was locked, and when Silva and Danusa rang the bell, they were admitted by an armed guard. Security cameras were mounted on the ceiling. The door was of bulletproof glass, the show windows divided into panes. Silva had no doubt they were bulletproof as well.

"Uneasy lies the head. . ." he said.

"Shakespeare?" Danusa said. "You continue to amaze me, Chief Inspector."

"I'm not just a pretty face."

"And now you're sounding like Arnaldo."

Before Silva could respond, a slim young man, twenty-something, emerged from a door. He was wearing a well-tailored suit and a Versace tie.

"I'm Uzair," he said to Silva in poorly-pronounced Portuguese while pointedly ignoring Danusa, "Please, come with me."

"And what, Uzair, do you do for Señor Al-Fulan?" Danusa shot back in fluent Spanish.

He hesitated before answering. "I'm his secretary."

"Really? A male secretary in Paraguay? That's a first for me. Your boss doesn't believe in hiring females?"

Uzair's response was a sniff.

Two men holding Heckler and Koch MP5s were standing in the corridor that led to Al-Fulan's office. One of them slung his weapon onto his shoulder and checked their documents.

It was only after they'd surrendered their weapons and passed through a metal detector, that Danusa and Silva were admitted to the great man's presence.

Al-Fulan snorted in disgust when he caught sight of the pendant around Danusa's neck.

"The Jewess will wait outside," he said to Uzair. "Not in the showroom, on the street."

"If the Jewess leaves," Danusa said, "we both leave."

"So leave."

"Nice try," she said, "but we know you got your marching orders from Chaparro. You're obligated to see us, so back off."

Al-Fulan blanched. "You should be whipped for speaking to a man like that."

"I'd rip off the balls of any man who tried it," she said.

Uzair's mouth was agape. No one ever addressed his boss in such a fashion. No one. Much less a woman.

"Close your mouth, you idiot," Al-Fulan said, "and get Kassim." Then, to Danusa: "Neither Chaparro nor anyone else tells me what to do. I don't take orders. I give them."

"You don't take orders? Don't make me laugh. You refused to see us. Then we dropped one little word with Chaparro, and the next thing you know"—she held out her hands, palms upward—"here we are. Doesn't that make you Chaparro's bitch?"

Even Silva thought she might have gone too far with that one. Al-Fulan's face turned purple. He had to take a few calming breaths before he could reply.

"Ask what you came to ask and get out," he managed to say at last.

The door opened. A man with a nose like the beak of a hawk walked across the room and took up a position about a meter behind Al-Fulan's chair.

Danusa waited, but no introduction was forthcoming, so she asked, "Were you involved in a car-smuggling scheme with Plínio Saldana?"

The newcomer said something to Al-Fulan in Arabic. Al-Fulan replied in the same language, then reverted to Spanish.

"I had no business dealings of any nature whatsoever with Plínio Saldana."

"Were you involved in his murder?"

"Your question is stupid. What do I care about some Brazilian politician? How could it possibly benefit me to be involved in the murder of one?"

"Perhaps because the two of you had a falling-out?"

"I've already told you. I had no dealings with Plínio Saldana. But let's suppose, just for a moment, that I did."

"I'm supposing," she said.

"It's likely he was going to be elected governor of the Brazilian state just across the river. A partnership with such a man would have opened no end of opportunities. We could have made millions together. So would I kill him? No, I certainly would not. As I said, your question is stupid."

"How about the bombings in São Paulo and Buenos Aires? Did you have any role in those?"

"I deny taking part in any bombings."

"Do you condemn them?"

"Not at all. They were done for legitimate political ends."

"How could you possibly know that? Up to now, no one has taken credit."

"That statement, too, is stupid. An American consulate? And a Jewish temple? They were actions clearly directed against the two powers colluding to commit injustice in Palestine. What else could it be other than an action carried out by a Muslim freedom fighters' organization?"

"So you believe," she said, "that the lives of innocent women and children should be sacrificed to political ends?"

"I do."

"I think that's the first honest answer you've given us since we came in here."

"I'm finding this conversation boring. I've said all I intend to say. Why don't you two leave?"

Danusa looked at Silva.

"Why don't we?" he said.

OUTSIDE, WALKING toward the taxi they'd kept waiting, Silva asked, "What went on between that thug, Kassim, and his boss?"

"Kassim called me a Zionist whore."

"Did he now?"

"He did. And Al-Fulan called you a pig fucker."

"A pig fucker, eh?"

"That's a loose translation."

"Anything else?"

"He made some kind of a reference to the 'other one,' but I didn't catch it."

Silva stopped walking, and took her by the arm. She turned to face him.

"As soon as we get back to the hotel," he said, "call Luis Chagas. Ask him if he has a photo of that man Kassim. If he doesn't, ask him to send someone over here to take one. Clandestinely."

"And, once we've got it?"

"Email it to Mara in São Paulo. Have her compare it with the images she received from Curitiba."

"What images?"

"She'll know what I'm talking about."

"But I don't. And I'd like to."

"There's a video recording of everyone who got off the elevators on Nestor's floor the night he was killed. One face couldn't be identified."

"And you think it might belong to this guy, Kassim?"

"I hope so."

"What if it does?"

"We do nothing. Not yet. Al-Fulan is the big fish. Let's give him a bit more rope."

"ALLAHU AKBAR," Mullah Asim said.

Hector was familiar with the *takbir*. He didn't wait for Ragab to interpret it for him.

"Tell him to stop spouting platitudes and answer my question," he said.

Ragab put Hector's statement into Arabic and rendered the reply in Portuguese: "I have forgotten the question."

They'd been sitting in mullah Asim's office for a quarter of an hour. Everything he'd said had been evasive, but the visit hadn't been entirely useless. The walls told their own story.

One was decorated with photos showing events, often multiple photos of the same event. Another bore photos of people.

The events included, but weren't limited to, aircraft striking the World Trade Center in New York, the carnage at Atocha Station in Madrid, the mayhem caused by British Muslims in the London Underground, the damage to the USS Cole in the harbor of Aden, and the attacks on the US embassies in Kenya and Tanzania. Some were clipped from newspapers, others from magazines. There were even a few that looked like they'd been printed from negatives. All had two things in common: destruction and death.

The people were Osama bin Laden, Khalid Sheikh Mohammed, Abu Nidal, Ayman Al-Zawahiri, Mohammad Atta and a succession of young men and women, mostly standing in front of green banners with inscriptions in Arabic.

"Ask him what he took off those walls while he kept us waiting."

Hector's query was purely provocative. He knew he wasn't going to get a straight answer.

Ragab translated the mullah's reply: "He says the walls are the same now as they were when you had the discourtesy to appear without an appointment. And why should you think differently?"

"Because there's a hook for another photo there, and two more over there. Salem Nabulsi, maybe? And the bombings in São Paulo and Buenos Aires?"

"He says he does not know the name Salem Nabulsi. And he has no photos of the bombings in São Paulo or Buenos Aires."

"Tell him Salem Nabulsi was one of his students, and we know it."

"He says he has many students. He does not always recall their names."

"Show him the photo."

Ragab showed Asim the photo they'd brought. The mullah gave it a cursory glance, and looked at his tea. Served by a young man of about twelve who'd come and gone, it had been standing on his desk for the last ten minutes, but he hadn't yet touched it. In addition to tea, the glass contained crushed mint leaves. Their smell perfumed the room.

"He says he doesn't recall ever having seen the young man in the photo. He also says he's busy. You should stop wasting his time and discuss these matters with his secretary."

"Tell him," Hector said, "that I prefer to discuss them with him."

The mullah picked up his tea, said something, and took a sip, watching for Hector's reaction over the rim of his glass.

"In ten minutes," Ragab translated, "it will be time for his prayers."

"Which still gives us ten minutes," Hector said. "How many students has he got over the age of fifteen? Ask him that."

The mullah shook his head and gave a terse reply to the question.

"He says he doesn't remember," Ragab said.

Arnaldo had yet to contribute to the interview in any way. Now, he did. "Tell him he's a lying sack of shit."

The pupils in the mullah's dark eyes dilated in anger.

Ragab grinned and started to translate what Arnaldo had said. The mullah interrupted him with the wave of an imperious hand.

"Get out," he said, in excellent Portuguese.

Chapter Thirty-Six

WHEN SILVA GOT BACK to his hotel, the Chief of Ciudad del Este's National Police was waiting in the bar.

Chaparro had chosen to leave his uniform in Paraguay. He was wearing a dark blue sports jacket, an expensive one by the look of it, and an open-necked dress shirt without a tie.

"If I've kept you waiting," Silva said, "I'm sorry."

Chaparro waved off the apology. "I came early," he said. "I like this place. Champagne?" Chaparro's flute was half full, the one on Silva's side of the table still empty. The wine was a non-vintage Krug. "I should, perhaps, point out you'll be paying for the bottle. I put it on your bill."

"In that case. . ." Silva said and signaled the waiter.

When the man had poured and left, Chaparro saluted with his glass. Silva followed suit and took an appreciative sip.

"The container of C4," Chaparro said, "arrived in our country on the nineteenth of July last year. It was shipped, in its entirety, to an army depot in Concepción. Do you know Concepción?"

"No."

"Quite a nice little place, really. Except in summer. From mid-December right up to the end of March it's far too hot."

"Where is it?"

"On the Paraguay River, about three hundred kilometers north of the capital."

"Who's in command of the depot?"

"A colonel by the name of Suarez. He's young, only twenty-seven years old, but destined for great things. He has a brilliant future ahead of him."

"Twenty-seven and already a colonel?"

"Indeed. Impressive is it not?"

"And he's the one who sold the stuff?"

Chaparro shook his head. "Of course not," he said. "Did you not hear me refer to his brilliant future? Colonel Suarez is the son-in-law of one of our most senior generals."

"And, therefore, clearly innocent of any wrongdoing?"

"Mario, Mario, do I detect sarcasm in your tone?"

"Who's going to take the rap?"

"The guilty party is a supply sergeant."

"Arrested?"

"Killed. This afternoon. In an attempt to escape."

"I see. And he was, I suppose, the sole perpetrator?"

Chaparro held his glass up to the light and studied the bubbles. "How prescient of you," he said.

"Matias, I hope you've got more for me than that."

"I do. Before the supply sergeant made a break for freedom, he dictated a full confession."

"And signed it, of course."

"Of course. And it is available for inspection by your government." Chaparro took another sip and emitted a contented sigh.

"What, precisely, did he confess to?" Silva asked.

"Firstly, that he sold only three drums. We have since verified that every other drum in the shipment is accounted for."

"How reassuring."

"Isn't it? And now that the perpetrator is no longer in a position to do further damage, there's no possibility of the terrorists being able to get their hands on any more of the stuff."

"None whatsoever?"

"None whatsoever."

"Thank you. I'll include that in my report."

"How much of the explosive do you believe to have been used in the bombings?"

"No more than forty kilos."

Chaparro frowned and scratched his chin. "So they have at least thirty-five left," he said. "Not good."

"Not good at all," Silva said.

Chaparro drained his glass. The waiter hastened to fill it. He topped up Silva's at the same time. Again, Silva waited until he was gone. Then he said, "Now the important question: To whom did your wayward supply sergeant sell those drums?"

Chaparro took a pack of Dunhills out of his pocket, lit one with his black and gold Dupont lighter, and expelled a jet of smoke before he replied. "All three drums were sold to a fellow who fits the description of a man who works for Jamil Al-Fulan. His name is Kassim Hamawi."

"Bingo," Silva said.

Chapter Thirty-Seven

DONATO AND VIRGILIO RETURNED to the hacienda at 4:30 P.M. and reported that Roque, in a rented car, was already on his way to the Hotel das Cataratas.

Donato, like a child with a new toy, was excited about the firearms they'd purchased.

"Taurus M975s, Senhor. Brand new. Never fired. All with silencers and seventeen-round magazines."

There is no weapon more suited to silent killing than the M975, a pistol especially developed for the Brazilian army's elite jungle fighting unit. When used with their 14-centimeter-long suppressors, the noise they make is negligible. Rounds fired in Silva's room might not be totally inaudible to his neighbors on either side, but it was unlikely they'd be identified as pistol shots.

"Don't fall in love with them," Muniz said, "because, just as soon as we're finished with them all four are going right to the bottom of the river. Go fill the tank for the outboard motor and hook the boat's trailer to the blue pickup. We'll leave in two hours."

Just before noon, he'd taken the same truck and gone down to the river to scout the departure location. It was, in every way, ideal.

The nearest house was two kilometers away. There was a stand of trees behind which they could park, and a beach of sandy soil where the riverbank shelved gradually into the water. The boat would have to be carried through some dense brush, but the capangas were strong men. And the motor could be unshipped and carried separately.

Other than the prospect of getting into the boat, there was only one thing that made Muniz uneasy: the Devil's Throat.

That fearful chasm, where half the river's flow disappeared over a precipice more than 80 meters high, was less than a kilometer away. Clouds of swirling mist hung above it; a hellish roar emanated out of it and, every now and then, a helicopter, coming from the direction of the Hotel das Cataratas, dipped into it. The passengers were tourists, plunging, for a full thirty seconds or so, into an abyss where they were surrounded, on three sides, by thousands of tons of falling water.

It was not Muniz's idea of fun, nor was a voyage, however short, on what most people would have regarded as a relatively placid river.

And yet, as he stood there on the margin of the stream, reviewing his plans for a final time, he sensed his powerful fear of the upcoming embarkation being tempered by something far more agreeable: a sharp sense of anticipation.

In just a few hours, he'd be looking into Silva's face, savoring the terror that would be written there when he came to realize what awaited him. Then he'd kill him. And, once it was done, who would dare, ever again, to threaten Orlando Muniz? The prospect of a long prison term would be forever lifted from his shoulders, and he would have proven himself, once again, a figure that rose above the constraints that governed ordinary men.

Wasn't that end worthy of almost any risk? And how much risk was there really? As long as they made the damned crossing early enough to have light to navigate by, late enough to be certain the helicopter tours had been suspended for the night.

In the midday heat, he'd spent more than an hour on the

riverbank, reveling in what was to come, studying the sun's progression, watching the advancing shadows as the sun dropped from its zenith.

The gorge, he noted, would fall into deep shadow long before sunset. That, coupled with the mist, might reduce visibility to the point where the helicopter rides were no longer attractive.

And that would be ideal, because then there'd be no danger whatsoever of their boat being spotted by the people in the aircraft.

THEY REACHED the stand of trees just before 7:00 P.M. The boat was on the riverbank, the motor mounted and the fuel line connected by 7:15. Sunset, according to the internet, would be at 8:14.

From 7:00 to 7:45, the helicopter came regularly, every fifteen minutes.

Then it came no more.

Muniz breathed a sigh of relief and hazarded a call on the radio. "Are you in position?"

Roque responded immediately. "Sim, Senhor."

"Keep radio silence. Sit tight. We'll push off just before dark. Click your transmit switch three times if you understood."

There were three clicks.

Donato took the mantle lantern he'd purchased in Ciudad del Este, lit it and hung it in a tree. It would serve as a beacon to guide their return.

The road was free of traffic. There were no boats on the river. The day was virtually wind still, the gentle breeze not even strong enough to rustle the reeds. The sound overpowering all others was the thunder of water pouring into the Devil's Throat.

As the sun began to sink below the horizon, lights twinkled

into life on the far shore. Muniz lifted his binoculars. Most of the illumination came from the hotel, standing in stately majesty on the brow of a hill.

He refocused on the riverbank and followed it to the right until he reached the T-shaped dock. While he was staring at it, a light on the far end blinked on.

"Perfect," he muttered.

He pointed it out to Donato. The *capanga* nodded.

"Shall we go now, Senhor?"

"Not yet. If we can see that dock, they can see us. But now we have a light to steer by. So we can wait until after dark."

Donato shook his head. "We have no compass, Senhor. If we just keep the bow on the light, without reference to a compass, and we can't see what the current is doing, we could be swept downstream and never know it."

"If you knew that, why didn't you buy a compass?"

"We agreed to leave before dark, Senhor. I didn't think we'd need it."

"How about on the way back?"

"By then, Senhor, we will have some idea about the strength of the current. It won't change much in the next few hours. We'll simply steer upstream of the light on this side. How far upstream will depend upon our experience as we cross over now."

"You really do know something about boats, don't you?"

"My father was a fisherman, Senhor."

"A fisherman? In Acre? Where did he fish? In a river?"

"No, Senhor. He fished the sea. And I fished it with him. I did not always live in Acre. When I was a child, we lived in Alagoas. But then, one day. . . ." Muniz wasn't paying any attention to his story, wasn't even looking at him, so Donato cut it short. ". . . He drowned."

"Too bad," Muniz said. "Let's get moving."

Chapter Thirty-Eight

SILVA, DANUSA, HECTOR AND Arnaldo gathered on the terrace at eight. Luis Chagas, once again invited to join them, was late.

Hector took the opportunity to report on their unsatisfactory meeting with the mullah.

"So," Silva said, when he was done, "in essence, you didn't learn a thing."

"We learned," Arnaldo said, "that Massri is a guy who shouldn't be allowed within a thousand kilometers of an impressionable kid."

"I think we knew that already," Danusa said. "And I wouldn't be at all surprised if the Qur'an isn't the only thing he's an expert on. Someone had to teach Salem how to put that bomb together. What happened with Chaparro, Chief Inspector?"

"I'll wait until Luis arrives," Silva said. "I want him to hear it."

"Speak of the devil," Hector said, and pointed.

"Sorry I'm late," Chagas said when he reached their table, "but Mara called just as I was leaving. The photo I sent of Kassim? The one she was going to compare to the mystery man in the hospital?"

Silva put down his glass and sat up straighter in his chair. "Yes?" he said.

"It was a match."

THE CROSSING went off without a hitch. They saw no one, and Muniz was relatively certain no one had seen them. The fast-flowing river was smooth, and the sound of their motor was masked by the roar of the falls.

But the current was much stronger than Donato had anticipated. They had to steer for a point well upstream to avoid being swept downriver. That lengthened the journey, and the last of the light faded from the sky a full five minutes before they reached the dock.

When he estimated they were about one hundred meters away, Muniz picked up the radio to call Roque, but his finger, soaking wet from nervous perspiration, slipped on the switch. He dried it on his pants, tried again, and got an immediate acknowledgement. The thug was on his way.

Donato throttled back and put the motor in neutral. It was nicely timed. They lost headway an arm's length from the pier. Virgilio, standing in the front of the boat, reached out, grasped one of the mooring cleats and made it fast to a line attached to the bow. Then he climbed onto the dock.

Muniz refused the hand that was offered him, not wanting Virgilio to feel the moisture. That was another of his rules when dealing with subordinates: never display fear.

When he was out of the boat, and his heartbeat was beginning to slow, he cast a glance over the dark water. The lantern on the opposite shore was clearly visible, and it seemed quite close. But he knew it would look far away again as soon as he was back on the water.

"Where the hell is our car?" he said.

As if in answer, a pair of headlights appeared, racing toward them down the dark road. A moment later, a Fiat Doblo 1.8 pulled up next to the dock. Roque hopped out of the driver's seat, and hurried toward them.

"Where have you been?" Muniz snapped.

"I saw him, Senhor."

It was the first time Roque had addressed him with any-thing other than a grunt.

Muniz's anger, and the residual near-terror of the last ten minutes, instantly gave way to eager anticipation.

"Silva? You saw Silva?"

Roque nodded. "That's why I'm late, Senhor. I circled around to the back of the hotel, and saw him on the terrace. I was there, in the garden, looking right at him, when you called. He was —"

"Wait. You mean we can get at him without passing through the hotel?"

"Sim, Senhor."

"Is he alone?"

"No. There are four of them, Silva, two other men and a woman."

BACK ON the terrace, the federal cops were still discussing Chagas's revelation—that Kassim had been the mystery man in the hospital.

"Maybe," Hector said, "Nestor's death had nothing to do with Plínio's. He was in a hospital bed, debilitated and defenseless. Al-Fulan hated him, was determined to make good on his threat to kill him and thought he might never get a better chance. Maybe it's as simple as that."

"Maybe," Arnaldo said. "But, if that's true, it doesn't bring us a step closer to solving Plínio's murder."

"No," Silva said, "If it's true, it doesn't."

"Kassim goes back and forth all the time," Chagas said. "I'll keep a lookout on the bridge and grab him the very next time he sticks his nose into Brazil."

"No, you won't," Silva said. "Not yet. There's no way we're going to be able to secure a conviction simply because he happened to be in the hospital when Nestor was murdered.

And besides, the man we *really* want is Al-Fulan. He's behind all of this. The bombing, Nestor's killing—"

"But not Plínio's murder?" Arnaldo said.

"No," Silva said, "I think not. The solution to that lies elsewhere."

"What happened with Chaparro?" Chagas said. "Did he show up as promised? Meet you in the bar?"

"He did," Silva said, and he told them about the dead sergeant's alleged confession.

"A pile of crap," Arnaldo said.

"Most of it," Silva agreed, "but I tend to believe the part about Kassim being the one who purchased the C4."

"So that's another nail in his coffin," Danusa said.

"But not enough to punish him the way he deserves," Silva said. "The sergeant's signed confession, and the depositions from the people who purportedly interrogated him, might be enough to convict Kassim of arms trading, but I doubt we'd be able to get a judgment against him for collusion in the bombing itself."

"And," Chagas said, "we still don't have any damning evidence against Al-Fulan."

"So Al-Fulan will walk?" Danusa said.

"Yes," Silva said. "As things stand at this moment, I'm afraid he will."

"I won't have it," Danusa said. "There's no way I'm going to let that happen."

Silva, nonplussed by her aggressive tone, was the first to look at her in surprise. The others weren't far behind.

"None of you get it, do you?" she said, looking at each in turn. "These people play by different rules. They're animals, and yet we keeping treating them like human beings, giving them the rights of human beings, wanting to bring them to trial like human beings."

In the uncomfortable silence that followed, she got to her feet.

"I have a phone call to make," she said and stalked off.

"What's with her?" Luis said when she was gone.

Hector told him about the circumstances of her father's death.

"I sympathize," Luis said, "but that's no reason to take it out on us."

"She's not taking it out on us," Silva said. "It's just the way she is. She can't abide terrorists, and she gets frustrated when she thinks one might be getting away with something."

"I can relate to that," Luis said. "I'm frustrated myself. Is Kassim guilty? Yes. Does he deserve to be punished? Yes. But, in the end, he's just a tool."

"Which was exactly my point," Silva said. "Danusa's as well. The person we should be concentrating on is Jamil Al-Fulan."

"And, at the moment," Hector said, "we haven't got a damned thing we can use against him.

Chapter Thirty-Nine

"WHERE'S THE WOMAN?" MUNIZ whispered.

He moved aside to allow Roque to look through the gap in the foliage. They were in the darkest part of the garden, about fifty meters from where the federal cops were gathered on the terrace.

"Gone," Roque said. "She was in that empty chair, next to where the blonde guy is now."

Muniz had brought a pair of binoculars. He elbowed Roque aside and raised them to his eyes.

"The big man," he said after adjusting the focus, "is Silva's shadow, Arnaldo Nunes. He never goes anywhere without him. The one in the blue shirt is his nephew, Hector Costa. I've got it in for those two bastards as well."

He put the binoculars in circulation. Each of the three capangas took a turn studying the people around the table. Meanwhile, Muniz considered his next move. By the time the binoculars came back to him, he'd reached a decision.

"This," he said, "is too good a chance to pass up. We'll kill all three of them, and we'll do it now, while we have the chance."

"And the fourth man, Senhor?" Donato said. "The blonde one? Who is he?"

"I have no idea. I've never seen him before, but if he interferes, kill him as well. Get out your scarves. Tie them on. Which one of you is the worst shot?"

"Roque, Senhor," Donato said, reaching for his makeshift mask.

"Then, if it becomes necessary, Roque will take the blonde guy. Virgilio takes Costa and you, Donato, take Nunes."

"Remind me, Senhor," Donato said, now speaking through the cloth that covered his nose and mouth. "Which one is Nunes?"

"The big one. Costa, the nephew, is the one in the blue shirt."

"There are only four of us," Donato said, "and four of them. Wouldn't it be better—"

Muniz didn't let him finish. "We're coming out of the dark. No one is looking this way. They won't even know what's hit them. If Silva pulls a gun, which he probably will, disable the bastard. Shoot him in his arms, his legs, anywhere but his chest or his head. Before it's over, I want to get close enough for him to see who's killing him."

As Danusa was emerging from the door between the lobby and the terrace, she saw movement in the garden. Four men, masked and armed, were emerging from the darkness.

"Guns!" she shouted.

The cops turned to face the threat.

The man in the lead, gray-haired, and with a pair of binoculars dangling from a strap encircling his neck, stopped running, took a two-handed stance and shot Danusa in the chest.

Blood bloomed on her white blouse.

The four cops dived from their chairs. The crystal wine bucket exploded, filling the air with shards of ice and glass. A chunk of masonry was blasted from one of the columns supporting the roof.

Silva took shelter behind a vase holding a palm tree, Arnaldo and Hector behind a concrete trough planted with flowers. Chagas was hit and went down.

Illuminated only by the light coming from the hotel, the

four attackers kept coming, their pistols shooting little stabs of flame into the night. But the weapons were silenced, and the reports sounded more like puffs of compressed air than gunshots.

Arnaldo and Hector started returning fire. Their waiter was cowering in the doorway. Silva made a frantic gesture to attract his attention.

"An ambulance," he shouted. "Call an ambulance."

The man scuttled inside.

Hector shot one of the assailants in the abdomen and, as the man bent over, followed up with another round to his head.

Arnaldo hit another in the throat. The gunman's blood, black in the night, started pulsing out of him in spurts.

Silva fired a shot, then another, missing both times.

"Back," the gray-haired man shouted. "Back to the car."

The remaining two assailants, apparently uninjured, retreated into darkness. Silva crawled to Danusa's side.

"See to Luis," he called to Hector.

"I'm okay," Chagas said through teeth gritted against the pain. "Just a flesh wound. How's Danusa?"

Silva didn't reply. He was bunching up fabric from her blouse, trying to use it to stanch her bleeding.

"A doctor," he snapped to Hector. "See if there's one in the hotel. And see if that waiter did what I told him to do."

Hector took off at a run.

"You hear that voice?" Arnaldo said.

"I heard it," Silva said. "Orlando Muniz. Hector was right on the mark." And to Danusa: "You're going to be all right. It's not so bad."

That part was a lie. There was too much blood.

"Who the hell is Orlando Muniz?" Luis said, looking at Danusa with concern while he fashioned a tourniquet for himself out of a napkin.

"A dead man," Arnaldo said, replacing the empty magazine of his Glock with one of the spares from the holster on his belt, "just as soon as I catch up with him."

"Don't even think about it," Chagas cautioned. "Odds are, he's waiting to ambush anyone who tries it."

"That cowardly *filho da puta?* No way! He's running. I guarantee it."

Car doors slammed, two in quick succession. Tires squealed on the road.

"See?" Arnaldo said. "There he goes."

The taillights of the car were red dots in the night—getting smaller as it moved away.

"I know that road," Chagas said. "It ends at the river. The bastards have a boat."

"First things first," Silva said. "Let's get Danusa attended to. Arnaldo, go find the pilot of that helicopter. I'll meet you on the pad."

There was a rivulet of blood dribbling from one corner of Danusa's mouth. She'd started panting for breath. Arnaldo, for the first time, seemed to notice how badly she'd been hurt. He stood motionless, staring at her, his face contorted with distress.

"Go," Silva said, angrily. "*Now.*"

Arnaldo started, as if he'd been awakened from a trance. Then he holstered his pistol—and ran.

Chagas knelt facing Silva, Danusa between them.

"Hang in there, *menina*," he said to the prostrate woman.

Danusa's eyes were closed, but she surprised them both by moving her lips.

"I screwed up," she said in a voice just above a whisper.

"Nonsense," Silva said. "If you hadn't spotted those bastards, we'd all be dead. Don't try to talk. An ambulance is on its way."

"You're hurting me," she said.

"Can't be helped. I have to maintain the pressure."

"It's bad, isn't it?"

"Not bad at all. You're going to be up and about in no time."

"Liar," she said. "How many? How many did you get?"

"Two."

"Only two?"

"The leader and one of his henchmen are making a run for it."

"Go after them."

"Don't worry. They're not going to get away."

"Promise?"

"I promise."

She tried to smile—but couldn't. Her breath rattled in her throat. She opened her eyes and looked at him. "Tell Amzi I'm sorry," she said.

"Amzi?" Chagas said. "Who's Amzi?"

Silva leaned closer to hear her reply, but there was none. A man tapped him on the shoulder. "Stand back," he said. "I'm a doctor."

Silva stood up and moved aside. The doctor took the position he'd vacated. Hector appeared at his side.

"Ambulance on its way," he said.

But the doctor was already shaking his head. He rose from his haunches, took a napkin from a nearby table, and wiped his bloody hands.

"I'm sorry," he said. "She won't be needing it."

Chapter Forty

ROQUE FLOORED THE CAR'S accelerator. A second later they were burning rubber. The *capanga* kept glancing in the rear-view mirror as they sped toward the dock.

Muniz, more calculating, was less concerned with immediate pursuit. The federal cops couldn't possibly beat them to the boat.

But what if one of them had recognized his voice?

Stupid! It had been stupid of him to cry out.

Wait! They may think it was me, but can they prove it?

He had ample fuel on board the Cessna. A ninety-minute flight would take him to his *fazenda* near Cascatas do Pontal. He had twenty-seven employees there, twenty-seven people who depended upon him for their livelihood. And, because they knew damned well what would happen to them if they didn't, they could all be made to swear he hadn't left the place all week. When it came right down to it, it was only the word of the federal cops against his—and the numbers would be on his side.

He'd have to get rid of Roque, of course. But that was easily done.

Muniz's breathing slowed. He began to feel better. It was a cock-up, but cock-ups happened, and there was always a next time. He'd kill the bastard yet.

When they screeched to a stop, the road behind them was still in darkness, and the lantern still glowing on the Argentinean shore. They hurried aboard. The boat's engine started immediately.

Muniz took it as a sign that luck was with them.

Roque cast-off the mooring line and rammed the throttle home. He hadn't said a single word since they'd turned to run.

But Muniz knew *capangas*.

Right now, he thought, *the greedy bastard is trying to work-out a way to turn this situation to his advantage.*

Roque was. But thinking was not his strong suit, and it took him almost a full minute.

"Donato and Virgilio had families," he said at last. "I am thinking, Senhor, of their wives and children."

He was like hell. Muniz saw through the subterfuge at once, but it wouldn't be prudent to tell that to a killer. Not on a boat, during a dark night, in the middle of a river.

"The wives," Roque said, as if the thought had just occurred to him, "should receive their husbands' shares of what you'd planned to pay us."

"They should," Muniz agreed. Then, before Roque could suggest it, "I'll give the money to you. You can pass it on to them."

"Of course, Senhor. You can trust me."

He couldn't, of course. The wives, if they existed at all, wouldn't see a *centavo*. But, then, neither would Roque.

The wind had risen since they'd crossed from the Argentinean side, and it had changed direction. Now, it was blowing downriver.

Wind and current were conspiring to push the boat closer to the falls. Roque perceived the danger and corrected his course to steer further upstream. And, if fate hadn't taken a hand, they would have landed only meters from where they'd left the pickup.

But then, without warning, disaster struck.

A tree, many times larger than the boat and adrift on the

river, appeared out of nowhere and smashed into their port side.

"Get away from it! Get away from it!" Muniz shouted, in a panic.

"I can't. I can't turn!" Roque shouted back.

He had the tiller hard over, trying to open space between the tree and the boat, but the water was moving too fast. The rough bark remained in contact with the stern, slamming the bow backward at every attempt to turn away. Meanwhile, the whirling prop was carrying them further along the trunk.

"My God," Muniz said, pointing ahead at a massive shape looming out of the dark "What's that?"

It proved to be a ball of roots protruding a full two meters from the base of the tree. The boat was headed straight for it. Roque threw the motor into reverse.

"Backward," Muniz shouted. "Go backward!"

"I'm trying, damn it!" Roque said, all subservience gone.

They gathered sternway slowly, had just passed their original point of impact, when a sharp *thud* was followed instantly by a metallic *snap*—and the motor began to run wild.

The whirling prop had struck something under the surface, probably a projecting limb. The shear pin had given way. The drive shaft was turning, but the propeller wasn't. The boat was dead in the water.

THE BELL 429 was tied down on a helipad less than one hundred meters from the hotel's main entrance.

Arnaldo found the pilot in the bar, seated at one of the tables, drinking guaraná and chatting up one of the female tourists. It was the work of only a moment to flash a badge and explain the urgency.

The engine on the aircraft still hadn't cooled from the

afternoon flights, and was already up to operating temperature when Silva joined them on the pad.

Arnaldo saw the expression on his partner's face, and the question he was about to ask died on his lips.

Less than thirty seconds later, they were airborne.

"THIS THING have a spotlight?" Silva asked, as their pilot turned the nose of the helicopter toward the river.

"This thing has the mother of all spotlights," the pilot said.

His name, he'd told them, was André, and he was no spring chicken, closer to sixty than fifty. He handled his machine with the easy familiarity of someone who'd been doing it for a very long time.

"Turn it on."

André threw a switch. He hadn't exaggerated. The spotlight was incredibly effective at turning night into day.

"Eighty million candlepower," he said, responding to Silva's appreciative grunt. "Okay, we're over water. Where to now?"

"Cross over," Silva said, pointing toward Argentina.

It took less than a minute.

They saw a blue pickup, a boat trailer, and a light hanging in a tree, but no fugitives.

"Go back to midstream," Silva said. "Follow the current."

ABOVE THE roar of the falls, Muniz could hear the snapping and cracking of wood.

The closer they got to the lip of the precipice, the shallower the river became. Below the surface of the foaming brown water, Muniz felt and heard the limbs scraping along the bottom, their branches clawing at every rock, every irregularity, as if the tree had become a live thing desperate to arrest its plunge to final destruction.

And then, with a shudder, their forward motion stopped.

The huge trunk slowly twirled into a position where it offered the least resistance to the current. The base was now pointing directly at the Devil's Throat, but the trunk was moving no closer.

Not so the boat. Their little vessel was driven forward until it smashed into the ball of roots. A pressure wave arose at the stern. Water spilled over the transom, the cold of it contrasting sharply with the warm sensation in Muniz's crotch as he pissed himself

"Bail!" Roque shouted and grabbed a bucket.

But it was the only bucket, and there was nothing for Muniz to bail with. He flashed back to what his grandmother had said, to her prediction that he'd die in a boat. Terrified, he clambered toward the bow, putting as much distance as he could between himself and the incoming flood.

It was the right thing to do. Shifting weight forward lifted the stern. They stopped shipping water.

Muniz pulled himself upright, high enough, now, to look over the tangle of roots. Ahead, and not far ahead either, he could see swirling clouds of mist.

And then he couldn't see much at all, because he was being dazzled by a light from above.

THE PILOT was the first to spot the fugitives.

"There!" he said, redirecting the light.

"Just a tree," Silva said.

"No. There, with its nose up against the roots."

André was right. A boat with two men aboard was nestled parallel to the trunk. The figure in the bow turned, shielded his eyes, and looked upward.

"That's him, all right," Arnaldo said. "That's Muniz."

"Whoever he is," André said, "he's in big trouble. I've seen this sort of thing before, trees as big as that one, some even bigger, adrift on the river. Right now, they're hung up on the bottom, but it won't last long. They'll start moving again any minute. And then. . ."

He let the searchlight speak for him, using it to illuminate the lip of a precipice not fifty meters from the boat.

"Cool," Arnaldo said. "So that's settled. Can you position this thing so we'll have a good view when they go over?"

"Not funny," André said.

"He's not joking," Silva said.

But André continued to take it as such. "That," he said, pointing to a microphone hanging from a hook on the control panel, "is the megaphone. Press to talk. I'm going to hover just above them. Tell them to grab the skids on opposite sides. Stress that. Opposite sides. We don't want both of them to cling to one side of the aircraft. I won't be able to compensate for that."

Silva and Arnaldo exchanged a glance.

"Let me tell you," Silva said, "what those people down there have just done."

"Later," the pilot said.

"Now."

"We haven't got a second to lose."

"Now."

"Jesus Christ, why does it have to be now?"

"Because when I finish," Silva said, "you'll understand why we're not going to do a damned thing to help the bastards."

"OH JESUS," Roque said, startled.

Muniz, from his perch on the bow, whipped around to look at him. "What?" he screeched in panic "*What?*"

"We just moved!"

Roque was right. They were in movement again, no doubt about it. The tip of a boulder, smoothed by the river, appeared in the water beside them and then slowly slipped away into the darkness astern. Muniz caught his breath.

Up above, the helicopter came no closer.

"What are they waiting for?" Roque said. "Why are they just hovering there like that? They gotta come now, low, so we can reach up and grab on. It's the only way we're gonna get out of this."

"THEY BOTH sound like right bastards," the pilot said, when Silva finished, "but I can't just hover here and watch two guys go over the falls."

"If they hadn't tried to kill us," Silva said, "it wouldn't be happening."

"I understand what you're saying, I really do. But no one deserves to die like that. Come on, grab that microphone. I think that tree just started to move."

"You haven't heard all of it," Silva said taking note of the little gold cross suspended from a chain around André's neck. "That guy in the bow? He murdered a priest."

"A priest?"

"A priest, an old man who never did any harm to anyone. Shot him. In cold blood."

André took a hand off the controls and crossed himself.

"And it isn't like we'd be killing them," Arnaldo chipped-in. "The river would be doing that. All we have to do is . . . nothing."

And nothing is what they did.

THE LAST few seconds of Muniz's life came in a terrifying rush.

He scrambled from the bow back toward the stern, trying to stave off the final moment for as long as possible.

Roque, in contrast, abandoned himself to the inevitable. He knelt down between the seats, clasped his hands, closed his eyes and, probably for the first time in many years, began to pray.

THE BOAT went vertical when it reached the edge. Muniz and his companion were catapulted forward and thrown clear. Separated from the hull by a meter or so, they seemed to hang in the air for a moment before they began to plummet.

André followed them with the light. Muniz's arms were flapping, flaying the air, as if he was trying to fly, while his legs moved back and forth, as if he was trying to run. He was still at it when he vanished into the swirling cauldron of water at the foot of the cliff.

"That was awful," André said after a moment's silence, and Silva could see he meant it.

But later, when Arnaldo related the story to Chagas and Hector, he described the scene he'd witnessed as "one of the funniest things I ever saw".

Chapter Forty-One

THE NEWEST AND LARGEST of São Paulo's Jewish cemeteries is in São Paulo's Butantã neighborhood, not far from the world-famous biomedical institute of that name. It was there that Danusa's parents had been buried, and there that her uncle, Simão Marcus, arranged for her to be laid to rest.

Seventeen of her colleagues from the Federal Police attended the funeral. Nelson Sampaio, the director, confirmed his attendance—but failed to appear.

After the service, a tall man with piercing blue eyes tapped Silva on the shoulder.

"Chief Inspector? Might we have a word? In private?"

"I'd welcome it," Silva said. He turned to Arnaldo. "Wait for me. I won't be long."

The tall man took Silva by an arm, as if they were old friends, and, like old friends, they began strolling between the graves.

"You seem to know who I am," the blue-eyed man said with a frown.

"I do. Your name is Amzi Ben-Meir."

The frown dissolved. "How, pray tell, do you know that?"

"I recognized you from your photographs."

"You maintain a file on me?"

"We do."

"So you already know I'm the cultural attaché at the Israeli embassy in Brasilia?"

"There's no need to dissemble, Senhor Ben-Meir. You're no cultural attaché."

"No? What am I then?"

"You work for the Israeli intelligence service."

"The Mossad? Really? Is that what you think? Should I be vexed or flattered?"

"Perhaps a little of both. I admire your department's professionalism. I don't like what you're doing in my country."

"Organizing concerts? Bringing in dance troupes?"

"Please, Senhor Ben-Meir, let's be frank with one another. I think Danusa would have preferred it."

The frown was back. "Why do you mention Danusa?"

"She left a message for you on the night she died."

"What was the message?"

"She said, *tell Amzi I'm sorry.*"

"Only that?"

"Only that. At the time, your name was unfamiliar to me."

"So you looked me up?"

"I did. And, once I had, I expected to see you here, so I waited until now to pass it on."

"And now you have. And I thank you for it."

Ben-Meir looked away, letting his gaze sweep across the monuments to the dead, dealing with an emotion he was finding hard to contain.

"Had she ever mentioned me before?" he said at last.

"Never."

"She respected you a great deal," Ben-Meir said. "She told me that."

"It was kind of her to say so."

"She meant it." He stopped walking. "Danusa and I were engaged to be married."

The catch in Ben-Meir's throat took Silva by surprise. He took a step backward to focus on the man's blue eyes.

"You have my heartfelt sympathy," he said. "She was a lovely girl."

Ben-Meir nodded. "Knowing of our relationship, of course, might cause you to question a possible conflict of interest. I mean, a Brazilian federal agent marrying an Israeli . . . cultural attaché, it wouldn't have been acceptable to you, would it?"

"No, Senhor Ben-Meir, it would not have been acceptable."

"Brazil was the land of her birth, and the land in which her parents are buried. She loved it. She would never have acted against the interests of this country. I assure you of that."

"Still, you can see my point."

"Of course I can. That's why I brought it up. She, too, was conflicted by the situation. She intended to tender her resignation upon the completion of the job in Foz do Iguaçu. I am about to be rotated back to Israel. She'd planned to accompany me."

"Under the circumstances, I think she was making the right decision. Again, I'm sorry for your loss."

"Thank you. This, too, you should know: She made it clear to those of us in the . . . cultural section that, as long as she was serving with the federal police, she would do nothing in violation of Brazilian law. To my certain knowledge, she never did. She would have wanted you to know that. Given the chance, she would have told you herself."

Silva extended a hand. "Thank you, Senhor Ben-Meir. I'm grateful you took the trouble to speak to me."

Ben-Meir took Silva's hand in a firm grip. "There's something else you might like to know," he said.

"And that is?"

Ben-Meir released him. "She spoke to me shortly before she died."

"I'd been wondering whom she went inside to call. So it was you?"

"It was. She told me about your visit to Al-Fulan and also

about that mullah in Foz do Iguaçu. She was quite convinced they were behind the two bombings, the one in Buenos Aires and the one here in São Paulo."

"So am I, Senhor Ben-Meir, but I have no proof."

"None at all?"

"None at all. The best I've been able to do is to trace the sale of the explosive to one of Al-Fulan's henchmen, and the bomber to the mullah's madrasa. Not enough, regrettably, to secure a conviction."

"Thank you, I appreciate your candor."

"I truly wish I could offer you more than candor."

"Believe me, Chief Inspector, your candor is quite enough." He looked at his watch. "And now," he said, "I must take my leave. We'll be speaking again before long."

"Will we?"

"Yes, Chief Inspector. We will. I assure you, we will."

With that, Amzi Ben-Meir turned on his heel and walked away between the graves.

Chapter Forty-Two

JAMIL AL-FULAN DIPPED A forefinger into his glass, removed a single drop of wine and shook it onto the table-cloth. The stain joined others on his side of the table.

"Why do you keep doing that?" Matias Chaparro inquired politely.

"The fact that you have bought me dinner," Al-Fulan said, "does not give you the right to interrogate me about my customs."

The smile on Chaparro's face didn't falter. Maintaining it, however, took some effort. "Quite right," he said. "It does not. Shall we get down to business?"

"By all means. What did you want to see me about?"

"The disposition of that plastic explosive your man Kassim bought. May I assume the purchase was made on your behalf?"

"You can assume anything you like. As to the disposition, it's none of your business."

"On the contrary, Jamil. The use to which that explosive was put is likely to bring down the wrath of four governments on our heads. It is, therefore, very much my business."

"*Four* governments?"

"The Argentinean, the Brazilian, the American and the Israeli."

"The *Israeli?*"

"Their ambassador to Argentina, his wife and two children were killed in the blast in Buenos Aires. Their representative in Asunción has been making inquiries about you."

"About *me?*"

"Yes, about you. Specifically."

"This is the doing of that Jewish bitch."

"What Jewish bitch?"

"The Brazilian federal agent killed in that shootout last week at the Hotel das Cataratas. The day before she died, she and her boss came to see me. A fact, I might add, which you well know, because you were the one who pressured me to accept an appointment with them."

"Yes, Jamil, I know that. But what I *don't* know is what you discussed. Why don't you tell me about it?"

Al-Fulan waved a dismissive hand. "It would be a waste of your time and mine. The conversation from their side consisted entirely of unfounded accusations."

"And from yours?"

"Truthful denials."

"So there was no truth, whatsoever, to any of their accusations?"

"There was not."

"Then you should have no objection to telling me the disposition of the explosive. So I ask you again, what did you do with it?"

"I? I did nothing with it. It wasn't sold to me. It was sold it to Kassim, remember?"

"Yes, Jamil. I remember. What do you suppose Kassim did with it?"

"I suppose he sold to the *Comando Vermelho.*"

"I submit to you that it was *not* sold to the *Comando Vermelho,* or to any other drug gang."

"No? What happened to it then?"

"It was used to commit the bombings in Buenos Aires and São Paulo."

"There's no way to prove that."

"In fact," Chaparro said. "There is." He took another sip of wine. "Do you know what taggants are?"

"What?"

"Taggants."

"No."

"Taggants are tiny pieces of plastic embedded into some explosives. They're as unique as fingerprints, and they're not destroyed by detonation."

"Wait. So you're saying—"

"I'm saying, Jamil, that the explosives used to bomb the American consulate in São Paulo, and the Jewish synagogue in Buenos Aires, have been traced back to those three drums of C4 sold to your associate, Kassim."

"Traced by whom?"

"The Brazilian Federal Police."

"They're lying."

Chaparro went on as if he hadn't spoken. "I don't think you realize," he said, "how injudicious you've been. Selling our C4 to a drug gang is one thing. Using it the way you did is quite another. It's unacceptable."

Al-Fulan held his glass in front of one of the candles as if to admire the color of the wine. Then he locked eyes with Chaparro.

"You have my answers," he said. "Do you have further questions?"

"No."

"Then our business of the night is concluded."

"Except for one small detail." Chaparro rubbed thumb against forefinger. "Need I remind you that it is, once again, that time of the month?"

Without breaking eye contact, Al-Fulan reached into

the breast pocket of his Zegna jacket and withdrew a white envelope. But, instead of handing it to his dinner companion, he contemptuously tossed it onto the table.

Chaparro, however, took no offense. "Thank you," he said—and pocketed it.

Al-Fulan put his glass aside, as if the contents had become distasteful to him. He looked at his watch. "My car will be waiting," he said, and rose to his feet.

His two bodyguards, seated at a neighboring table, rose with him. A young couple, hugging each other and laughing, were being bowed out by the headwaiter. The sole remaining customer was Chaparro.

But he didn't intend to be hurried. "My car," he said, "will come when I call it."

The wine he'd ordered to accompany their meal was a magnum of fifteen-year-old Cheval Blanc, and Chaparro was in no way pleased that Al-Fulan had chosen to waste an entire glassful of it.

Jamil buttoned his jacket and nodded to his men. One preceded him out the door, the other followed.

Chaparro was reaching for the bottle when the shooting started. He added the last of the wine to his glass, and savored it, before going outside to view the carnage.

Chapter Forty-Three

". . . AND then he heard shots. By the time he got out there, he said, there was no sign of either the assailants or Jamil. But, knowing Matias, I doubt he hurried. He's not the kind to involve himself in a gunfight if he can possibly help it."

Luis Chagas was recuperating in his hometown of Porto Alegre. After a jubilant Abasi Ragab had rung with the news, he'd called Matias Chaparro for a first hand report. Now, he was passing on what he'd learned to Silva in Brasilia.

"Witnesses?" Silva asked.

"Three. A doorman and two valets. It was past ten, and it's a quiet neighborhood. There was no one else on the street."

"How did it go down?"

"A young couple came out of the restaurant and asked for their car. A moment later, Al-Fulan stepped out of the same door. He was preceded by one bodyguard, trailed by another. The woman waited until the second bodyguard passed her, took out a pistol and put a bullet into the poor bastard's head. Her companion did the same to the other bodyguard. While that was happening, a gang of guys in black, wearing balaclavas, materialized out of the night."

"How big was this gang?"

"No agreement there. More than six, less than a dozen. Two grabbed Al-Fulan and wrestled him to the ground. One cuffed him. One went directly to the car window and shot the driver. It was Kassim Hamawi, by the way, the guy who killed Nestor. They singled him out for special treatment, shot him over and over in the head."

"Six times?"

"Yeah, as a matter of fact, six times. What do you know that I don't?"

"Israeli execution teams generally leave a signature when they kill enemies of the state."

"And it's six bullets in the head?"

"It is. Remember that Amzi fellow, the one Danusa mentioned just before she died?"

"Yes?"

"He's Mossad. I spoke to him at Danusa's funeral. He said we'd be hearing from him again. I think we just have."

"You think Chaparro collaborated with them? Set Al Fulan up?"

"I wouldn't be at all surprised. How's your wound?"

"Mending nicely. Ready for some more big news?"

"Go ahead."

"I got a call from Stella Saldana."

"And?"

"And she offered me a job, one I can't refuse: State Secretary for Security."

"Congratulations, Senhor Secretary. Does the Director already know you're leaving our nest?"

"Not yet, and I can't tell you how much I'm looking forward to telling him."

JUST AFTER midnight, the telephone in the living quarters on the second floor of the Escola Al-Imam began to ring. He was not accustomed to receiving calls at that hour, and the mullah picked it up with a sense of dread.

"Yes?"

"Asim, is that you?"

There was no mistaking his patron's voice.

"Yes, Jamil, yes! You're all right?"

"I was kidnapped by the Israelis."

"Yes, yes, I know."

"But I escaped."

"Praise God."

"He is truly great."

"You didn't . . . tell them anything about me?"

"Of course not. What do you take me for?"

"I'm sorry, Jamil. I should not have asked. I know that you, of all men, can be trusted. How did you manage to get away?"

"There's no time for that now. We have to meet."

"Of course, of course. Where? When?"

"At the mosque. Immediately. Bring your passport and all the money."

"All of it?"

"All of it."

"Are we leaving, Jamil?"

"We must. Hurry!" Al-Fulan hung up.

And Asim Massri wasted no time in doing what he'd been told.

Twenty minutes later, and ten meters shy of his destination, three females rounded the corner in front of him. Their clothing was too tight, their voices too self-assured, their laughter too loud. Not whores, no, but they might as well have been. They were looking at him as if he was a piece of meat, a male creature created for their pleasure. And one was drunk. She was carrying a large paper cup and slurring her speech. They were coming toward him, occupying the full width of the sidewalk as if they owned it.

Asim's lip curled in disdain. They were, like most Brazilian females, beneath contempt. Flaunting their sexuality. By no means subservient. He would *not* step into the gutter to avoid them. *They* would have to avoid *him*.

He put his head down and quickened his pace, charging

at them like a bull. One stepped off the curb. He elbowed his way through the narrow gap between the other two.

That's when they grabbed him.

Hard hands gripped his forearms and twisted them behind his back. A steel-tipped shoe connected with his knee, causing his leg to collapse. While he hung there, supported between two of them, the third, the one he'd thought was drunk, put the cup she'd been holding over his nose and mouth.

"Don't fight us, Mullah. Just take a deep breath, and go to sleep."

She said it without a slur—and in perfect Arabic.

THE MULLAH awoke naked and tied to a chair. His mouth had been taped shut. They'd stuck some kind of a gag behind his teeth. The space around him was damp and smelled of mold.

A cellar?

What illumination there was came from a dim bulb mounted within a conical shade. It dangled slightly in front of him and a mere ten centimeters above his head. He couldn't see walls, or furniture, or any other details. The extremities of the space were in darkness.

He heard rustling and low voices.

What is this? Where am I? How many of them are out there?

A man stepped into the pool of light, a tall man with piercing blue eyes.

He ripped off the tape. It hurt. He plucked out the gag. It was a blessed relief. Asim's mouth was as dry as the desert, his throat parched.

They'd anticipated that. A hand reached out of the darkness. It was holding a tumbler of water.

"Drink," the tall man said, "and you'll be able to talk."

He took the glass and held it to Asim's mouth. The mullah swallowed greedily, spilling a good deal onto his chest and belly in the process.

"Who are you?" he managed to croak when the glass was empty. He said it in Portuguese. The answer came back in flawless Arabic.

"My name is Amzi Ben-Meir."

A *Jew!* he thought.

"What do you want with me?" he said.

"I think you know."

"I do not. And you have no right, no right to do this to me. You're in Brazil."

"Don't you talk to me about rights, you butcher. If you lived in Israel, you'd have rights. You'd have the right to a trial and an execution. Here, we intend to give you as many rights as you gave your victims."

"I have no victims. I'm a teacher and a scholar of the Holy Qur'an."

"And four things more: a terrorist, a bomb maker, a corrupter of young minds, and a man who preaches and practices violent jihad."

"You lie! I'm a man of peace."

"You're the one who's lying, Asim. We know you brainwashed Salem Nabulsi into going to São Paulo and blowing himself up. We know you personally placed a bomb in that synagogue in Buenos Aires. We know you were the mastermind behind both bombs, and that you intended to build another one. We even know where you intended to use it."

The man was bluffing. They couldn't possibly know! "No," Asim said.

"Yes," Ben-Meir said. "You were going to use it to blow up the *Cristo Redentor*."

The *Cristo Redentor*, a great statue of Jesus Christ with his arms outstretched, stands high on a peak overlooking the City of Rio de Janeiro. It is probably the best-known of all of Brazil's man-made icons.

And what Ben-Meir was saying was true. They *had* planned to blow it up.

But aside from Asim, there was only one man in the world who knew that.

They must have tortured Jamil, he thought.

"Thank God he escaped you," he said.

"Jamil? He didn't."

Asim's mouth opened in surprise. He couldn't believe his ears. "You mean the call I received, the one from Jamil was. . ."

"A trap? Yes, Asim, he set you up, sold you out. But, before he did, he told us everything he knew."

"Damn him!"

"On that point we agree. And I'm sure you'd like to tell him that to his face. We'll give you that chance. But, first, we have some questions."

"If it's true what you're saying, there's no need for questions. The traitor Jamil has already told you everything."

"Everything he could. But there are things he doesn't know."

"It's not true. What I know, he also knows."

"He doesn't know where you received your education in bomb making. He doesn't know who taught you. He doesn't know who your fellow students were. He doesn't know the names of all the other terrorists you're acquainted with."

"I know no terrorists, I only know freedom fighters. As to the other matters, I will tell you nothing."

"You will. You will tell us everything."

"Never!"

Ben-Meir scratched his chin, shook his head and looked at someone beyond the range of the light. "Begin," he said.

Chapter Forty-Four

WHEN ASIM FAILED TO appear for classes, the father of one of his younger students, a man who shared the mullah's radical views, went to look for him.

The door of the Escola Al-Imam was locked, but when he knocked it was answered by Ghalib, one of the mullah's servants. He was a recent immigrant from Palestine, a man of an indefinable age with teeth as crooked as the gravestones in an ancient cemetery.

No, he said, he had no idea where the mullah was. Yes, he agreed, his absence was most noteworthy. No, he had no idea when Asim might be back. Yes, he would contact the head of the parents' association straightaway if he received a message from the mullah.

On the following day, when the cleric still hadn't appeared, Ghalib went to the police and reported him missing.

It was noted, on both sides of the river, that Asim's patron, Jamil Al-Fulan, had also disappeared. This provoked some consternation in the Muslim community, but also a great deal of clandestine satisfaction.

As for the Israelis, they were not surprised when Asim turned out to be more resilient than Jamil had been. Fanatics, they had long ago learned, were reluctant to part with their secrets.

But Lev, Ben-Meir's interrogation expert, had cracked harder nuts. And when Asim started talking, he held nothing back.

He told them about the training camp he'd attended in

the mountains of northwest Pakistan, a graduate school for bomb makers. His recall of the surroundings was absolute. Ben-Meir was confident his description would enable the Americans to pinpoint the location—and take appropriate action.

He furnished them with the names of other students. One was in Madrid, another in London. Emails went out, immediately, to the security services in Spain and the UK.

He told them, in detail, of his participation in the bombings. How he'd rigged the timer for the bomb in Buenos Aires. How he'd placed it. How he and Salem had rehearsed the assembly of the one destined for São Paulo, using pencils instead of detonators and modeling clay instead of plastic explosive. How he'd demonstrated the technique of cutting a throat. How they'd practiced on a pig.

The baby, he revealed, had suffered an injection to ensure that it wouldn't cry. The drug was propofol, provided by a veterinarian, a co-religionist in Ciudad del Este.

The remainder of the C4 was in a cache under the floor of his office.

Zivah, Amzi's bomb specialist, was sent to recover it. Some members of the team were in favor of using it to blow up the madrasa, but Amzi forbade it.

"The building isn't the problem," he'd said. "The mullah is the problem. Let's give them a chance to replace him with someone better."

AUTOMOBILES HEADING west across the Friendship Bridge are never searched. No one has any interest in smuggling anything *into* Paraguay.

Getting Asim to Ciudad del Este was, therefore, a simple matter of gagging him, binding him, and driving him there in the trunk of one of the rental cars.

Less than an hour after leaving their isolated safe house, Ben-Meir and the two associates who accompanied him were safely across the border. Fifteen minutes later, they arrived at the back door of Al-Fulan's auto dealership.

It was 2:15 in the morning. The narrow lane was deserted. The four men who'd entered the building to subdue the guards were expecting them. The guards themselves had already been drugged and transported to a distant location.

Ben-Meir's men hustled Asim inside, tied him to one of two chairs nailed to the floor in Al-Fulan's office and removed his gag.

The mullah, talked-out and exhausted from his ordeal, looked around him with bleary eyes. Then he closed them for a while—and dozed.

He awoke, an hour later, with the arrival of Jamil Al-Fulan.

"Do not bring that traitorous filth close to me," he said angrily. "Even the air around him is polluted."

Al-Fulan made a show of attempting to advance on the mullah. But it was no more than that, a show. "How dare you?" he shouted as they bound him to the other chair. "How dare *you* call *me* a traitor?"

"Because that's what you are!" the mullah shouted back. "They told me what you did. You lured me into a trap."

"And am I any worse than you? You, who betrayed everyone and everything."

"I? Betray?"

"Don't play the innocent with me, Asim. I know what you've done."

"You believe the lies these Zionist pigs have told you?"

"I believe the recording they made of your interrogation. They played it for me. You spilled your guts and gave up your friends. You are despicable!"

"Despicable? I? You are—"

Ben-Meir interceded. "Quiet," he said. "One more word from either of you and the gags go back in."

Neither wanted that. They fell silent.

The chairs had been positioned to face Al-Fulan's desk. Ben-Meir stepped behind it and sat down. The other members of the team gathered around him.

For the first time, Al-Fulan and the mullah could see the extent of the force the Israelis had marshaled against them: an even dozen, eight men and four women. The oldest was Ben-Meir himself; the youngest, a youth who looked to be no more than eighteen.

"As you have undoubtedly guessed by now," Ben-Meir said, "we are members of Israel's secret intelligence service."

"I knew it!" the mullah said.

"I told you to be quiet. You will have ample time to respond when I have finished."

The mullah's eyes narrowed in hatred. He started to curse.

"Do it," Ben-Meir said. "Gag him."

A gag was stuffed into Asim's mouth. Ben-Meir waited until it had been secured with tape and continued. "Our government does not tolerate attacks on its representatives or their families. If you were in Israeli territory, you would be tried for the murder of our ambassador to Argentina, his wife and children."

Al-Fulan opened his mouth. A minder stepped forward, gag in hand. The Paraguayan pressed his lips together and shook his head.

"But," Ben-Meir continued, "you are not in Israel, and neither one of you has the prominence of an Eichmann, so we're not going to the trouble and expense to take you there. In cases like yours, we have an established procedure: confession, condemnation, execution. You have confessed. A quarter of an hour ago, the President of Israel signed your death warrants. You've been duly informed. Now, you may speak."

Al-Fulan licked his lips. His voice came out in a croak. "Let me go," he said, "and I will make you rich."

Ben-Meir shook his head.

"No, wait," Al-Fulan said. "Let me finish."

"Go ahead. Finish."

Al-Fulan inclined his head in the mullah's direction. "He prepared the bombs. He sent Nabulsi to São Paulo, and he did the job in Buenos Aires. All I did was to supply the money. He's the one you really want, not me. Why don't you just kill *him?*"

The mullah's face turned bright red, and a vein in his forehead began to throb.

Ben-Meir shook his head.

"Think about it!" Al-Fulan said. "Think of the money! If you let me go, you'll all be rich, and I'll disappear. You'll never see me again. No one need ever know."

"Gag him," Ben-Meir said, "and remove the gag from the other one."

When it was done, the mullah tried to spit in Ben-Meir's face. The spittle fell short.

"Say your piece," Ben-Meir said. "I will give you fifteen seconds."

"You are all doomed," Asim said. "There are one point six billion of us and less than fourteen million of you. And except in your Zionist state, your numbers shrink from day to day. We, however, grow more numerous each year. You are surrounded on all sides by enemies. You cannot stand against us. We will destroy all of you and return your cities to dust—"

"His fifteen seconds are up," Ben-Meir said. "Put back the gag and let's finish this. Zivah."

She took a step toward him. "Yes, Amzi."

"Put it where they can see it," he said. "Set it for four hours. We don't want to awaken the Chief Inspector too early."

At 3:27 in the morning, the Israelis filed out of the room, leaving the two condemned men tied to their chairs, staring wide-eyed at a digital timer moving inexorably toward zero.

At 7:25, the numbers ran out, and the remaining C4, all thirty-seven kilograms of it, exploded.

Afterwards, the Paraguayan National Police concluded the two terrorists had accidently blown themselves up while assembling a bomb of spectacular proportions.

But at 7:30 A.M., while the ruins of Jamil Al-Fulan's auto dealership were still smoldering, Mario Silva's telephone rang.

And Amzi Ben-Meir told him what had really happened.

Chapter Forty-Five

ON THE THIRD OF January, seven weeks to the day after the deaths of Jamil Al-Fulan and Asim Massri, Stella Saldana was inaugurated as the new governor of Paraná.

By that time, the former governor, Abbas, was already ensconced in his new house on Saint Barthélemy, counting his money and plotting a return.

Madalena Torres was in São Paulo transforming a senator into a governor.

Braulio Serpa was still looking for a job.

And the federal cops were no closer to discovering who'd planned the murder of Stella's husband.

The solution came in early February—and from an entirely unexpected direction.

The telephone rang in Silva's apartment at eight o'clock at night. Irene, as usual, was well into her cups. And Silva, as usual, was the one to answer it.

"Hi, Mario. Heard about old man Saldana?" It was Luis Chagas.

"Hello, Luis. How's the new job?"

"I'm in heaven. Stella is a dream to work for."

"When you say *old man Saldana*, I assume you're talking about Plínio's father? Orestes?"

"I am."

"What about him?"

"His son, Lúcio, is up on charges of defrauding his clients. It's going to be the first time a Saldana ever got convicted of anything in the State of Paraná. Not that they haven't done a lot of nasty things—they have. But it's never gone farther than vague accusations. Not this time. This time, Stella is all over it. Lúcio's going to do jail time for sure. And, when they told Orestes about it, he went ballistic. He had a stroke. Then, while he was still in his hospital bed, and unable to talk, his mother had him declared mentally incompetent. He's been committed to the same institution he committed her to."

"Ha! And is he? Mentally incompetent, I mean."

"The judge said he is."

"What do you say?"

"Who am I to argue with a judge? Recently appointed, by the way, and an old law-school colleague of Stella's, so they tell me. But all that's just a bit of gossip I thought you might be interested in. It's not the reason I called."

"No?"

"No. My boss and I are in Brasilia. She'd like a word with you."

"About what?"

"That's between you and the governor."

"All right. Where?"

"We're at the Meliá."

"The Meliá is fine. When?"

"Four o'clock tomorrow afternoon?"

"Works for me."

"And Mario. . . ." An element of caution had crept into Luis's voice.

"Yes?"

"Come alone."

GOVERNOR STELLA Saldana's suite was one of the best, just two floors below the rooftop swimming pool. Chagas answered his knock and ushered him inside.

The window in the living room looked out on the television tower. Stella had coffee and croissants waiting. Silva accepted the coffee and passed on the croissants. Chagas excused himself and left. Stella set down her cup and tilted her head at the door from which he'd made his exit.

"He didn't want to be here for this," she said.

"I noticed."

"But it's at his insistence that I'm talking to you now."

She picked up her cup, took another sip of coffee, let the silence stretch out. Silva, wisely, said nothing. After a while, she continued. "Before I spoke to Luis about this, I was the only person alive who knew."

Silva frowned. "Knew what, Senhora?"

"Knew what really happened to Plínio. I will not repeat this anywhere or at any other time. And if you go public with it, I'll deny it."

He raised a curious eyebrow. "Then why, Senhora, are you going to tell me anything at all?"

She took one breath, two, and then the plunge. "So I'll have it off my conscience—and so you can stop wasting your time."

"Wasting my time?"

"Any further investigation of Plínio's death is a complete and total waste of time. There's no one left to punish, and without my help, you'll never get to the bottom of it."

"He was your husband, Senhora. And he was murdered. How can you possibly—"

"He wasn't murdered."

"What?"

"Plínio's death was an accident."

"An accident?"

She'd said it. Now, she wanted to get it over with. She hurried forward.

"It was supposed to be a stunt, a ploy to capture votes. Cataldo was supposed to shoot at Plínio, but he was never meant to hit him. It was all Plínio's idea. He planned it, and he convinced Nestor to help him pull it off."

Silva sat back in his chair. "Maybe you'd better tell me the whole story."

"I just did. The rest is detail."

Silva crossed his arms, thought of the waste of time and energy, thought of the time he'd taken away from the bombing case, thought of the fact that Danusa might still be alive had he not been misled by the lies. Most of all, he thought of Jessica Cataldo and her orphaned children.

"Then tell me," he said, "the detail."

"The polls suggested the election could go either way. And when Plínio thought Abbas was about to embarrass him with that girlfriend of his—"

"Wait. You mean to tell me you knew about Eva Telles?"

"Of course I did. It's not as if she was making any secret of it."

"You confronted your husband with it?"

"I did. Eva Telles is a greedy little gold-digger. She thought she'd captured his heart, but it was a dalliance on his part, nothing more. He'd had his fun. Even before we spoke about it, he'd made up his mind to tell her it was over. I think, in a way, he was relieved I found out."

"So you had no intention of leaving him?"

"I did not. We had plans, he and I, for the State of Paraná. Good plans. We'd been cherishing those plans for years. I wasn't about to let his sordid little affair get in the way of fulfilling them."

"But?"

"But if Abbas did what my husband suspected he was going to do, if he divulged to the press that Plínio had been cheating on me, it was sure to cost us votes, maybe even cost us the election. Plínio was worried. He felt he had to do something."

"And what he did was?"

"I told you. He staged an attempt on his life, a completely bogus one. At least, that's what it was supposed to be. No one was going to get hurt. Cataldo wasn't going to come out and say it, but he was going to imply Abbas was behind it."

"So Abbas would get the blame, and your husband would get the votes?"

"Exactly. An attempted assassination trumps cheating on your wife. The votes Plínio stood to gain would put him safely over the top."

"I see. How was it supposed to go down?"

"Cataldo was to shoot and miss, after which Nestor would wrestle him to the ground. That was all."

"Why would Nestor Cambria, a cop who was honest his whole life long, go along with something like that?"

One of the prints on the wall of the suite was an artist's interpretation of how a village street must have looked in colonial times. Diamantina, Ouro Preto, someplace like that. She stared at it without seeing, and shook her head.

"I asked him that," she said. "I had to know. It was one of the reasons I went to the hospital on the day he . . . died."

"And?"

She looked back at Silva.

"Nestor wanted to be the State Secretary for Security. He reasoned the same way Plínio did. Even if they had to play a dirty trick to win the election, it was for the good of the people."

It was Silva's turn to shake his head. It wasn't the Nestor he knew, but he'd been exposed to that kind of thinking before. The lust for power did strange things to people,

changed them in ways that was difficult to predict. After a
moment he said, "How about Cataldo? He'd be accused of
attempted murder."

He'd be arrested, charged and convicted. Then he'd be
pardoned."

"Pardoned?"

"Part of the deal. Plínio, once he'd been elected governor,
could pardon him. Forgiving the man who'd tried to kill him
would make him look even better."

"But Cataldo would still wind up doing jail time. And after
it was all over, he'd be classified as a convicted felon. Why
should he go along with a crazy scheme like that?"

"You used the key word. Crazy. To kill a man like Plínio
in front of thousands of people, in front of television cameras, would be crazy. That's the way they intended to play
it. Cataldo wouldn't be cast as a villain. He'd be cast as a
deluded soul in need of medical attention. He wouldn't go
to jail. He'd go into an institution for psychiatric care. Then
he'd be cured. And he'd make a public apology. And Plínio
would see to it that his record was expunged."

"Could Plínio do that?"

"Probably not, but he was perfectly willing to lie. He convinced Cataldo he could."

"And if, later, he went back on his word?"

"Cataldo would have had a history of mental illness by
then. Who'd listen to a man with a record of delusions?"

Silva scratched his head. "Why would Cataldo even consider doing it at all? Was it for money?"

She shook her head. "No."

"No?"

"Cataldo was an idealist. He believed in Plínio. He was
naïve, and my husband had a silver tongue. Plínio convinced him the end justified the means, convinced him

he'd be acting in a good cause, and convinced him that, together, they'd be able to realize the things Cataldo had been fighting for all his life, everything from gun control to saving the whales. The money was nothing more than icing on the cake."

"How much money?"

"I don't know. I wasn't involved. I got the essentials of the story out of Nestor that night in the hospital, but I had people waiting for me, and I couldn't leave them milling around in the corridor for too long. I'd planned to go back, talk to him again, question him about the rest, but I never got the chance."

Silva fell silent, mulling it over.

Outside the suite an elevator pinged. They heard voices approaching, but the people, two women engaged in a heated discussion, passed and moved on.

Stella's attention had been diverted by the noise, and she was looking at the door. Not so Silva. He hadn't taken his eyes off her. "Who else knew about this?"

She looked back at him.

"No one. Only Cataldo, Nestor and Plínio. That's why I told you you'd be wasting your time trying to get to the bottom of it."

"But you knew as well, Senhora. You just told me you did."

Again, she shook her head. "I was brought into it at the last minute. By the time Plínio told me what he was planning to do, it was too late to do anything about it."

"What do you call 'too late'? Surely—"

"Plínio knew I wouldn't agree to a scheme like that, knew I'd try to argue him out of it. So he didn't tell me a thing until we were together, in the car, before he mounted the podium to give his speech. He made the driver get out. And then he told me."

"If he hadn't told you before, why did he tell you then?"

"Don't you believe me, Chief Inspector? Do you think I was actually involved in orchestrating any of this?"

"Please answer my question, Senhora."

"He told me to spare my feelings. He didn't want me to be shocked when I saw Cataldo taking out a gun. And I think, too, he wanted to prepare me, so I wouldn't go all to pieces, and I'd be poised when I spoke to the press."

"What did you do when he told you?"

"I objected. I protested. I told him he was crazy."

"And he?"

"Said it was too late. Said Cataldo was already in the crowd, waiting for him to finish his speech. That trying to stop it would ruin his candidacy; ruin everything we'd worked for. And besides, if Cataldo didn't go through with it, he'd always be a risk. But, if he did, he'd have to keep his mouth shut."

"I see."

"I don't think you do. If you did, you wouldn't be looking at me like that. Do you think I haven't been over this a thousand times in my head? Do you think I haven't asked myself what else I could have done? It was a moral choice, Chief Inspector, a question of the greatest good for the greatest number. I did what I felt was right. And, remember, no one was supposed to get hurt."

"Yes, you said that before. So what happened then?"

"After Plínio and I spoke?"

"Yes. After you spoke."

Stella toyed with her empty cup, considering her reply. Outside the window, between the television tower and the hotel, an executive jet glided by, descending into its final approach to the nearby airport. When she finally spoke, it came out in a rush.

"I stayed in the car. I refused to participate, refused to mount the podium with him. Ask the bodyguards. Look at the videos. You'll see I wasn't there, the first time in the whole damned campaign I wasn't there. I sat, turning the situation over in my head, until I heard the shots. Not the single shot I was expecting, but four. I got out of the car to see what had happened. They let me through. I cradled Plínio's head in my lap, but it was too late. They didn't announce he was dead until after he'd arrived at the hospital, but I knew it even then. There was only a little hole in his forehead, but the wound in the back was a lot bigger. It blew out a piece of his skull. He was already gone by the time I got to him."

Fiction or truth? He'd probably never know, Silva thought. And, in the end, did that part of it really matter?

"What else did Nestor tell you?" he said. "How did he come to shoot Cataldo? How did he come to be shot himself?"

"He saw that woman. What's her name? The one that gave all those interviews?"

"Nora Tasca?"

"Yes. Her. She was elbowing her way forward. He saw her strike Cataldo's arm, throw off his aim just as he pulled the trigger. Cataldo wasn't more than two meters away, and Nestor could see this shocked, horrified expression on his face when he realized what he'd done, how he'd screwed up."

"And?"

"And, to hear Nestor tell it, his training kicked in. He reacted instinctively, shot Cataldo before he gave it conscious thought."

"And Cataldo, realizing he'd been shot, which wasn't supposed to happen, acted to defend himself?"

"That's right. He shot Nestor."

"At which point, Nestor shot him again and killed him."

"That's what he told me, yes."

"Had you reason to disbelieve him?"

"Well. . ."

"Well what?"

"It occurred to me, Chief Inspector, as it has undoubtedly occurred to you, and as I'm sure it occurred to Nestor, that Cataldo had become a threat."

"You think Nestor might have killed him to keep him quiet?"

She paused, and he could see the doubt in her eyes.

"Nestor said he didn't."

"And you believed him?"

She smiled faintly. There was no humor in it.

"We'll really never know, will we? So that's it. That's the story. Coming forward with it now wouldn't do anyone any good. My husband ended his life with many faults, but he began it with many virtues, and I'm not about to destroy his legacy."

"I have to tell you, Senhora, that there was some talk of him becoming involved in the smuggling of automobiles into Paraguay."

She showed no surprise, grimaced in distaste, but also nodded, as if it was old news.

"It was stupid. We'd gone into debt, deeply into debt, during the campaign. He thought he saw a way out. I convinced him it would undermine everything he'd ever stood for. In the end, he agreed with me."

"So he was going to back out of the deal with Al-Fulan?"

"He was. I'm sure Senhor Al-Fulan would have been bitterly disappointed."

"Did Nestor know about their negotiations?"

"No. And that was another factor. Nestor hated Al-Fulan, and the feeling was mutual. He never would have stood for it. I think Plínio knew without me telling him, but I told him anyway. The deal was dead in the water."

"Does Nestor's wife, Bruna, know anything about this? About the plot? About your husband's conversations with Al-Fulan?"

"No. And you mustn't tell her. There's Nestor's memory to consider. How do you think Bruna would feel if she knew? As for me, I'd have to resign, so I'd be abandoning my chance to do any good in Paraná, and leaving the field to Abbas and his gang of crooks. What's done is done. I'd change it if I could, but I can't. So all I can do now is to make the best of it."

"How about Cataldo's widow? His children?"

"Collateral damage, Chief Inspector. I can't help that."

"I think you can, Senhora, and you must."

"Is that some kind of threat?"

"Senhora, I've been in the service of a corrupt legal system for all of my working life. I'm nothing if not a pragmatist."

"That's what Luis said. That's why I'm telling you all this."

"But I'm also an idealist. And any evil I do, I attempt to do for the greater good."

"I feel the same way. You see? We're alike, you and I."

"So let's say I accept all your arguments," Silva said, and his tone was cold. "Let's also say I accept that you weren't involved in your husband's schemes and that you discovered the plot when it was too late to stop it—"

"You still don't believe me, do you?"

"—and that I further accept that no good can be done by sullying the memory of Nestor Cambria, and even that your motives for accepting the mantle thrust upon you are entirely philanthropic."

"Assume it," she said, setting her jaw and attempting to stare him down, "because it's true."

Silva didn't break eye contact.

"I have already given you all of that. And yet a problem remains."

"Which is?"

"The position you've left Senhora Cataldo in."

Both of her eyebrows moved toward her hairline. She seemed genuinely surprised.

"The position *I* left her in? I've just explained to you that I had nothing to do with it. To participate in the plot was her husband's decision. He's to blame, not me."

"So you're an innocent victim of circumstance, while she and her two children are not?"

"All three of them may well be innocent, but I can't help that. At this point, there's nothing I can do to help them."

"I think you can."

"You have a suggestion?"

"As it happens, Senhora, I do."

Chapter Forty-Six

ARNALDO LOOKED AT SILVA over the rim of his coffee cup. "You're not going to tell the Director, are you?"

"Not on your life," Silva said.

It was an hour later. He was back in his office. The door was closed, and they were alone.

"If I mentioned any of this to Sampaio," Silva said, "he'd only start thinking about how he could use it. And, in the end, he *would* use it. And it would all come out."

"You think Bruna knew?"

"I don't think so. I hope not."

"She's not in on the money deal, is she?"

"No. She doesn't need it. Bruna's family is wealthy. It was Senhora Cataldo I was worried about."

"So what's Stella going to do for her?"

"There's an insurance company, based in Curitiba. Cataldo had a policy with them. They've been refusing to pay out on it, told the widow he'd committed suicide by cop."

"So?"

"Stella's going to get them to approach Jessica Cataldo, tell her they've reconsidered their position about suicide by cop, tell her, too, that Cataldo brought the value of the policy up to a million Reais the week before he died."

"They're going to pay Cataldo's widow a *million* Reais?"

"Uh-huh."

"After initially telling her they wouldn't pay at all? What possible excuse could they offer for having changed their minds?"

"A lawyer is going to accept Senhora Cataldo's case pro bono. And he's going to find a loophole in the new policy."

"What lawyer?"

"A friend of Diogo Mariano's, Stella's new Chief of Staff."

"What loophole in what new policy?"

"The loophole Stella's going to write into the policy Cataldo squirreled away and nobody's been able to find."

"But if nobody's been able to find it—"

"It will be discovered, by one of their sterling employees, in the company archives. That employee, in turn, will bring it to the attention of a concerned directorate. It'll be a nice public relations ploy for the company, show how honest they are, how dedicated to their policy holders."

"Jesus Christ, Mario, you *do* have a devious mind."

"Thank you."

"What makes you think Senhora Cataldo will believe all this claptrap?"

"Why should she not? Why should she look a gift horse in the mouth?"

"Where's the money coming from?"

"Plínio had a policy, a big one. If it wasn't with the same company as Cataldo's new one, Stella will make sure it's transferred. She's not giving Senhora Cataldo all the proceeds, though, just half."

"Sounds to me like there are too many people involved in this little scheme. What if someone talks?"

"Stella isn't worried."

"Why not?"

"Because, if it comes out at all, which it may not, everybody's going to think she's a wonderful person for treating the family of her husband's killer with such charity and tying herself into such knots to do it."

"And Stella would come out smelling like roses."

"Sure. The money is hers. She can do whatever she wants with it. There's no real fraud, only a subterfuge to help the widow Cataldo."

"Pure genius," Arnaldo said with admiration. "You know, Mario, I sometimes think you should have been a politician yourself."

"What a rotten thing to say," Silva said.

Author's Notes

Poor Paraguay.

In the nineteenth century, she suffered the bloody War of the Triple Alliance, which cost her 70% of her population and 140,000 square kilometers of her territory.

In the twentieth, she suffered Alfredo Stroessner, the longest-ruling dictator in the history of South America.

And now, in this book, she might seem to be suffering calumny.

Not so.

In fact, I wish there were more fiction in what I have written about her in these pages.

The contribution of smuggling to Paraguay's economy cannot be overestimated. It exceeds by five times the country's official GNP.

More than half of everything brought legally into Paraguay is exported as contraband.

Seventy percent of the 600,000 automobiles circulating in the country are there illegally.

Her factories produce more than 65 billion cigarettes a year, most of which go directly to Brazil, where they drain the equivalent of US $2.5 billion a year from badly-needed tax revenues.

Paraguay is the continent's biggest importer of whisky from Scotland. Only 5% of it is consumed locally.

She is Brazil's principal source of illegal weapons. As of this writing, a criminal can walk across the Friendship Bridge, enter any one of the 32 specialized shops in Ciudad del Este, buy a fully automatic AK-47 without showing any form of identification, and have it delivered to him in Foz do Iguaçu. The whole process takes less than 24 hours and costs US $400, a mere trifle for the drug dealers who are the illicit arms industry's major clients.

More than US $1,000,000,000 a year is laundered by Paraguayan banks and exchange businesses.

Along one strip of the river forming the border between the two countries, a strip barely 200 kilometers long, more than 3,000 clandestine ports have been identified by the Brazilian authorities. Identified, but not controlled—partly due to insufficient staffing and inadequate resources, but also due to corruption. Many customs agents, and many cops, earn more in bribes than they do in salary.

The porosity of its borders has allowed Brazil to become the principal conduit for the supply of cocaine to Europe and Africa. It enters Paraguay by way of Peru and Colombia, and enters Brazil by way of Paraguay. From there, it moves eastward by ship and airplane.

The area where Paraguay, Argentina and Brazil meet, often referred to as the Tri-Border-Area (TBA), is home to one of the largest Muslim communities in all of South America—and the one most closed to outsiders. Documentation concerning the TBA has been found by U.S. forces searching captured Al Qaeda facilities in Afghanistan.

Islamic terrorist groups with a presence in the region reportedly include Egypt's Al-Gamaá Al-Islamiyya and Al-Jihad, Al-Muqawamah, al Qaeda, Hamas, and Hizballah.

In March of 1992, a TBA group linked with Hizballah staged an attack on the Israeli Embassy in Buenos Aires. Two years later, in July of 1994, they followed up with an action against a Jewish community center, also in Buenos Aires.

From the sketchy information law enforcement authorities

were able to piece together, there was disagreement about both actions within the TBA's radical community. One wing, the more pragmatic one, wanted to reserve the area as a safe haven. They defended the position that operations traced back to the TBA would call down the wrath of the authorities. The other wing, the more idealistic one, held that actions shouldn't be prohibited for fear of reprisal.

The debate was settled when the pragmatic group's position got a stamp of approval from Osama bin Laden.

Reports of a visit to the region by bin Laden himself remain unconfirmed, but Khalid Sheikh Mohammed was there in 1995, a fact that came to light following his capture in Pakistan in March of 2003.

It is unclear, at this moment, how much trouble might be brewing in the region, but all it would take to tip the balance would be the emergence of a few dedicated fanatics.

Santana do Parnaiba, SP
Brazil
April, 2012